# ONE WINTER AT THE
# FRENCH CHALET

MANDY BAGGOT

Boldwood

First published in Great Britain in 2024 by Boldwood Books Ltd.

Copyright © Mandy Baggot, 2024

Cover Design by Alexandra Allden

Cover Photography: Shutterstock

Every effort has been made to obtain the necessary permissions with reference to copyright material, both illustrative and quoted. We apologise for any omissions in this respect and will be pleased to make the appropriate acknowledgements in any future edition.

A CIP catalogue record for this book is available from the British Library.

Paperback ISBN 978-1-80549-391-4

Large Print ISBN 978-1-80549-390-7

Hardback ISBN 978-1-80549-389-1

Ebook ISBN 978-1-80549-392-1

Kindle ISBN 978-1-80549-393-8

Audio CD ISBN 978-1-80549-384-6

MP3 CD ISBN 978-1-80549-386-0

Digital audio download ISBN 978-1-80549-387-7

Boldwood Books Ltd
23 Bowerdean Street
London SW6 3TN
www.boldwoodbooks.com

*To the best friends a girl could have:*

*Sue*
*Rachel*
*Karen*
*Jane*
*Michelle*
*Angela*

*Thank you all for being there for me when it mattered most!*

# 1

## LONDON, UK

'Put your guess in here!'

Orla Bradbee flinched in her office chair as the A4 piece of paper was whisked in front of her and slammed down on her desk.

'Alan!' she exclaimed, cupping her mug of hot chocolate in fear that his frenetic energy was going to upend it all over the Christmas cards she shouldn't be writing on company time.

'Be quick!' Alan ordered, looking over his shoulder. 'Because Sharon is chasing me, desperate to guess ten, but she has insider knowledge so I don't think I can let her compete.'

Orla had no idea what was going on. She looked at the sheet of paper. 'What *is* this?'

'Oh, Orla, I knew you had your head stuck in work this week! You should be ashamed of yourself.'

'For working too hard?' she clarified.

'It's nearly the end of December,' Alan said, as if this explained everything. 'Anyway, it's the long-awaited sweepstake. How many Cadbury's Heroes can Sonil fit into his mouth in one go!'

Orla shook her head. What was it with Alan and his need to make a challenge out of every event on the calendar? Last month, allegedly for Movember, he'd made everyone grow cress heads with moustache cut-outs and there'd been a prize for the thickest one. After a particularly intense meeting she'd been starving and had ripped the cress from hers and eaten it. She picked up the pen. 'Sonil doesn't celebrate Christmas.'

'That's the beauty of it, though,' Alan continued. 'Cadbury's Heroes aren't just for Christmas, and it makes it an inclusive event for him, doesn't it?'

There was so much wrong about that sentence, but Orla didn't have any energy to unpick it. She had already promised that after work tonight she would take her sixteen-year-old sister, Erin, for some extortionately priced coffee at the place their mother said 'exploited the youth of today' and 'did nothing but encourage rich rivalry'.

She wrote a number down on the paper and passed it back to Alan.

'Fifteen!' Alan exclaimed in horror. 'Are you sure you don't want to guess something else? I don't think you're considering the length of those miniature Twirls.'

'Well,' Orla began, eyes already back on her computer screen. 'If you really want me to make my guess based on the science of it, I'd have to ask whether the sweet selection was random or pre-determined. And who is making that choice because then they have to be completely neutral in the contest and it absolutely cannot be Sonil.'

In the reflection of her computer screen, she could see that Alan had not thought about any of these things and, now someone had pointed them out, the likelihood was he was imminently going to go home with a migraine to rethink the whole thing. She was about to luxuriate in a few seconds of joyful abandonment as Alan backed away, when her mobile erupted. It was Erin. What could her sister want now when they were going to be meeting in less than an hour? She picked up.

'Hello.'

'Bruh, do you think blonde highlights would suit me?'

'Sorry, what did you call me? This is your sister, not Central Cee.'

'Answer me, 'cos hair appointments in December are like table reservations at Club Class.'

Club Class was the latest night spot everyone wanted to be seen at. Their mother called it 'tits and ass' and Erin was banned from going there or anything like there since her not-known-about tattoo was exposed on the club's social media and their dad's old building crew had made him aware. And there was also the fact she was only sixteen and shouldn't have ever been going there in the first place.

'Erin, we're seeing each other in approximately fifty-six minutes, can't we talk about it then?'

'Yes or no?'

'I don't know.'

'I didn't give you that as an option. Yes, or no?'

'Aren't highlights expensive?'

'Boring and still not a yes or a no. Quick!'

Now Orla felt like she was in the middle of a countdown on a gameshow with the top cash prize about to slip through her fingers.

'What happens if you don't like it?' Orla answered. 'You know your hair as it is, right? You know it and you're comfortable with it and it looks nice. I'm not saying a change wouldn't look nice too, but if it's a lot of money and—'

She was cut off by the dial tone that said this conversation was over. Erin had hung up. Rude, yes, but not unusual. Orla returned her mobile to her desk and then jumped in her seat. Standing right behind her was Frances, her boss. Erin knew from the look on her face that Frances had heard enough of the conversation to know it wasn't work-related.

'Not interrupting anything, am I?' Frances asked, that look of superiority on her face Orla had rarely seen her without since the day she'd joined the magazine.

'No,' Orla said quickly. 'A cold caller. Very cold actually. Very demanding of my attention. Had to cut them off.'

'And give them hair advice,' Frances said. 'That was way too kind.'

Orla just smiled and hoped Frances would move on. Her boss had a piece of paper in her hand.

'And talking of kindness...' Frances continued.

Oh no. This meant this was a donation to charity moment and Orla had zero paper in that respect until she visited a cash point.

'You're going to France. Tomorrow. Think of it as a pre-Christmas treat.'

'What?' Orla said, not really computing any of the sentence she'd just heard.

'Could be the biggest scoop of the year that GMB would probably want live in between a shouty politician and the latest comedian doing something ridiculous for a good cause. Equally, it could also be nothing, but it's intrigued Roger enough to sign off on the flight, and your time so...'

Orla was still none the wiser. 'Did you say tomorrow? Where in France? For how long? I mean, I haven't actually finished the article on the Greek otters yet.' Her interest was piqued at the words 'biggest scoop of the year' though.

'OK, Orla, perhaps I haven't been clear.' Frances leaned in close, a little too close perhaps. 'You are on a flight in the morning. The woman was very insistent – over the last three or four weeks actually, insistent that she wanted *you* to do the interview, quoted from your article about ice fishing. But then, this morning, she dropped the real clincher. There's a pregnant reindeer, due to give birth at any minute. So, I want the interview with the mute guy, I want photos and video of that four-legged furry and I want it done and dusted and on the website for Christmas Eve with the hope the baby drops out in alignment with the nativity story. We need the traffic. We need the subscriptions. And I need to end this year on a high!'

Had she said 'cute guy' or 'mute guy'? This wasn't sounding very Pulitzer prize now. It was actually more in line with someone a lot less senior at the magazine, surely!

'You want me to stay until a reindeer gives birth,' Orla said. 'And it's imminent, but it might not be until Christmas Eve? But, that means I won't get back for Christmas Day and I have plans for Christmas Day.'

'Oh, I know,' Frances came back. 'Those same plans you have every year. Well, apart from, let me see, was it 2019 you had that ridiculous turkey en croute and lunch was served two hours later than Bradbee tradition? Turkey emoji, laughing with tears emoji, wind emoji – not sure what that one means without a sprout emoji, if that's even a thing.'

Orla couldn't stop her mouth from falling open. She knew Frances came into any battle forewarned and forearmed, but she'd stalked her Christmas Facebook posts to see she got up to nothing but the same thing every year?!

'I… don't know what to say,' Orla said. Perhaps she could suggest giving the job to someone else?

'Good,' Frances said. 'I've emailed you the details – the subject heading is "don't fuck this up".' She waved the piece of paper in her hand. 'And now to this.'

She planted the A4 sheet on Orla's desk and grabbed a pen from the pot. Was this going to be more details that weren't in the 'don't fuck this up' email? Perhaps background info on the pregnant reindeer or the alleged cute guy or, better still, something that warranted the magazine sending one of its most senior reporters to France so close to Christmas?

'It's a sweepstake,' Frances informed her. 'How many Cadbury's Heroes will Sonil fit into his mouth before he chokes and needs medical attention?'

Orla looked at the form. Rita had guessed twenty-five. Samuel had said thirty. 'But this is—'

'Just a little riskier than Alan's fun, right? And Sonil does deserve a bonus this year, if you know what I mean.'

Orla didn't know whether to feel appalled, marvel at the ingenuity, or worry for Sonil on every count. But, apparently, what she should be thinking about was packing a cabin case for another country...

She picked up the pen. 'How much have you bribed him with?'

'Hush, Orla, that's a scandalous suggestion.'

'Well, I'll need a ball-park figure if you really want me to pay for a guess and fly to France in the morning.'

Frances's expression said she was mentally assessing the question and wondering if there really was a chance that Orla wasn't going to head to the airport *tout de suite*.

'I might have offered him 20 per cent more than Alan's bonus. And reassured him I have the ambulance service on standby. That's all I'm saying.'

'Fine,' Orla said, writing her guess in the column next to her name. 'But if this email doesn't give me all the details I need for the trip, I will be using WhatsApp and I will be expecting your prompt reply.'

'WhatsApp away,' Frances said. 'I'll reply. But after my brother has opened whatever flavour Baileys is en vogue this year I can't guarantee the quality of the copy.'

Orla nodded, knowing that, sadly, it was about as good as she was going to get.

## 2

'How many calories are in a flat white again?'

'Does coffee even have calories?'

That sentence earned Orla such a disparaging look from Erin it could probably have turned her to stone if she hadn't looked away. She changed her focus to the twinkling lights making everything gleam with prestige at this uber-contemporary coffee shop where it seemed even the steam came out in elegant bursts, rather than something from Thomas the Tank Engine's funnel.

'I was being serious,' Erin reiterated, her eyes now grazing the menu on her phone – no paper here, just a QR code to zap. 'I'm trying to make sure I fit into the size eight dress I bought that won't quite do up at the minute.'

'Why didn't you just buy a size ten?' Orla asked.

'Are you a hundred like Mum?' Erin said accusingly. 'Why would I do that when the other size almost fits and that's the size Danica and Tania bought in colours that look aesthetic together?'

Orla had no answer. She had never thought the ten-year age gap between them was that much, but it seemed she had little idea how to converse with Erin and her generation without sounding like she was Mary Berry describing a thriving garden and pairing it with a festive trifle.

'I'll just have an Americano. And don't get milk. Ooo... and I'll have a triple chocolate muffin, if *you're* paying.'

'I'll have the same,' Orla said. 'Do you want to order it on there and I'll give you my card to pay and—'

'Done. I used your PayPal,' Erin said, putting her phone on the table, screen down.

'Oh,' Orla answered. She was going to follow it up with asking if Erin used her PayPal account a lot, but challenging her sister never worked well if she wanted her to open up. And a text from their mother between the chocolate sweepstakes, reading Frances's France email and buying some 100 ml liquids in Superdrug had suggested that Erin was hiding something more than her appearances at Club Class and Orla had been tasked with trying to find out how deep she was in with a guy on Insta.

'So, have you ordered the turkey yet?' Erin asked, picking up her phone, looking at the screen, then putting it right back down again.

A chill ran down Orla's spine. She wasn't in charge of buying the Bradbee's turkey. She had done it last year. This year it was Auntie Bren's turn, wasn't it?

Then Erin burst into fits of laughter. 'Oh my God, your face! I thought you were gonna piss yourself. You haven't, have you? 'Cos that's what old people do. I loaned Auntie Bren my phone for ten minutes last Christmas and I was served ads for Tena Lady for weeks.'

It wasn't funny. But it was presenting her with an opportunity to address the fact there was a chance she might not be back for the annual festive lunch, the Boxing Day Banana Bonanza and the New Year New Stew evening...

'Actually,' Orla began tentatively. 'I'm probably not going to be at Christmas dinner this year.'

Erin laughed again. 'Sorry, what? That's better than any joke out of the Poundland crackers. Wait, that doesn't make sense. They were shit.'

'I mean it. I have to work.'

'You've had to work before. One time you were actually working and Mum poured custard on your laptop.'

She sighed heavily. 'I have to work away.'

'You were working away hard when Mum poured custard on your laptop.'

'I mean... I'm not going to be in the country.'

Now she watched her sister's eyes light up like they could take centre stage in a festive display. 'You're leaving the country? Is it Dubai? Tell me it's Dubai.'

'It's not Dubai.'

'Where then? Bora Bora? Thailand at least?'

'It's France.'

'Oh my God! Paris! Well, that's it! I'm coming with you! I'll need more clothes, acrylics and a Brazilian!'

'Erin—'

'Wait until I tell Burim. It has to be a lot easier to get to France than here, right?'

*Burim?* Was this the guy their mum was worried about? She should be trying desperately to dull Erin's excitement, because there was no way her little sister was coming with her – and it wasn't Paris she was going to either – but maybe she could use this current travel effervescence to her advantage...

'So, Burim, you... haven't told me about him,' Orla said as their drinks and muffins arrived.

Erin shot her a straight look. 'How do you know Burim is male?'

'What?'

'Well, it's not like I just said "David", is it? Burim could be a female name, so why did you assume it was male?'

Orla always seemed to underestimate exactly how whip-smart her sister was. But, in her defence, Erin did tend to go from going full-on dreamy eye-lash-lifted eyes over anything the colour pink to laser-focussed-on-the-details top barrister in a miniscule amount of time.

'*Is* Burim female?' Orla asked.

'Are *you* asking me? Or is Mum?'

Damn, she was good. And, as a journalist, Orla ought to sharpen up her ability to get people to divulge things they hadn't planned to. *Travel in Mind* magazine was an eclectic mix of *National Geographic* meets *Time* with a spattering of *Condé Nast Traveller*. Although, this past year, most of her features had been about places or animals, not people. She'd been getting to the heart of heathlands and the apex of the animal kingdom, finding those unique stories that made their magazine stand out amongst its peers. Perhaps if she focussed much more on the pregnant reindeer than the mute man, it would be more in her comfort zone...

'You don't have to answer that,' Erin said when Orla hadn't immediately replied. 'I saw Mum's message to you earlier.'

'You read Mum's messages,' Orla exclaimed, a whole catalogue of things she had sent her mum about Erin raining down on her mind like the stringy ribbons from party poppers.

'Who doesn't have an app that reads people's messages these days?' Erin rolled her eyes.

'I don't,' Orla replied. 'Because that is an invasion of privacy.'

'As is Mum getting all pretending like she cares over someone I'm in a situationship with.'

'So, Burim *is* a guy.'

'Sorry, do you even know the word "situationship"?'

'I'm aware of its meaning and that it's usually not of a platonic nature. I also know it's generally ended by the guy who, five messages before, has called you "ml" and said he hopes you sleep well and the rest of the chat is the girl saying "good morning", "wyd", "is everything OK?", "have I done something wrong?" until we get to "Merry Christmas" and "Happy New Year" when eventually she dries her eyes, picks up her self-respect and moves on.' She took a breath as all those oh-so-relatable phrases she'd just spewed out gave her flashbacks.

Erin looked impressed. 'That was so accurate to what Marla's been through at least seven times now.'

'Erin,' Orla said. 'Mum's worried you're spending a lot of time focussed on Burim and not concentrating on college.'

'Mum should spend less time poking her nose into what I'm doing and more time focussing on Dad and his drink problem.'

'What?'

'Hmm,' Erin said, picking up her coffee. 'I bet she didn't tell you anything about that, did she? Got so drunk last week he fell down the steps outside the chip shop and ended up in A&E with concussion.'

Orla knew her dad liked a few pints at the weekend with his friends and there was nothing wrong with that. Everyone did it, didn't they? And who hadn't had a little slip of their footing when on a night out? It usually happened right before kebab sustenance was required then on to the Uber home.

'Well, Keith can go a bit over the top on their nights out and he encourages Dad to try drinks he isn't used to,' Orla reminded.

'Oh, sorry, didn't I say? This was ten in the morning. Keith was probably at work. You know, the thing our dad doesn't do any more because he took early retirement?'

Shit. Why hadn't her mum told her anything about this? This

was far more urgent than Erin talking to a guy on Insta. Then she had a thought: maybe that was why she'd been sent down this rabbit hole, as a distraction technique.

'I know what you're thinking,' Erin whispered like she was a conspirator in a government overthrow plot. 'You think Mum has given you the task of asking about Burim as a distraction technique from the real shit that's going down with Dad.'

'No,' Orla said immediately. 'Of course not.'

'Ha!' Erin replied. 'Not even the muffin believes you.'

And how had she lost control of this conversation? She was finding out nothing from Erin, she now had a new problem to worry about and tomorrow she was heading to France.

Erin bit into her muffin and smiled. 'So, as Mum hasn't been honest with you either, we should put that boring shit to one side and plan a little stop in Primani after here. I could do with one of those cropped puffa jackets, but furry – perfect-Paris-chic-meets-UK-drip.'

Orla didn't know how to respond so she simply bit into her muffin too.

## 3

'Thanks, Orla.'

Erin had said this through a mouthful of hot chips covered in vinegar that were currently making *her* eyes water on the walk from the bus stop to the family home on the outskirts of Ruislip. Orla had had no plans to visit her parents tonight, but what Erin had said about their dad had worried her. There was no way she could leave for France without attempting to address it. And trying to get more information out of her sister had already cost her a furry puffa jacket, fake eyelashes, a Kylie Jenner lip kit and the chips...

'Call it an early Christmas gift as I might not be here,' Orla said, watching her breath dance in the cold of the winter air. There was still a chance she could be in and out of France in no time. If the mute man really had nothing to say and the reindeer had a premature birth. She needed to know how long reindeer were usually pregnant for... But where were the real guts to this story? At the moment it just sounded so *The One Show* rather than *Planet Earth*. And it definitely didn't sound like it was going to be *the* breakthrough story she wanted to put on her résumé and email off to *Time* magazine.

'What, so, you haven't got me any other presents?'

'Erin!'

'Just kidding. I know how disorganised you are. That and the fact you almost burst a kidney when I mentioned the turkey earlier.' She laughed.

They arrived outside the house and it was in complete darkness, like no one was home. It wasn't unusual. Both their parents were on the wear-three-jumpers-and-gloves-before-the-heating-gets-switched-on side of frugal and all unnecessary energy went off between May and October regardless of the layers concept. However, Christmas was different. That was when the lights were strung up outside and their mum did everything she could to make their home the festive showstopper of the street.

'Where are all the lights?' Orla asked Erin.

'Oh,' Erin said, biting into a chip. 'She'll be sat around some fragranced tealights that probably cost more than having the electric on. Helen has one of those parties every month and Mum feels compelled to buy something so no one thinks we're poor.'

Were they poor? Were their parents struggling financially since their father took early retirement? The golden handshake was supposed to be weighty enough to see them to the grave even if they outdid the Queen's ripe old age.

'No, the Christmas lights,' Orla clarified. 'It's December. They're always up on the first of December no matter what day that falls on and no matter what the weather.'

'Yeah, well, do you want Dad up a ladder when he's pissed dangling from a winking snowman?' Erin asked. She pushed open the gate. 'Are you coming in?'

Orla didn't really have time. There was still so much to do

before her flight... like look into exactly what time the flight was and where she was actually going. But she stepped forward.

Erin stopped her. 'A few things before we go in. *Don't* mention *Sky Sports. Do* mention Mum's hair, but you have to say it looks nice when really it looks like someone plugged her into the National Grid. And if Dad's in there just... let him sleep.'

Now her sister's fierce outer coating was cracking just a little, like an iPhone screen protector – signs of destruction but still holding it together. Before Orla could make any reply, Erin strode towards the front door, chips in the crook of her elbow, key in the lock and turning.

The very first thing Orla noticed when she stepped into the hallway – apart from the darkness – was it was actually colder *inside* the house than on the street. She put a hand to the radiator – lukewarm at best, but at least it was on.

'OK, well, good luck,' Erin said, back to munching her chips and beginning to mount the stairs.

'What?' Orla said. 'Where are you going?'

'To my room. I've got people to speak to, to let them know I'm gonna be in Paris soon.'

Shit. She hadn't actually clarified that she wasn't going to Paris and that Erin was in no way able to come on this trip.

'Erin, wait, listen—'

'I'll message you later.' The response was accompanied by Erin's Nike Air Force trainers thumping up the stairs and then the door to her bedroom slamming shut.

'Erin! What have I told you about slamming doors?'

Orla jumped as her mum, Dana, appeared in the hallway from the lounge. She wasn't sure if it was in reaction to the shout or to the new hairstyle that did look like a poodle had been weaved with Russell Brand. Nice things, she had to say nice things...

'Oh, Orla, what are you doing here?' Her mum put a hand to her chest like Orla's appearance was as crazy as someone turning up with a National Lottery winning cheque.

'Your hair looks great,' Orla said, a little too fast.

'Your sister told you to say that, didn't she? Where's she gone? Because I want a word with her about your dad's favourite beer glass.'

'She's... on the phone,' Orla said, suddenly feeling the need to protect Erin as their mum looked like she was about to mount the stairs.

'Of course she is,' Dana answered. 'It would take surgery to remove that thing from her hand; it's like a second palm.'

Her mum retreated back through the living room door as if the conversation was over. Until... 'Are you coming in here or not? Because I don't want to leave this door open.'

Orla took a deep breath and then followed her mum's path. But what lay beyond the door stole the air from her lungs. The living room was nothing like the last time she had visited only four weeks ago. It was practically bare. Gone was the large dresser that had housed her grandmother's china, absent was a chaise longue Dana had bought from an antiques fair and re-covered, and where was the DVD player?

'Don't stand on ceremony, Orla. Sit yourself down,' her mum ordered.

On the one chair remaining or squeezed up to her mum on a two-seater sofa she had never seen before? What was going on here?

'Mum,' Orla began, opting for the chair. 'Where has all the furniture gone?'

'You mean that old cabinet and those ancient plates of your grandma's?'

'Yes.'

'It took up so much space! You get Bren in this room as well as all of us and you're fighting for room like cats in a litter tray.'

'But, Mum—'

'And that sofa thing I bought *years* ago was practically threadbare.'

'You re-covered it.'

'And what a waste of time that was. Now, tell me, do I need to get a fancy Waitrose trifle this year or will a Bird's one do? I was thinking we could mix it up a bit and get raspberry.'

'Mum,' Orla said. 'What's going on?'

'I don't know what you're talking about,' Dana said, hands in her new hairdo. 'What's wrong with raspberry? Or is that the latest mid-life crisis trigger word or something?'

She had no other choice but to get straight to the point. She knew her mum liked to do a word dance around difficult topics but now she'd seen with her own eyes that there were issues here, there wasn't time to skirt around them.

'Mum, Erin says Dad has a drink problem. And, I don't care what you say, you loved that dresser *and* the chaise longue. So, I'm asking again, what's going on?'

Dana opened her mouth to reply and Orla waited for the torrent of words about anything other than the big question she'd asked. Except that didn't happen. Instead her mum sat very still, her mouth open, but nothing coming out. This was bad.

# 4

Orla could count on one hand the number of times she had seen her mum cry. Three funerals and one very bullish parent/teacher meeting at Erin's school. Dana Bradbee was not a crier. But the tears were soaking her cheeks before Orla could get off the chair and make moves to put her arms around her. She had hesitated though, hadn't committed to it, knowing the show of physical affection would likely make her mum batten the hatches rather than the other way around. Instead, she had offered a cup of tea. There was a bottle of Baileys next to the kettle and although Orla was tempted, alcohol was not the solution right now. It also set to remind her of Frances and France. How was she going to break that to her mum now? Maybe she could embellish the assignment a little. Make it sound like it had some kind of gravitas...

'Here we are,' Orla said, holding the steaming mug out to her mum.

'I'm all right. Don't make a fuss.'

'It's just a cup of tea,' Orla said. 'No fuss.'

'I hate tears,' her mum said, wiping her eyes with a tissue. 'Such a waste of energy.'

'Well,' Orla said, sitting down next to her mum. 'Some people find it therapeutic. To get the negative feelings out.'

'Soothsayers.'

'So,' Orla said, not wanting to lose what momentum she had. 'Is Dad really struggling with alcohol?'

Her mum sighed. 'I'm not sure, to be honest. I thought it was a phase, you know, boredom after the greenhouse project and the brief spell as a Yodel driver, but then, money started to get tight. And I know your sister's beauty regime claws away at the budget but I'm not going to have a child of mine not having what everyone else has and being bullied for it, so I indulge it to a certain degree by making personal sacrifices. Except for the luxury of the scented candles but that's to give Helen a boost, you know.'

Orla swallowed. She'd had no idea about any of this. Why hadn't her mum told her before things had got to this crying point? Or had she missed signs?

'Have you asked Dad about it all?'

'Are you mad? What do you think he'd say? "Oh, my love, yes, it's true, I can't get through the day without a tot of Captain Morgan's at dawn, the rest of the crew throughout the day and a final Famous Grouse before I turn in for the night."' Dana sighed, 'And he doesn't acknowledge that money is tight. He says it's a lean spell, then mumbles things about pensions maturing.'

'But ignoring it isn't going to solve anything. It isn't just going to go away.'

'I wish it would.' She sighed. 'Because worrying about a beautiful sixteen-year-old girl who's just ripe for being taken advantage of is hard enough as it is.' She raised her eyes to meet Orla's. 'Did you ask her? About the Moroccan?'

'Burim's Moroccan?'

'Ah! Is that what he's called?'

She suddenly felt she had been duped into giving up a secret. 'Does he live in Morocco?'

'Not a clue,' her mum replied. 'Let's be honest, he could say he lived anywhere, that he's called anything, it wouldn't be the truth. I read an article that said 85 per cent of men on social media tell lies within the first three messages. So you have "hello" and "how are you?" and then it's straight down to "I've never seen a girl as pretty as you before". Utter bollocks.'

Orla swallowed, ripples of her last situationship playing on her mind. Henry. Someone she'd given months of her online life to. Another failure. The dating game wasn't so much of a game any more, it was more like full-on warfare where it seemed everyone was your enemy, even the person you were legitimately trying to get to know. How did that work?

'Maybe *you* could speak to your dad.' The topic had turned again.

'Me?' Orla said, like the idea was as crazy as eating mussels with their shells still on.

'You've always had that way about you that says "friendly" but with an undercurrent of "serious" that you can't miss.'

Had she? And did her mum mean in confrontation or all things? Now she was starting to overthink the whole of her personality.

'I don't think I'm the one who's best placed to raise the topic,' Orla answered.

'And now you've gone BBC newsreader on me.'

'No, but I'm not here all the time like you are and I'm going away tomorrow so—'

'You're what?' Dana cut in, tea almost sloshing into her lap.

Orla hadn't meant to drop it quite like that. She sighed. 'I've been given a last-minute assignment and—'

Suddenly her mum's eyes widened, and the tea mug was

quickly dispatched to the one table that used to be part of a nest of three... 'This is it, isn't it? This is the assignment you've been waiting for. The one that's going to get you to *Time* magazine and New York! Oh, Orla, this is big news! The biggest! Much more important than a few silly drinks too many and Dad getting a bonk on the head, because I expect your sister told you that too!' She finally drew breath. 'I always knew you'd get there! Always knew it! Your sister got all the beauty but you got all the brains! This is something to be celebrated!'

As Dana bounced up out of her chair and took a couple of steps towards the mantelpiece Orla ignored the backhanded compliment and knew she should stop this train of thought before it pulled into a station. Because on first email glance, this trip to France was the very opposite of something that was going to further her career dreams. In fact, it had all the potential to be a nightmare. 'Mum, it's not exactly—'

'Look!'

A switch was flicked and Orla's gaze was drawn to one string of white fairy lights now glowing across the family photos and a resin duck ornament Erin had made in pre-school.

'I know they don't seem much,' her mum said. 'But they change rhythm – there's twenty-nine different settings. I don't know why there's not thirty but there we are. Oh, Orla, you're making me so proud. Just knowing you're really on your way now is making everything seem a tiny bit brighter. Maybe I will call the doctor in the morning, see if she can have a chat with your dad, perhaps make up some middle-age check-up he should have and get to the root that way.'

'That sounds like a good idea, Mum. But this assignment, it's—'

'So, tell me more about it, if you're allowed to that is. But, if you can't tell me everything now, make sure you get the go-ahead to tell everyone all the details over Christmas dinner because Bren's still crowing that her godson's daughter got into Cambridge and I swear the length of time she's been talking about it, the degree must be done by now.'

And, after that sentence, Orla knew there was no way she was going to be able to miss Christmas dinner at home this year, no matter how long the reindeer took to give birth.

# 5

## SAINT-CHAMBÉRY, FRANCE

Jacques Barbier could always tell when he was being watched. Call it a survival instinct. Whether the watcher had malintent or not, it didn't matter. Any kind of attention whereby someone felt the need to look and not be seen to be looking warranted your guard going up. It didn't often happen when he was between the aisles of this convenience store/café though. Ordinarily, this was one of the places he felt most comfortable. Except now, as well as feeling eyes on him, he could hear whispered voices. There was only one thing for it. Grabbing a tin of chopped tomatoes from the shelf, he whirled round at speed and held the can in the air like he might be about to launch it somewhere.

Shop owner Delphine gave a shriek and Gerard, the owner of the one bar in town, who was standing next to her, dropped a carton of *jus de pomme* to the floor. The apple juice started to leak out, but instead of anyone dropping to attend to it, Jacques was statuesque, staring at the pair and they were solemnly looking right back at him wearing the kind of expressions that told him he *had* been the subject of their hushed talk.

'Are you going to throw the tomatoes?' Gerard asked eventually. 'Because, if you are, could you aim for something other than my left knee? My arthritis is playing up again.'

Jacques looked at the tin in his hand and wondered what he had been thinking picking it up in the first place. This wasn't the forest and this pair weren't bears. They were civilised people. People who had been nothing but kind to him since he had arrived here with nothing but a backpack and a whole lot more mental baggage two years ago now. He placed the tin back where it belonged and looked to the contents of his shopping basket. What was he thinking about the things he'd put in here too? Bread, OK. Cheese, also OK, but he'd been indulgent about the type today. Muesli, no; he liked it, but it was full of hidden sugars. But this was worse, a particular brand of biscuits. Square. Plain on one side, thick chocolate on the other. He could almost taste them. He picked them out of the basket, looking at them like *they* might be his latest enemy.

'Are you going to throw those instead?' Gerard asked. 'A wiser choice. Less chance of anything breaking. Produce… or flesh.'

'No one is throwing anything,' Delphine said, bending to pick up the juice that had fallen from Gerard's hands. Jacques noticed the lack of fluidity in the movement, the slight jar in the woman's rise and fall. Was she suffering with her hips again…?

Jacques put the basket down on the ground and before Delphine got to the carton, he picked it up for her.

'I will pay for this,' he told her, handing it back to her.

'There is no need,' Delphine said quickly. 'I will tip what is left away. No problem.'

'I said I will buy it,' Jacques insisted. He took it back from her and before she could protest any further he put the carton to his mouth and began swallowing the rest of its contents.

'I do not know what is wrong with everybody today,' Gerard remarked as Jacques finished the juice and moved to put the empty carton into his basket. 'It is like people go crazy the day the Christmas lights are switched on.'

Jacques grunted. He didn't need another reminder about the annual festive light switch on. There were enough signs and posters from here to his cabin and beyond. There wasn't even civilisation beyond, but still there were notices pinned to trees, in case perhaps a family of racoons wanted to come along.

'They go crazy for my *sablés de Nöel* I hope,' Delphine said. 'I have made over a thousand of them.'

Jacques felt his mouth water. Perhaps there was one good thing about the Christmas light switch on: Delphine's exquisite shortbread cookies. Decorated by hand – some with icing, others with all variations of chocolate, nuts or sweets pressed into the top – he could probably eat a thousand of them himself.

'Will you save some for me?' he asked her.

'I am afraid I have already had people try to bribe me for them in advance, but you know the rules. Not until the ribbon is cut on the opening of the celebration fête do I start selling them.'

'Then I guess I will live without them,' Jacques replied, turning into another aisle and trying to remember what exactly it was he had made the trek here for.

His turn wasn't sharp enough to miss seeing the elbow nudge Gerard gave Delphine, however. This time he decided to ignore it and return to perusing long-life products so he didn't have to come here so often over the festive period.

'You're not coming?' Delphine exclaimed. Jacques could hear her footsteps quickening up behind him, sticky with spilt apple juice.

'Why would I come to something I do not like?' Jacques answered.

'But I am premiering my alcohol-free Christmas beer,' Gerard began, moving closer too. 'Like with Delphine's shortbread cookies, I cannot guarantee how long stocks will last.'

Jacques shrugged. 'Then I guess it will be something else I will live without. Now, please, can I shop in peace?' He hastened down the aisle. He was going to put the flat chocolate biscuits back on the shelf where they belonged.

'But you can't not come!'

The insistence in Delphine's tone gave him concern enough to turn around again. As if realising she had been too loud and too eager, she put her head down and her hands into the pockets of her apron.

'Why,' Jacques began, 'do I have to be there?'

'Delphine didn't mean you *have* to be there.' Gerard spoke quickly. 'Only that, you know, everyone in the village and the neighbouring villages will be here. And Pierre from Bousie... he is coming to do his world-famous walking-on-stilts performance.'

Jacques now didn't know if he should laugh or cry. Only this area of France would brag about having someone with an allegedly world-famous walking-on-stilts routine. It would be terrible. It was always all kinds of terrible. From the out-of-tune singing to the axe-throwing demonstration. And the latter always infuriated him because Luc did not know how to throw an axe properly at all.

'I feel my imagination has already filled in all the blanks that I might miss. But thank you, for thinking of me,' Jacques said, preparing to stride off again.

'Reindeer!' Delphine blurted out.

Why was he here? There was enough to do in and around his cabin. Why had he sought provisions instead of work and solitude today? He turned around.

'What?'

'Delphine,' Gerard said, seemingly with a note of caution.

'There is a reindeer. Coming here, tonight, to the fête,' Delphine continued.

'And you and the rest of the committee are going to let the village children pull at its ears and stick carrots up its nose for a few euro?' Jacques asked.

'No,' Delphine said. 'And last year that was only the sheep that tried to bite everybody.'

'I really am very busy,' Jacques said, looking at his watch.

'It needs to be looked after,' Delphine continued.

'Then the very last place it should be is the Christmas fête.'

'It is going to give birth!' Delphine blasted.

Her words ricocheted off the packets of flour, flavoured jellies, sponge cake bases and silver and gold edible decorative balls they were standing nearest to.

'What?' Jacques said.

'Delphine, let us leave Jacques to finish his shopping and if he feels he wants to come tonight then—'

'It cannot be about to give birth. Whoever has this reindeer is lying to you,' Jacques said, cutting Gerard off. Though he couldn't deny he was intrigued. Although Delphine didn't always get things completely right.

'No,' Delphine said with authority. 'It is true. The baby... the cub... whatever it is called—'

'A calf,' Jacques said.

'It is due to come out... very soon,' Delphine concluded.

Jacques eyed her with suspicion. Her hands were out of her apron now, fingers of one hand toying with the other. He turned his attention to Gerard.

'You know about this?' Jacques asked the bar owner.

'Well... I...'

Gerard was looking decidedly nervous. Something was amiss

here. However, if there was an ounce of truth in the rumour he needed to know more.

'Reindeer calves are born in the summer,' Jacques told them both. 'May or June. Not December.'

Delphine was already shaking her head. 'I do not know about the planning of childbirth in the animal kingdom but what I can tell you is there is a pregnant reindeer coming tonight that needs your help and—'

'*My* help?' Jacques clarified.

'Wolf, apart from the vet in Grenoble, you are the only one who knows about animals.'

Wolf. *Le loup.* That was what he was sometimes known as here. At first a title he'd received for being crazy, weird, a loner. The man who'd moved to the mountains and lived in a tent, until he'd built his own cabin. But then slowly, almost as if he and they had both begun to thaw to his sudden appearance, the name was said less with jest, more good-naturedly. He sighed. But he still held back from village events, valued his peace. But, a pregnant reindeer in December was piquing his interest. Not a phenomenon perhaps, but unusual nonetheless.

'And, Gerard, you will need some help if there is a rush at the bar, yes?' Delphine continued.

'I... well... yes,' Gerard answered.

Jacques had made his decision. 'I will be here. For two hours and no more. I will help you, Gerard. And I will take a look at this reindeer. That is all.' He then strode away from them, down the aisle, at speed.

'The ribbon-cutting is at 6 p.m.!' Delphine called after him.

Already he was regretting it.

# 6

## LONDON GATWICK AIRPORT, UK

'So, what do we think? Black Opium? Or Good Girl?'

Orla was wondering if she was actually awake, or if all of this was some crazy nightmare she was going to be aroused from by her neighbour's Take That addiction that began through the walls at 6.30 a.m. every weekday. Surely she hadn't got up at 2 a.m. Definitely she could not have last night somehow agreed to take Erin with her so their mum and dad could have crisis talks. Absolutely she can't possibly have got Frances to sign off on a second seat on the plane. But the reality was, Erin was here. Currently waving tester perfume strips in front of her nose.

'I... don't know,' was the only reply Orla could muster. She really needed coffee, but she also knew if she mentioned that out loud, Erin was going to want Starbucks and in Erin's world, a simple Americano was not enough and every coffee had to be infused with syrup, chocolate, every seasonal flavouring the brand had to offer and very possibly edible glitter if it was an option. Suddenly two coffees were adding up to the price of a moderately generous festive gift for a loved one...

'Ugh! You're no good! What time is it?' Erin asked, grabbing another perfume bottle and a third stick.

'A-quarter-to-I-don't-know-what-the-hell-I'm-doing?'     She couldn't believe she had said that out loud.

'That was almost funny,' Erin replied. 'I like 3.30 a.m. Orla. Except she can't make a perfume decision.' She sighed. 'And it's like only five-thirty with Burim so I can't ask him either. And he wouldn't be able to smell them so he would judge it on the designer logos or just choose the most expensive.'

Now Orla's head was thumping, full of noise and energy and random snippets from the very sparse information she had about this upcoming trip that her mother now thought was her golden ticket to her dream job, a penthouse in Manhattan and Michelle Obama on speed-dial...

They were flying into Grenoble and being met by a driver who would take them to a village called Saint-Chambéry. It was so small it warranted only the faintest dot on the map. What wasn't absent were the lines that indicated mountain terrain and the dense patches of forest. It looked almost as remote as it got. Not that Orla had an aversion to remote. She had visited many challenging locations in her role as 'animals and anthropology' at the magazine, from a lighthouse in the middle of the ocean – home to a family who had never once left their cylindrical nest – to bedding down with beavers in Alaska. Since she had joined the publication, website hits on her articles were second only to the celebrity news pages and she really *really* wanted that number-one spot. Not easy in a world where gossip and fame were currently king. But if her articles could be the magazine's most popular content surely it had to lead to bigger things. And then she wouldn't have to maintain a half-truth just because her mother needed something to be enthused by while she fought her way through tough times, both emotionally and financially.

'Maybe I should get them both,' Erin said. 'And this one for Burim.' She was holding a silver bottle now that was shaped like a robot.

Financial tough times did not equate with spending a fortune on perfumes, even the airport discounted ones. And where was Erin getting her money from when she wasn't hacking into Orla's PayPal?

'Let's put them back and... get a Starbucks,' Orla suggested.

'Really!' Erin said excitedly, scrambling to place the perfume bottles back and almost knocking a stack of Dior off in the process. 'I didn't ask because we had coffee yesterday and I know you get a bit overwhelmed by all the options.'

Overwhelmed by how much the options cost really. But less than three bottles of designer perfume hopefully – unless Sir Keir Starmer had unleashed more cost-of-living hell she was oblivious to.

'Hey,' Orla said, nudging her sister's arm. 'I'm not a hundred like Mum.'

Minutes later Orla watched Erin suck at a hearty-something-cold-ending-in-'cino' while she nursed a plain-but-very-nice-and-badly-needed Americano.

'So, tell me about where we're going,' Erin said, straw leaving her mouth, thin layer of cream on her overlined lips that she had redone in the toilets when they'd arrived here. 'How many night-clubs? Cool places to be seen that I can Insta and make Tania and Danica jealous of?'

She had forgotten that Erin knew even less about this trip than she did now. Her sister, however, did know that they weren't heading to Paris. But how was she going to cope with rural-perhaps-bordering-on-wilderness?

'I mean, it's France, isn't it? Home of Mbappe and, mmm all the good chocolate and mmm Chanel.'

Or perhaps Erin didn't need to know exactly how far away from civilisation they were going to be just yet. And it could just be that it was exactly what her sister needed. Maybe there wouldn't even be constant 4G. It could be time to reset, spend days without connecting with anything but the environment.

'It's going to be an adventure,' Orla assured her.

'And I'm not going to have to... you know... rub myself with mud to make the local wildlife accept me as one of their own?'

She hadn't actually told Erin about that. That was something she had done in Namibia with warthogs. It meant...

'You read my article,' Orla said, unable to keep the surprise out of her voice. 'About the warthogs.'

'Calm down,' Erin answered, rolling her eyes. 'I might give your articles a quick skim after I've read about what the latest past season Love Islander has got up to.'

Ugh. *After* the celebrity gossip not before. Still, Erin showing interest in something other than fashion, brands and guys with tattoos was a good thing.

'What did you think?' Orla asked, sipping her coffee.

'That you're mental. That there's no way I'd cover myself in mud for anyone.' She sucked at her drink. 'But that when you're out there doing that weird stuff I think you're really sick.'

Orla smiled at the high praise.

'You know I don't mean ill, right? Sick as in—'

'I'm not a hundred like Mum,' Orla reminded her. 'I know what you meant. And, you know, you could work towards getting out there and doing your own kind of weird stuff.'

'Oh, I am, don't you worry,' Erin answered.

'You are? College is going well?'

'Ha, you're funny.'

Orla hadn't been aware she was making any kind of joke. 'No,

I mean, I know college work is tough, but you know you can always, I don't know, run things past me if you want.'

'You didn't do any of my subjects and it was many, many, *many* years ago, right?'

OK, there was way too much emphasis on the manys there. Orla knew there was ten years between them, but it wasn't ten centuries. But, also, she hadn't meant the subjects. College, for her, had been a fusion of study, difficult social elements to weigh up and navigate and the real beginnings of turning from just a teen to a full-blown adult. It had been a lot.

'It wasn't easy for me,' Orla admitted, cupping her hands around her coffee.

'Really? Didn't you get all As?'

'I got one A,' Orla said.

'And failed the others?' Erin laughed.

'No, but sometimes teachers put a lot of weight on performance and results and they forget that there are humans behind it all.'

That was at the heart of why she did what she did. She sought out the intricacies in behaviour – animal and human, the whys and the why nots – some of which never even had a definitive answer. It was the spirit of something that mattered most, not the results according to some often-manufactured worldwide agenda, wasn't it?

'Are you studying me?' Erin asked. 'For an article?'

Orla shook her head. 'No. Don't be silly.'

'Because forget the inside bits, I would make a great cover model, don't you think?' She pouted, the cream from the drink still on her top lip.

Orla went to reply but Erin quickly continued.

'We should take our drinks and check the board. We don't

want to miss the flight.' She got up, drink in one hand, trolley case handle in the other.

And that was how Erin Bradbee ended the conversation about college. Orla sighed. Well, it wasn't like she didn't have time to try again.

# 7

## SAINT-CHAMBÉRY, FRANCE

'You know what's gonna happen, right?' Erin began in a whisper. 'We are going to be taken to a log cabin and it's gonna be all hot chocolate and niceties until he turns... and the sweet middle-aged-man act is gonna drop and you and me are going to be killed like this ferrety weasel thing over my shoulder and he's gonna turn us into snow mummies.'

Erin gave a muted yelp as the rather unique vehicle they were travelling in bucked over what Orla assumed was a rut in the road. There might be the carcass of a dead something on the parcel shelf but Orla hadn't ruled out it being a shawl, no matter how anatomically incorrect that might be. But, so far, everything was as it should be. They'd been met at the airport by their driver, Gerard, as it had stated in Frances's email, and they were on their way to Saint-Chambéry where they were going to be staying at a small hotel with the name 'Delphine'. Once there, Orla's remit was to report on the pregnant reindeer and meet the mute man who had developed a special bond with the animal. She was already hoping the 'special bond' included a unique way of communicating, as she had experience with

Navajo Code and she'd found that fascinating. However, Frances had written:

I'm envisaging Vincent from *Lost* meets Rudolph the Red Nosed Reindeer and hoping the guy looks like Ian Somerhalder. Heart-warming, factual and sexy – the holy trinity.

'Shh,' Orla said to her sister, looking out of the window at their surroundings and glad for the Christmas music Gerard had put on over an hour ago.

'Shh?' Erin said in whispered shouting. 'It's freezing! I can't get internet *at all* and the friendly barman/postman/Santa's buddy or whatever he called himself is gonna murder us. Here. In this cold, cold place.'

Orla looked at Erin then, squished next to her in the back seat of this weird three-seat vehicle where their cases were in a footwell next to the driver's position. Was she seriously a little bit scared? Her sister had her acrylic nails between her teeth and Orla needed to remember that despite all Erin's swagger, she was still so young and obviously home was not currently the comforting sanctuary it was supposed to be. Perhaps Orla had a chance to provide some sisterly reassurance here in France, make her feel safe.

'Erin, everything's fine,' Orla said calmly. 'The very last place a murderer would take us is to where he lives and we're heading exactly where we're supposed to be going.'

'But how do you *know*? He could be driving away from where he lives *and* where we're supposed to be because everything looks the same. Look!' Erin put the flat of her hand to the window as if she was trapped in a transparent box.

Orla *did* look though, and it was spectacular. Towering fir trees as far as the eye could see, the road like a slippery white snake slithering a path through the density, craggy mountains specked with snow, white mist hiding their peaks. It was the epitome of a winter wonderland. Quiet, simple, but she knew the potential of what quiet and simple on the outside could hold. Maybe it wasn't so much what the brief of the assignment here was, perhaps it was more about what she could make it...

'I know,' Orla said to Erin. 'Because I'm following our route on Google Maps.'

'You have service?' Erin exclaimed, thoughts of murder temporarily forgotten.

'How long until we get to the village now, Gerard?' Orla asked, leaning forward a little.

'*Vingt minutes.*' He paused. '*Désolé.* I will speak in English. It is twenty minutes. It has to be twenty minutes because I have many things to do before the opening.'

'Opening?' Erin was leaning forward now too. 'It sounds like an event. Is there an event? Will there be a red carpet?'

'Erin, do you have your seat belt on?' Orla asked.

'Yes,' Erin said, tugging at the strap to prove it.

'I have blue carpet,' Gerard answered. 'Not red.'

'Sorry, Gerard, my sister just means what kind of event is it?' Orla asked, the car still bumping along.

'And will there be a DJ?' Erin added.

'Is first Christmas fête in Saint-Chambéry. We switch on winter lights. We eat. We dance. We drink my homemade beer. Everyone is happy.'

Erin flopped back into the seat, arms folded across her chest. 'Not everyone. Not me. Sounds lame.'

'Well, I heard eating, beer and dancing,' Orla said, nudging her sister's arm. 'And, I have the company credit card.'

'Really?' Erin said, brightening up considerably.

It *was* true, but she would have to account for each expense and use it sparingly, for necessities only. But Erin didn't need to know that in this particular moment.

'I think we are going to like the fête, Gerard,' Orla assured. 'Very much. *Trés beaucoup.*'

'Well, I hope there are enough cookies,' Gerard said with a grunt. 'We were only expecting one of you.'

Yes, she hadn't actually told anyone on this side of the Channel that she was travelling with a companion now and she hoped it wasn't going to cause problems. Surely whatever room Frances had booked would accommodate a five-foot-five, almost size eight, addition.

'And here we are,' Gerard announced almost twenty minutes later. 'The start of Saint-Chambéry. Here is the luxury spa hotel. Then, on the left there is the designer shopping village and modern mall.'

'Where?' Erin asked, body snapped into staying still by her seat belt.

Orla knew Gerard was joking but she also knew that wasn't going to go down well with Erin. They were not even at their final destination and she was already worried that Erin being here wasn't going to be easy.

'Ha! I am joking with you!' Gerard said, bursting into laughter as the steering wheel seemed to be swayed by the terrain.

Erin went very quiet. The worst kind of non-appreciation when it came to her. An annoyed and feisty Erin was always preferable to the silent version who was doing more thinking than shouting. *Reassurance.*

'Don't worry,' Orla whispered to Erin. 'I mean, I do have to work but if this village *is* as dead as a cemetery then I am certain we can find the nearest city at some point and have a night out.'

'Nearest city is Grenoble,' Gerard butted in. 'Where we have driven all this long *long* way from.'

Erin shifted in her seat, turned to completely face the window like she could be looking at a brick wall instead of a snow-festooned town. Knowing there was nothing she could say to help in this moment, Orla looked out of the other window as a few buildings began to appear. Most were wooden, like chalets, some on stilts. There were strings of lights hanging from their roofs, lanterns glowing amber and yellow, the only lights that seemed to just about differentiate the road from the not-road. But as they travelled, people began to appear, walking, wrapped up in thick coats, hats and gloves like burritos packed for the Ice Age. Orla had checked the temperatures before they left, but was now wondering if she had underestimated the clothing needs. A side-eye to her sister confirmed that Erin was wearing leggings just about fit for autumn in the UK not minus temperatures in the mountains.

'Oh, there is a roadblock,' Gerard announced, pulling the car to a rather skiddy halt.

'A roadblock?' Orla asked. One glance through the wind-screen showed old wooden barriers with orange beacons flashing on and off and two large men looking official standing in the way. Were they policemen? What was going on? 'Has there been an accident?'

'*Non*,' Gerard replied. 'It is the Christmas fête. No traffic in the village square. I thought we would arrive before this time but...'

'But?' Orla asked, hoping they were very close to where they should be or that their driver had a plan.

'But your plane came late,' Gerard reminded her. 'It is OK. I will park the car and we will walk.'

'Walk!' Erin exclaimed as though the word was really code for 'do a marathon'.

'I don't think snow is particularly good for pulling luggage,' Orla said, empathising with her sister. It was freezing. She needed to clarify the length of this walk before anyone opened any car doors. 'So, Gerard, how far do we need to go on foot because—'

Suddenly, the car was spun around like it might be about to take part in a high-octane street race and Orla's words were taken from her as she smashed into Erin.

'It is not far,' Gerard answered as he morphed into Charles Leclerc. 'You have good walking shoes, *non*?'

Why Orla felt the need to look down and check what she had on her feet as the car raced away from barriers, people and towards towering pines, she had no idea. But her usual not-anything-special trainers might not cut it if 'not far' was further than a catwalk runway...

'Orla,' Erin said through gritted teeth. 'I feel sick.'

Oh no! Suddenly Orla was cast back in time to a visit to the fair when her sister was eight or nine. Erin had suffered with motion sickness for a few years after a frantic fling-around on the Waltzers and Orla had never been able to look at popcorn in the same way ever again. But she had outgrown it, right?

'Stop the car,' Orla demanded. 'Erin, take a slow deep breath.'

'I... am trying to stop the car... it does not... seem to be working.'

Now Gerard sounded just a tiny bit panicked and Erin was doing a very good impersonation of a bleached sheet... There was only one thing for it.

Orla grabbed the handbrake and pulled on it hard. Instantly the car slipped into a sideways skid and suddenly there was something or someone now in their path. Big, black, getting closer. Orla was torn between taking the handbrake back off or grabbing the steering wheel from Gerard. Erin let out a shriek and then...

*Thump.*

The noise was loud, the impact hard, but suddenly the car was stationary and Orla realised exactly how quiet everything now was. The car engine was idling, Erin was silent apart from a few panicky breaths and Gerard seemed like he was dazed and confused as to what had occurred. But beyond all that Orla felt something was wrong. The dark apparition. Had they hit something? Hit *someone*? She was reaching for the door handle, unconcerned for the cold outside now.

Her trainers crunched down into snow that was a couple of inches thick but she barely noticed, eyes searching the darkness that was only less like night because of the bright white of the ground.

'Hello!' Orla called. 'Is anyone there?'

She couldn't see anything but snow, trees and the top of the mountain in the distance. They couldn't have slid that far away from civilisation. And where had the dark figure/thing gone? Now she felt the cold. It was already penetrating her apparently inadequate puffer jacket.

'*Où est ton chapeau?*'

Orla jumped at the sound of a man's voice, hand going to her chest.

'*Vous n'avez pas de gants?*'

What little French Orla knew consisted of the niceties of meeting someone and 'do you sell ice cream'. Neither were appropriate for now. She turned around and lost her breath to the freezing air. The man was huge. Tall, broad, dressed head to toe in black from his woollen hat to thick sturdy boots. He had some kind of wrap across his face, the only stand-out was his eyes. Large, deep, dark brown and staring at her.

'*Parlez-vous Anglais?*' She didn't know where she had remembered that from, but her GCSE teacher would have been proud.

'Yes, I speak English,' the man answered. 'I asked you where your hat and gloves are. You cannot be out in these temperatures without them here. In the centre of the village, maybe, especially tonight with all the crowds of annoying people, but definitely not here.'

She had a hat and gloves. In her case. Just not on her head or hands. And why was he talking about that when someone could be injured?

'What?' the man asked her, presumably because of the confused expression even *she* could feel she was wearing. 'Is my English not understandable?'

'No, I... I thought the car hit someone and—'

'Yes,' the man answered. 'It hit me.' With that said, he walked past her and around to the driver's side of the vehicle.

'Sorry, what?' Orla said, following the man. 'But you're... walking.'

'Yes,' the man answered as Gerard emerged from the car. 'Strangely enough I have been doing this since I was around a year old. And it never stops amazing me. The one foot in front of the other. The balancing.' He spoke in French to Gerard and Gerard replied. Orla had no idea what they were saying except the odd '*oui*' and a name – Jacques.

'But we hit you,' Orla said, breaking into their conversation. 'I heard the impact and—'

The two men started to laugh, still speaking in their native tongue, apparently finding this accident utterly hilarious. And now she really was feeling the cold.

'Fine!' she announced. 'Be rude! Be not injured! Just show me and my sister the way to walk to get to the hotel I'm meant to be staying in!'

More laughter and now it was starting to get on Orla's nerves.

'Right, well, thank you for the lift most of the way here, and the added hell ride at the end, but we will be fine from now on!' She wrenched open the back door. 'Come on, Erin, let's go.'

'Orla,' Erin mumbled as if she had something stuck in her throat.

The smell. The visual. Orla didn't need an explanation but Erin managed one anyway.

'I've been sick.'

## 8

Despite all her bullishness about being perfectly capable of walking out into the winter-near-wilderness on her own and finding her way, Orla was still not quite in the zone of what was happening right now. Her trainers were filling with snow, her feet both feeling like the straw in a Slush Puppie and her brain didn't seem to be working properly. Because, if her brain *was* working properly, she would have been finding the fact that a vomit-covered Erin was being piggy-backed by a stranger something to comment on. Instead, she was saying nothing. It seemed every bit of energy had to be conserved for simply existing in this environment. And she should have known this. She was not a rookie when it came to travelling to climate-challenged places! All she could do was blame the lack of preparation she'd made. Not her fault.

'Are you still alive?'

The question came from the stranger who was carrying her sister on his back.

'I... don't know,' Orla answered. Why had she said that? Apparently close-to-brain-freeze made you dumb.

'Ha! Very good. But at least you are now aware that death is always a possibility on this mountain.'

'What?'

This had come from Erin who had said nothing until now, even when the stranger had lifted her out of the car with one arm and hoisted her onto his back like she was a rucksack.

'You are inappropriately dressed for the weather,' the stranger reiterated.

'OK!' Orla exclaimed. 'We get it! But, to counter that, we did not know that the person picking us up from the airport was going to end up having no control over his vehicle, cause a collision and leave us to walk in these conditions.'

Gerard had remained in the car. He had already been wearing a base layer, two jumpers, a thermal coat and had produced a flask of something from the glove box. His preparation was much better than theirs. A vehicle was being sent to pick them up and go back for him but the stranger had already told them that staying still was not an option and they may as well begin the walk that was only a mile or so and they would flag down their aid when it appeared.

'Ah,' the stranger said, striding on like he wasn't carrying anything on his back at all. 'You are one of those people who blames everyone else for the situation they find themselves in.'

'What? No, I do not! I—'

'You are getting angry,' the man said, a hint of amusement in his tone as Orla tried to keep up with his lengthy steps.

'If you think this is angry then you are so, so wrong, believe me.'

'I am never wrong,' the man answered. 'So, we will see.'

'Now, wait a second—'

'She is getting kind of angry now,' Erin said, her arms around the neck of this man, face half buried in the hood of his coat. 'Her voice gets like a politician when they're spitting lies to cover their arse.'

The man laughed at Erin's comment and Orla could feel her body begin to fizz with annoyance. The laugh wasn't an unattractive sound, but it wasn't stopping. He was reacting like Erin was the best comedian who had delivered the killer one-liner to end all one-liners...

'Right, well, where's the vehicle meant to be coming to get us and where is this village?! The roadblock to secure the sanctity of the square can't have been this far away... and we didn't wheel spin for miles!'

The man stopped walking then, turning a one-eighty with Erin, until he was looking at her.

'Are you going to stamp your feet?' he asked. 'Scream until it echoes? Maybe cry a little? Boo hoo hoo?'

For the last sentence he had put on a voice akin to something someone might use if they were talking to a three-year-old or their most cherished teddy. Just how patronising was this Frenchman? And why was she even here when she should be in the office, in the warm, watching Sonil shove chocolates in his mouth until his airway was compromised! Because her boss had ordered her to. Because she'd had literally no choice in bringing her sister with her. Because her dad was struggling with retirement and possibly addiction and there were money issues. Because the universe was not currently giving her a break, it was giving her a pregnant freaking reindeer!

'Now I'm mad!' Orla shouted. 'I'm so mad! *Madder* than mad! I do not want to be here!' She then let out a ridiculous scream/shout, the likes of which had never left her before. And it *did* echo. And now she was breathing heavily, feeling that *whoosh whoosh* of her heart as it worked on whatever anger chemical she had unleashed.

'Good,' the man said with a nod. 'Anger will keep you warm.
But we need to keep moving, as I said.'

He turned around and began striding off again. Wait, what?
He had *purposefully* riled her to make her angry so she wasn't so
cold? Who was this guy? Before Orla could deliberate any longer,
she realised she would have to start making moves herself or risk
being left far behind. She tried a jog, easier said than done in
snow but it was getting her heart working.

'Do you know where Hotel Delphine is?' Orla asked, finally
catching up to the back of Erin and the man.

'*Hotel* Delphine?' he queried.

'Yes,' Orla said. 'It's where we are staying.'

'There is no Hotel Delphine,' the man answered.

'What?' Erin bleated.

'Yes, what?' Orla asked.

'It is as I said. There is no Hotel Delphine. There is Delphine,
the owner of the village store. That is all the Delphine in Saint-
Chambéry. Are you sure you have arrived at the right
destination?'

There were so many answers to that question and Orla was
getting more confused as to her remit here. As much as Frances
flew by the seat of her pants if it was necessary for a scoop, she
wasn't usually so lacking on critical details like a roof over her
employee's head in an icy landscape.

'I... don't know.' There was real doubt in her mind now. Not
about the destination – after all, Gerard had been waiting for
them as planned – but about everything else that came next. Feet
moving on autopilot, she looked to the mound that was her sister,
gripping on to the tall stranger's back, shivering. She had to take
care of Erin. Before anything else, no matter what this assignment was, her sister's well-being came first.

'Do not worry,' the man said, his voice no longer condescending. 'I am certain everything will be in order. Delphine, she will know where you are meant to be.'

Finally, a little bit of upbeat from Mr I've-Been-Hit-By-A-Car-And-Am-Apparently-Iron-Man.

'But, if she does not, then you really are in trouble.'

Great.

# 9

Idiotes. That was what these two were. Another couple of tourists here for the quaint Christmas village atmosphere and the skiing that was substantially more affordable than Aspen. In this current cold snap they would be lucky to even make it to the slopes without a blistering wind chill destroying their skin and going to town on the inside of their lungs. And Delphine knew they were coming? She hadn't mentioned she had visitors arriving and she knew how he felt about strangers, how he tried to avoid the tourist elements of Saint-Chambéry, kept a low profile. And where was Milo with the rescue car? They were in the village now, but someone needed to go back to Gerard. Jacques scanned the crowds, hoisting the girl on his back a little higher to keep his grip. Would Delphine still be in the store? Or had she already begun to man the stall where she would be selling the cookies?

'Wow, there's a fire!' the girl on his back remarked.

'Yes,' Jacques replied. 'It is where we put the tourists with bad coats close to to thaw out. Then, if that does not work, we destroy the evidence that they were ever here.'

He felt the girl shudder and was struck with a little remorse for his tone and his words. When had he got quite so blunt and brutal with everyone?

'Come,' he said, striding towards the thick orange flames licking up into the night sky. 'Let us get you warmer.' He looked over his shoulder. Where was the other one? He couldn't see her amid the growing groups of people in the square waiting behind a thick bronze ribbon. That stupid ribbon! It was always treated like it was some kind of religious icon, fête-goers almost bowing at its presence. Ridiculous!

'I... can't let anyone see my front,' the girl said, sounding like her teeth were chattering.

'What?'

'Where I was sick,' she continued. 'It's rank.'

'I do not know what that means, but I do know your mother was very thorough with the wet wiping before you left the car.'

He had thought that was crazy, standing in the cold, getting a packet of damp *mouchoirs* out and wiping more cold onto a jacket. Left alone, these two would be halfway to the ER already. Ironic as that was many, many miles away and they would never make it there on foot...

'My mother!' the girl exclaimed. Then she laughed.

'I have made a joke?' he asked her.

'Orla isn't my mum,' the girl answered. 'I know she looks dead old, but she's my sister. I'm the one our parents didn't expect. Our mum always blames the big bang theory and no one ever knows if she's talking about the TV show or not. I really hope she is.'

Jacques had no idea what she was talking about either but it was good to hear her talking. He had been worried by how quiet and pale she had been in Gerard's car.

'Are you ready to get down?' he asked her as they got to a

reasonably uncrowded area behind the rope cordon no one really took much notice of.

'If no one looks at the front of my coat,' came the reply.

He swung her down and steadied her as her trainer-clad feet hit the snow and she rocked a little, looking slightly unstable. 'OK?' he checked.

'I think so,' she answered, unconvincingly.

Where *was* the other woman? And, also, where was this pregnant reindeer he had been promised? He was beginning to think the whole thing was a ruse just to get him here in the midst of the community on one of the busiest nights of the year. He knew he should have been integrating a little more now but old habits died hard and there were always those dark memories at the back of his mind...

'Stand here,' Jacques ordered her. 'By the fire. Do not move. I will be back.'

He was going to get the girl a hot drink and then he was going to find the woman he seemed to have lost. Why was he even concerned? He had zero responsibility for any of this. And that was exactly what he had wanted when he'd moved here. It was just him, his dog, Hunter, and the mountain. He strode fast, towards the stall selling coffee and an alcoholic drink that tasted as bad as it smelled, which he had only ever had once. Then suddenly...

'Oh!'

Someone had walked into his path and sideswiped him and was now rocking on their feet. He acted quickly, pulling them towards him before they fell into the queue waiting for hot beverages. It took him a second to realise who it was. Who he was looking for. The sister of the smaller one.

'You,' he stated. 'What are you doing? And why can none of you tourists stand up in the snow?'

'You walked into me,' the woman replied. 'And now you're crushing my arm. Please let go.'

Jacques did as she asked and she stood still very briefly until her trainers seemed to disappear fast into a clump of snow and she was losing her balance again. He reached out to save her.

'I'm good!' she answered roughly, steadying herself and quickly planting her feet on more secure ground. 'Perfectly OK.'

She didn't look perfectly OK, she looked angry. Her eyebrows were narrowed over her large blue eyes. There was frost in her shoulder-length blonde hair. And then the look in her eyes intensified, quickly turning from mad to concerned.

'Where's Erin?'

'Who?'

'My sister,' she said. 'The person you had on your back and obviously isn't on your back now. You didn't leave her on her own, did you?'

'Relax,' he answered. 'She is fine. But she could use a coffee. I was just—'

She was moving now, pulling her feet out of the snow and making moves through the gathering crowd. He tutted and followed. This was the best plan. To reunite them while he found Delphine and got away from the whole mess of the situation. Except, as his eyes found the spot he had definitely left the girl, he realised she was no longer there. *Merde.*

'So, where did you say Erin was?'

The blue eyes were looking kind of accusing now.

'Just over there,' he answered and pointed in a very vague way. Simultaneously he was scanning the features of every person around, looking for the girl in the puffy jacket. *Come on, Jacques.* This was slack. But finding people in a crowd, recognising faces, it was one of his specialities. And he needed that ability to kick in fast now before the next question came.

'Over where?'

'Er, not far.' Where could she have gone? Yes, there was a crowd here, but it was scores rather than hundreds. And, with his skills, he should be able to pick out a tourist at this time of year from the others around.

'How far?'

'Just... a little further.' *Come on, Jacques. Look. Look hard.*

'There is no further,' the woman answered, sounding very concerned now. 'There is rope!'

*Merde. Merde.* Where was the girl? And why had she wandered off? He had left her where it was warm. Where she could regroup. No one here would have...

'Someone might have taken her.' The woman's words were almost whispered, like if she said them too loudly it would make them come true.

'No,' he answered with fierce reassurance. 'Not here. Saint-Chambéry, it is very nice.'

'You could say that about anywhere. Just because a place seems nice, doesn't mean bad things don't happen.' There was definite panic in her tone now. She was already drawing her phone out of her pocket. 'God! Is there *any* signal *anywhere* around here? I need to phone her! I need to find her!'

'There is no need to panic,' Jacques told her.

'Is there not? Because, so far, since I've been here, I've been in an RTA, walked in freezing conditions and now my sister is missing! I'd say I should have started panicking the minute I got off the plane!'

'Orla?'

The girl's voice sent a shot of relief down Jacques's spine. There she was, a steaming cup of something in her hands.

'Oh, Erin! Thank God! I thought you'd been taken by... wolves or... something worse.'

'Do not hug me!' the girl responded, drawing the drink towards her body as if to prevent contact.

'OK,' Jacques said, clapping his gloved hands together. 'You are reunited. *You* have a hot drink. I am out of here before Gerard turns into an ice sculpture.' He turned away from them. He was going to find where the hell Milo had got to.

'Wait!' the woman called. 'Which way is... Delphine?'

He turned around. 'Over there. The store.' He pointed and then took off again. He couldn't wait for this night to be over.

## 10

'Please, take another cookie before I put them on the stall!'

They were inside a grocery shop that seemed to double as a café at one end. Everything in here was made from wood, from the beamed ceiling, the shelves stocking household essentials and gift items – small pots of honey, soaps, deer milk – and the café tables and chairs. It was quintessentially Alpine.

'Can I have another two?'

'One, Erin,' Orla said as her sister reached out to the stack of beautiful and frankly delicious-smelling biscuits Delphine was holding on a wooden tray. They had found Delphine, no thanks to Jacques's vague finger-pointing, and Orla had quickly introduced them. The woman was in her late sixties, petite, short dark hair highlighted with just a little grey and big glasses on her face that kept slipping down her nose. She was also a bustler. She didn't seem to be able to keep still, energy flowing from her. It wasn't a bad thing, but it was a little frenetic given they'd just arrived.

'But I'm hungry!' Erin complained, a little colour back in her cheeks now.

And she *had* thrown up the Starbucks...

'I know,' Orla answered. 'But I thought we'd have a nice meal at one of the restaurants.'

'Oh!' Delphine exclaimed, glasses slipping down her nose on cue. 'There are only two restaurants in Saint-Chambéry and they are both closed tonight. Because of the fête.'

Of course they were. Orla forced a smile and imagined Frances around her indoor firepit sipping a Baileys and scrolling through TikTok...

Erin took two cookies and shoved one into her mouth in one go. 'These are so banging.'

'Could you help?' Delphine asked Orla. 'Bring some of the boxes out?'

'I'll take one,' Erin said, shoving in the second cookie and putting her hands around a box.

Orla frowned. That coffee her sister had had seemed to have not only restored her warmth of temperature but also of temperament. Perhaps *she* needed to have one...

'Could you open the door?' Delphine asked. 'I can only get through it with this tray if I turn to the side.'

'I'll get it,' Erin said, forging ahead with the box and bumping her back against the wood and glass frontage to open it. As her sister disappeared outside, Orla sensed Delphine holding back.

'I do not wish to appear rude,' Delphine began. 'But we were only expecting there to be one of you.'

'I know,' Orla said quickly. 'I apologise for that. I don't usually travel on work assignments with my sister, but there was a last-minute... family emergency and, well, this assignment itself was somewhat of a last-minute thing too so...' She left the sentence open ended as she picked up a box as well.

'So...' Delphine said, as if she wanted Orla to add more.

'Oh, well, I just meant that, you know, usually I have time to plan trips away for a bit longer than twenty-four hours and—'

'I have been in contact with your magazine for almost six weeks now,' Delphine interrupted. 'It was very difficult to get anyone to reply to me at all.'

'Oh, well, I apologise for that too but, well, I am here now and I can't wait to meet the reindeer.'

'And Wolf,' Delphine stated.

'A wolf? Gosh, I was only joking with my sister about wolves. Are there really wolves here?'

'Wolf is a person. I told the woman at your magazine all about him.' Delphine tutted and shook her head, her initial very friendly exterior melting somewhat.

'Ah, yes, the man who doesn't speak.' She offered a smile. 'I've not done an interview like that before but obviously I will give it a go and—'

'Good,' Delphine interrupted, the friendly smile back. 'So tonight you will both stay here. Tomorrow, I will take you to see Wolf. *Allez.*'

'Sorry, what?' Orla asked as Delphine barrelled out of the door at a hard right angle.

'Please, I am behind schedule and people are cold and hungry.'

Those were the last words Orla was obviously going to get for now as the woman whisked out into the night.

\* \* \*

'This place is wild!' Erin announced, waving a hand in the air as they gathered around the bonfire now the fête was officially open.

It had turned out that as well as being the owner of the only bar in Saint-Chambéry, Gerard was the mayor of the village and until he had been rescued from the car and given cognac, the fête could not begin until he cut the bronze ribbon. But then accordion music and guitars had filled the night, fireworks had gone off and the hubbub of chat and laughter had enveloped the village that looked like it was made of gingerbread. Despite the unorthodox beginning of their being here, the place was all kinds of winter magical and could have been photographed for centre space on a Christmas card. The fire was the focal point tonight, but south of that was a snow-speckled, cobblestone square with a fountain they had been told had been spurting mountain water up until this icy spell that apparently was going to last for a few more days at least. There were benches and fir trees decorated with strings of lights and a large wheelbarrow that seemed to be a particular focus for people to stop and pay homage. Orla had made a mental note to ask their host about that. There was also a beautiful small church made out of wood with a star glowing from the top of its steeple. She tuned back into her sister who seemed to be bopping to the Christmas accordion like she was front row at a Stormzy gig... It wasn't what she had expected, as Erin liked to moan about everything that wasn't absolutely perfectly curated to her.

She *was* on her third coffee though. And who knew what this French coffee was like. Erin was used to the kind with more cream than caffeine. Maybe Orla needed to watch her sister's intake, suggest water.

'I took some photos,' Erin informed her. 'Of the man with the funny hat playing the weird small piano that sucks in and out. And the Christmas tree. And the man on stilts. And the sausage stand.'

Orla was still making her way through her hot dog. It was one of those long, thick, bratwurst-style sausages that was seasoned with garlic and herbs, topped with caramelised onion and served in a proper crusty baguette. Right now she frankly had never tasted something so good.

'I would send them to Burim,' Erin carried on. 'But I have no signal. Like there's no Wi-Fi and there's no 4G. And if I don't check in with him soon he will call the emergency services.'

'I'm sure there will be Wi-Fi at Delphine's place. We'll just need the password.'

'Well, I might need to go and do that now,' Erin said, checking her phone screen. 'Because I can't leave it more than six hours.'

'What?'

'Which bit of "Burim will call the emergency services" didn't you get? I wasn't playing. He called an ambulance once when I went to Club Class and didn't message him. He said whatever guy I was talking to would need it when he found out who he was. Aww! Look! There's Father Christmas.'

As Erin went to take photos of someone in a red suit on skis, Orla swallowed a mouthful of sausage and tried desperately to digest that and the conversation. So, Burim sounded quite the controller. Their mum was right to worry. And Orla was going to make sure she found out much more about him over the coming days. She was well aware of men and what they said online being very different to what they were actually thinking and doing in person. She was an intelligent person, but even *she* thought that someone who messaged you with every tiny update of their day for weeks was someone making an effort to grow a situationship into something much more. How was a sixteen-year-old meant to navigate that when a twenty-six-year-old was struggling…?

'Ah, you have tried one of Pierre's sausages.'

It was Delphine, looking a little calmer, a steaming cup of something in her hands.

'They are very good,' Orla replied, gesturing with what was left of her baguette.

'I know,' Delphine answered. 'I taught him how to make them. The first year he tried to, they tasted like... well, I cannot tell you what they tasted like. *Dégueulasse*. Disgusting.'

The description wasn't making these last bites taste the best. She looked around for a bin.

'So, you have a big family?' Delphine asked, sipping from her drink.

'Sorry?'

'You said you have a family emergency. I wonder how many people in the family.'

'Oh, well, it's my mum and dad really.'

'They are getting a divorce?' Delphine asked.

'No... nothing like that.'

'You do not believe in divorce?'

'I... don't have an opinion one way or the other and—'

'Because you have never been married?'

'Well, no but—'

'So, you *have* been married?'

This was a bit much. It felt like Delphine was giving her an inquisition or behaving like the reporter in this situation. It was an odd line of questioning too and Orla knew better than to give up personal details to someone who hadn't yet shown them more than cookies...

'Are *you* married?' Orla asked the woman, turning the tables.

'Me?'

'Yes.'

'Only to my supermarket now,' Delphine answered.

'I am only married to my job too,' Orla said.

'Oh,' Delphine said, disappointment evident in her tone. 'You do not want a family of your own.'

Delphine had said the sentence like it was a fact rather than a question. It was as if Orla not being married yet had made her into a spinster for life who would only be looking after knitting needles and cats. She wanted her career to shine and any partner to complement that, working towards their own individual goals as well as joint ones. The truth was she didn't know if she wanted children. And, as she was having a hard enough time trying to find a man who hung around long enough to ask if he was a pizza or a burger guy let alone anything deep, who knew whether children were ever going to be in the picture? And she wasn't about to divulge any of this to someone she had just met. She needed a distraction.

'What's the wheelbarrow about?' Orla asked, indicating the garden equipment in the square.

'A what?'

'A wheelbarrow. The wooden carrying thing with wheels everyone is looking at and touching.'

'Ah! That is a *brouette*. Here in Saint-Chambéry it is like an icon. In days long ago, our ancestors built the village by hand, using only wooden *brouettes* to move tools and stones and wood. We honour this at Christmas time, at a festival in the summer and we look to the *brouette* whenever we need guidance. The oldest surviving *brouette* is now in the church. It does not deal so well with the weather.'

Orla's story radar was clicking like a Geiger counter had encountered toxic substances. This was more like it. A community with slightly off-the-wall traditions, paying homage to something you'd buy in B&Q. Perhaps she could make something substantial out of this after all.

Delphine took a gulp from the cup in her hands and sighed, satisfied. 'Ah, the *vin chaud* is very good this year.'

'It's wine?' Orla asked. 'I thought you were drinking coffee.'

'It is a little more than wine here in Saint-Chambéry,' Delphine informed her. 'We like to add a lot of *crème de cassis*. It is the blackcurrant and the alcohol and the spices that really make you feel warm again.'

Orla felt a creeping feeling envelop her shoulders now as she focussed on the little brown paper cup in Delphine's hands. The woman wasn't the only person she had assumed was drinking coffee... And then her eyes found Erin, leaning against a snowboard that was upright in the snow, a manic grin on her face. She didn't wait to make her excuses to their host.

# 11

It was official. This morning Orla felt like Heidi. It might have been the French mountains she was looking out at from the window of the room above Delphine's café-shop, but this setting was definitely giving all the Swiss vibes from the white-topped peaks to the chalet-style buildings all around. It would have been peace and serenity in this loft-style room, if it hadn't been for the fact that she had got little sleep. It had taken actual coffee to bring Erin down from the high of at least three cups of mulled wine and then it had taken what had seemed like hours to connect to Wi-Fi. And there had been fifty-five notifications on Erin's phone. Thirty-two of them from Burim, which her sister had been highly delighted with, proudly claiming he was 'so down bad'. Thirty-two sounded excessive to Orla, but she did remember the high excitement and that fizzing sensation in her stomach when a new notification arrived from Henry. He had sent photos from the bookshop where he worked – the cloth-bound classics she liked – his beautiful hands around Lewis Carroll's finest. It had been different to the other connections. They had more in common – or so she'd thought...

Her phone made a noise. An iMessage rather than something from Insta and she picked it up from the windowsill, looking at the screen. *Mum.* Usually her mum's name on the screen of her phone would make her feel warm, comforted, a little nostalgic even. But as circumstances were, currently all she felt now was concern. And, as she had managed to get a message through last night that she and Erin were here in France and safe – excluding any mention of car crashes, the freezing climate and Erin getting pissed – who knew what this was going to be? There was only one way to find out. She pressed on the message and read.

> Dad sold your grandma's eternity ring. I have no words. That's a lie. I do have words. Right now I don't know whether I want to help him or let him drink himself into the ground. What time is it in France? Have you eaten frogs legs yet? Don't let Erin sleep without her retainer in. Don't worry about me.

The 'don't worry about me' was something her mum always used in texts as a joke, but today the humour wasn't hitting. Orla *was* worried. About her mum *and* her dad. She hovered her thumb over the keyboard, wondering whether to reply or make a call.

'What time is it?'

Erin's voice made Orla jump and her phone dropped to the wooden floorboards. She couldn't afford for her phone to be broken! They had sparse enough means of communication as it was without losing the scrap they *did* have. 'I don't know. I...'

She picked up her phone, thankfully unscathed, and looked at the time on the screen. 'It's almost eight o'clock.'

'Are you sure?' Erin asked, as if the question was life defining.

'That's what my phone says.'

'Yes, but is it on French time or English time?' She was out of bed now, her phone in her hand.

That was a good point. Did these things update automatically?

'I don't know.'

'And how many hours ahead is France from England? Or is it behind?'

'One,' Orla replied confidently. 'One hour ahead.'

'Oh, that's the same as... aww, it *must* be nine o'clock there because I've got my morning photo.'

Orla watched the biggest smile take over her sister's face as she gazed at the screen of her phone all bed hair and big eyes. Her sister was in another world, or perhaps just another country, very much oblivious to anything in this room, including the cold. Orla shivered as she looked at Erin's tiny bed shorts, inappropriate given the fact that the small heater-cum-air-conditioning unit mounted above the window was only giving out a breath of raised temperature.

'He's eating avocado again,' Erin continued, eyes still on her screen. 'He has an avocado obsession. He's always using the emoji too.'

Orla made a mental note to google what using the avocado emoji in messaging meant. There was always a double meaning. You thought your talking-stage guy was being cute and really he was telling you deeper stuff about himself – or you – than you could ever imagine. She had shivered when she found out the taco emoji wasn't an invitation to the Mexican restaurant...

'Can I see?' Orla asked, stepping closer.

'Ugh! No!' Erin exclaimed in horror, hugging the phone to her chest. 'Why would I let you see a photo of my guy half-naked.'

'Half-naked?!'

'OK, Mum, calm down. He's wearing what he wears to bed. Like, Lacoste trunks.'

And did Erin share similar photos with Burim? Snaps of what she wears to bed? These small barely-there shorts? Less than that? But Orla had to play it cool...

'OK,' she said. 'Well, maybe when he shares a photo and he's dressed, I could... you know... see what he looks like.'

'Why?'

'Because it would be nice to see the guy who's messaging you every minute and... making you smile.'

'He does make me smile,' Erin replied with more smiles.

The expression on her sister's face now was so like the little girl who used to make salt and vinegar crisp sandwiches for her Barbie doll parties. It was different to the pouty moody expression she seemed to wear on all her social media posts lately. But was that a good or a bad thing? Henry's messages had made *her* look like that. Henry had talked about actually meeting. Who said that if they didn't mean it?

'And he's so fine,' Erin said, fingers tapping on her phone, the noise of acrylic nails on screen protector sounding like an old-fashioned typewriter.

Before Orla could make any response there was a brief knock on the door before it opened wide and there was Delphine, bustling in without waiting for an invitation.

'*Bien*! You are awake!' Delphine announced.

'And not dressed!' Erin exclaimed, making a dive back for the sanctuary of the blanket layers.

'Breakfast is downstairs in the café,' Delphine said, picking up the remote for the climate control and pointing it at the machine. 'Your table is the one with the winter irises in the centre. Would you like tea or coffee?'

'Coffee,' Erin said quickly.

'Could I have tea?' Orla asked.

'I will make coffee,' Delphine replied, putting the controller back down on the thick windowsill.

'Do you have avocado?' Erin wanted to know.

'*Avocat*,' Delphine said. 'The French practically invented it.'

'Oh, that's good! I can take photos!'

'But we do not have here,' Delphine said firmly.

Orla watched her sister deflate.

'I could order, with my next delivery, if you like.'

Erin offered their hostess a smile. 'Yes, please.'

'*Bien*,' Delphine said. 'So, breakfast will end in thirty minutes and then I will take you to see Wolf.'

'Thirty minutes!' Erin exclaimed.

'Delphine, we haven't had time to shower yet and—'

Orla's sentence was cut off by the firm closing of the door as Delphine departed as swiftly as she had arrived.

'Fuck,' Erin said, scrabbling back out of the bed. 'It takes me forty-two minutes to do my make-up on a good day.'

As her sister began to tip the contents of her airport liquids bag onto her bedside table, Orla really hoped she wouldn't have to wait forty-two minutes for a coffee she was going to wish was tea.

# 12

## JACQUES'S CABIN, SAINT-CHAMBÉRY

It was still bitterly cold outside. When Jacques's alarm had gone off at 5 a.m. he had considered going for a run, but one look at the temperature and the face of his husky dog, Hunter, and he had opted for an indoor workout. Now, holding his form, balanced on the gymnastic rings, in this dojo/home gym he looked out through the window to the freezing landscape and focussed on keeping his form. *Peace. A quiet mindset. No distractions. Strength in silence. Forgetting about the past.* His core trembled as soon as his brain worked with the word 'past'. He loathed that it did that. Yes, it would be easy to erase that line from his thinking when he did this combination of a workout for the mind as well as the body but if you didn't ever even internally confront your demons then you were leaving no room for positivity to occupy that space.

Hunter whined and Jacques was immediately distracted, even more so when his dog got up from his blanket and headed towards the body of the main house. It was the move Hunter made when someone came within fifty feet of the house. Except no one came here, apart from reluctant delivery drivers or lost hikers and if hikers were out at this time of the morning, in these conditions, they were crazy. He refocussed, holding the rings tight, sucking in his abdomen, pulling taut...

Hunter barked once. Then two short sharp ones. It couldn't be, could it? Jacques took one last long breath and then jumped down, grabbing his towel and wiping his torso.

'What is it, boy?' Jacques asked when he had reached his dog. Hunter was parading up and down by the window, stopping then starting all over again. He put his hand on the dog's head, ruffled his fur, but Hunter didn't flinch, didn't acknowledge, didn't turn to receive the affection. The animal was a lot more focussed than Jacques had been on the rings.

Hunter barked in the same rhythm as before and, being unable to see anything against the white of the snow on the ground nor the grey/white of the cloudy sky, Jacques reached for his binoculars.

As Hunter carried on barking in the same way, Jacques finally saw what his pet had sensed. There in the distance was a vehicle and it was definitely heading his way.

\* \* \*

'I can't feel my face!' Erin squealed.

'You're supposed to have the scarf around your face, Erin,' Orla called back.

'What?'

'I said—'

'What? I can't hear you with that scarf over your mouth!'

This was impossible! And it was cold like she had never experienced before. Why she and Erin were riding a tractor-type vehicle that seemed to be spraying up snow more than it was making headway to wherever they were going she didn't know. But this was apparently Delphine's mode of transport and they hadn't had a lot of say in anything much this morning. Breakfast had been approximately eight minutes long with the coffee scalding the roof of Orla's mouth as she rushed it down. And, as nice as the freshly baked croissants were, there hadn't been a second to savour them before their host was telling them to dress in many layers, cover their faces and come outside.

Despite the extreme cold, the landscape was breathtaking. So far, Delphine had driven them through pine woodland and skirted a frozen lake but now they were heading up a steep incline that seemed never ending when the engine of this thing sounded like it was one noisy sputter away from a breakdown. But the thing nagging at Orla's mind was the lack of research she had done before embarking on this trip. Research was her forte. She found out everything she could about what she was stepping into, from the terrain to the possibility of local tyranny. Except she hadn't done *any* of that, and she was about to meet a mute man and a pregnant reindeer, neither of which she had any experience with. Unless you counted ghosting as being mute...

'Oh my God! Is that a wolf?'

Next, Erin screamed. And the grip of acrylic nails through gloves her sister had been forced to put on pressed into Orla's shoulders. She saw what Erin was talking about. It was furry, grey and white, with four legs, and it was running towards them at speed, barking. Did wolves bark? Why didn't she know the answer to that? She did. She'd spent time with wolves in Russia. They were largely misunderstood animals who weren't usually aggressive to humans. Where possible, they would avoid human interaction, not sprint towards them with what she could now see was a fierce look in its eyes.

'We are very near to Wolf,' Delphine shouted over the engine noise.

'I know!' Erin screamed. 'I can see it! And it's getting closer! I want to get off!'

Erin's last words had Orla panicking. Although their ride wasn't going anywhere close to street-race speeds, Erin jumping from it to the snow wasn't wise. And her brain was firing off all kinds of flight versus fight scenarios in this moment.

'You can see Wolf?' Delphine shouted again. 'Your eyes must be very good!'

'It's right there!' Erin screamed, leaning back into Orla. 'Looking savage!'

Delphine laughed and the engine of the tractor idled, quietening and slowing, the wolf bearing down on them.

'Orla! It's going to come and bite me! I don't want blood loss and I definitely don't want a scar!'

'You think the dog is Wolf?' Delphine said, the tractor stopping completely.

'It looks like one! An angry one! Orla!'

'Delphine, could you please reassure us that we aren't about to be attacked?' Orla said as calmly as possible.

'Attacked?' Delphine asked, getting off the vehicle. 'I do not understand this English word.'

The animal sped the final few metres and then it leapt into the air and landed on Orla's lap. Erin let out a scream that echoed down the valley and Orla just froze, a weighty four-legged beast mounted on her. She looked into its eyes and it looked into hers while it panted, tongue lolling, and, as her heart hammered against her chest, she wondered which one of them was going to make their next move. Apparently, it was neither of them. A loud piercing whistle hit the air and the wolf/dog sat stiller than she was, mouth closed up, breath now inaudible. A second whistle, this time in a different tone and rhythm, and the dog leapt off, down to the snowy ground where it sat, paws elevated like it was begging.

'Aww, Hunter, you want some treats? I have biscuits in my pocket.'

Orla watched as Delphine pulled off her gloves and dipped a hand into the pocket of her coat.

Another whistle blasted and this one was so severe, Erin rocked on the tractor and toppled off into the snow.

'Are you OK?' Orla asked, quickly getting off and going to her sister.

'No! I'm in the snow! And now everything is wet!'

'Here, Hunter, but do not look obvious,' Delphine carried on. Orla watched Delphine scatter the biscuits on the ground, but her actions seemed to be earning more whistling and it was so sharp Orla wanted to reach for her ears.

'Make it stop!' Erin groaned, wiping snow from her jacket.

Delphine shouted in French, gesticulating to ahead a little. It was then that Orla saw a dark figure standing out against the bright white mountain backdrop. Tall, wide, slightly ominous? She watched the figure move his arm and then there was another whistle blast. This one set the dog off and it jumped up, turned tail and began sprinting back across the snow.

'That is Wolf,' Delphine said.

'I thought you said it was a dog!' Erin exclaimed, teeth chattering.

'Not the dog,' Delphine said. 'The man! *Là-bas*! There!'

Orla looked again at the figure. This was the person she was going to be interviewing. He looked formidable even from this distance and there was an instant disturbance in Orla's gut that her ill preparation was going to come back and bite her harder than any dog might…

'Is that how he has learned to communicate? With the whistle?'

'*Comment cela*? What do you mean?'

'The man. He does not speak? That was what I was told,' Orla attempted to clarify.

'Oh... well... yes... he is a man of very few words but... loud whistles, they can speak too, no?' Delphine said.

Was it Orla's imagination or did Delphine sound slightly tense?

'What are we doing now?' Erin asked. 'Apart from turning into ice?'

'We must walk,' Delphine announced. 'The tractor will not go up the hill without missing gears so...'

The 'so' was left hanging with no more being offered. Orla waited for Erin to start complaining about the lack of transport but when she looked to her sister she was already making moves forward. Orla felt out of control and that was something she never liked to be. Not only was she here when surely a more junior reporter could have managed what seemed like a fluff piece on paper, but she had a vulnerable teen with her too. It could all so easily go pear shaped. But with Erin striding ahead, there was no more time for contemplation. It seemed Orla had no other option but to follow her.

## 13

Within a five-minute brisk breath-stealing hike they were standing outside a large cabin, the only building anywhere in sight apart from an adjacent barn. It had large windows with shutters and an absence of anything that said anything about the person who might live here. There was no car outside, no wheelie bins, no plants or personalisation. The dog wasn't even around either. If it hadn't been for the fact Orla had had the dog on her lap and her ears were still ringing from the whistling, she would think this place was deserted. Except there was a wisp of smoke coming from a small chimney that she was taking as a sign of perhaps an open fire inside. And fire equalled warmth, right?

'What are we waiting for?' Erin asked, stamping her feet. 'The dog to come back and change its mind about eating us?'

'I am sure Wolf will invite us in soon. He knows we are here,' Delphine said, unperturbed and just standing like she was waiting for a bus to show up.

'But it's cold,' Erin moaned. 'And I need to check my phone.'

Orla knew Erin had looked at her phone on the ride over here so checking it wasn't a necessity, but she did agree about the cold.

'In Saint-Chambéry we have a tradition. You cannot enter a house until you are invited,' Delphine told them.

'God, this has turned a bit *The Vampire Diaries*,' Erin said.

'OK,' Orla said. 'Well, that's very nice but it's very cold and—'

There was a buzzing noise then and Delphine clapped her hands together. 'So, now we have been invited. Come.'

Orla watched Delphine make short work of the last bit of the walk and then Erin was at her shoulder, nudging.

'What the fuck is going on?' Erin whispered. 'Because I don't know what's a wolf and what isn't, I'm freezing cold and I'm sure I've got croissant stuck to my windpipe because I had to eat it so quickly!'

'I know,' Orla said. 'It's not ideal. But hopefully once I've started this interview I can get a better feel for why I needed to fly here for this story. I know the publication wouldn't have sent me here if it wasn't going to pull huge volume to the website.' And, even though the timing wasn't ideal, now she was here she had the opportunity to make *sure* it went well, for *Travel in Mind* and for her career aspirations too. Another success on her CV and soon it would be time to take a chance on *Time*…

'So how are you going to interview someone who doesn't talk, again? Talk me through it,' Erin said.

'Well,' Orla answered. 'Maybe he can write his answers down. No one's told me he can't hear.'

'This is crazy! Are all the places you go like this? Because I remember your photos from UAE and there were definitely chandeliers in the hotels and wall-to-wall Balenciaga.'

'That report was on consumerism and the gender pay gap,' Orla said. 'It was meant to be Austin's article but he… said he wasn't going to do it unless he got a pay rise.' She didn't usually take other people's jobs but she'd thought she'd step up and step outside the box, widen her remit, show another side to her writing. It was all about the bigger picture. Small term sacrifice for long term gain...

Erin laughed. 'Oh my God, I'm so cold it's making me think you're funny.'

'Come on,' Orla encouraged. 'Let's go in, get this started and then we can find something fun to do this afternoon.'

'Can we eat Pringles?'

Orla led the way to the imposing solid front door that was slightly ajar and gave it a push. Immediately the dog was there, padding along a wooden hallway, but this time looking more friendly than fierce.

'Hello,' Orla said, stretching out a hand to see if petting could be a thing.

'We are in the kitchen!' Delphine's voice carried through.

The dog then led the way and Erin followed its trail while Orla mentally took in details about the house. Despite the abundance of wood it was made from creating an outward appearance of warmth, it felt somehow clinical. The living area wasn't bright, white or sterile, but it lacked any form of individuality. There were pictures on the walls, but they were prints that looked like they had been bought in sets of three from somewhere like Habitat. There were no photos of friends or family, no ornaments that had been passed through a generation or two, everything there had a purpose. A TV. A wood burner that was roaring in front of a big tan leather sofa devoid of decorative cushions. There was a coffee table but no magazines nor coasters, missing knick-knacks that would ordinarily say someone actually lived here.

'Is that coffee machine for real?' Erin exclaimed, wandering into the kitchen area and looking like she might want to take a photo.

'Ugly thing,' Delphine said, dismissing it. 'Like a spaceship.'

'It's amazing!' Erin carried on. 'Is this made from that?' She picked up one of the mugs on the clutter-free countertop.

'No,' Delphine answered. 'It is made with a kettle.'

Erin pulled a face as she drew her mouth away from the cup. 'But why though?'

'Because the spaceship does not work.'

Orla looked up as someone came into the room, tall, dark-haired, a pile of logs resting on his forearms as he made his way past them and towards the lounge area. Instantly recognisable. *Jacques*.

'You!' she exclaimed. 'What are you doing here?'

'I live here,' he answered. 'What are you doing here? Another ill-prepared for trip when it is high minus figures outside?' He looked her up and down. 'At least you are wearing more layers today.'

Orla felt her cheeks flush. How did he know she was wearing layers?

'We're here to meet a wolf,' Erin answered. 'Not a real one. Some guy who doesn't speak. Does he live here too?'

'No one is drinking the coffee except me,' Delphine butted in, rushing to pick up the tray that was now holding the mugs. 'Let us warm ourselves up.'

'Delphine,' Jacques said, dropping the logs to the hearth and putting his now empty hands on his hips. 'What is going on? First yesterday you tell me about a pregnant reindeer and now you tell people I cannot speak?'

'Wait, what?' Erin exclaimed.

'You're the mute man?' Orla said.

'I'm so confused,' Erin said, taking a coffee from the tray Delphine was now desperately brandishing.

'You can speak,' Orla said. Although why she was stating

what was blindingly obvious now she really didn't know. And she was rapidly losing any hook for the basis of this assignment!

'*Café?*' Delphine asked, moving across the open-plan area at speed and poking the tray towards Jacques/Wolf.

'No, Delphine. I do not want a coffee. I want to know what's going on! There is no reindeer and there are strangers in my house!'

'There's no reindeer?'

Orla had said it before she had even realised it. But now she was more than confused, she was annoyed. There seemed to be a whole lot of misinformation going on here and it didn't appear to be down to any of her inadequate research when these were fundamental facts from the brief brief she'd been given. This was a waste of time and there were far more important things she could be doing! Repairing her family for a start!

'*Non*,' Delphine said firmly. '*Non*. There *is* a reindeer. She is coming.'

'If she's pregnant I would have thought that had already happened many months ago,' Erin said.

'Really?' Jacques said, walking away from the fire and snatching the tray from Delphine. 'There is a pregnant reindeer coming here to Saint-Chambéry. How? By Fed-Ex?'

Erin laughed. 'That was funny.'

'I do not know why you are all making such a fuss,' Delphine said lightly. 'The reindeer is late. What can I say? There are some things that I cannot control here in the village. Like whether the delivery man will ever turn up with the cinnamon cereal I ordered for the season. Or Gerard's addiction to pickled vegetables. Or Madame Voisin.'

There was a silence as if they were all waiting for Delphine to conclude her sentence. Nothing was forthcoming.

'And these people?' Jacques finally said, putting the tray on

the coffee table and waving a hand rather rudely in Orla's opinion. 'Are here because?'

'Bruh, we do have names,' Erin said with sass. 'And you do
know them.'

'You have met?' It was Delphine's turn to look surprised.

'We ran him over,' Erin elaborated.

'He's fine,' Orla continued. 'Obviously you can see he's fine.'

And the more she said the word 'fine' the more she realised
she was looking at Jacques like he was the very definition of 'fine'
– the way Erin used it to describe hot guys. Well, it had been a
while and all this going from freezing weather to roaring wood
stack was bound to do something to a woman's temperature. It
was getting quite warm in here...

'Gerard did not tell you he crashed the car?' Jacques said to
Delphine.

'He did not!'

'Well,' Jacques said, picking up a mug from the tray. 'More
secrets in Saint-Chambéry. What a surprise.'

Orla needed to step in. Right now she was feeling there were
more reasons for her *not* to be here than the other way around.

'OK,' she began. 'So, maybe we need a more formal introduction.
My name is Orla Bradbee and I work for *Travel in Mind* magazine
and I was told to come here to interview someone called Wolf who
can't speak and find out about the pregnant reindeer. So, is any of
that going to happen or should I get the next taxi back to the airport?'

Delphine snorted. 'There are no taxis in Saint-Chambéry.'

'And Gerard drives like he's Albanian,' Erin announced.

And none of those responses were getting Orla closer to
answers. She opened her mouth, ready to say exactly that except
someone beat her to it.

'You're Orla Bradbee?'

It was Jacques and he had said her full name like it was somehow familiar to him. An involuntary shudder rolled through her and she had no idea why.

'Yes,' she replied. 'Were you expecting someone else? Because I'm literally the only one crazy enough to get on a plane in December and I had to bring my sister with me.'

'Oi! Don't make it sound like you don't totally love me!'

There was something written in Jacques's expression now that was pinching at Orla. His dark brown eyes seemed veiled, a pulse reacted in his jawline. He was looking at her but not looking at her, seeking some kind of visual clarification that she existed. Finally, he took a deep breath and his attention went to Delphine.

'I do not know what this is, Delphine, but you need to leave. All of you.'

'Wait, what?' Erin exclaimed. 'We just came. On a tractor. And your dog basically attacked us. And it's freezing. And this coffee is terrible when you have a machine that could run Starbucks. And you haven't let my sister ask you one question yet! And... did I say it's freezing?'

'Jacques, we are your guests. And you are French. You have to extend hospitality,' Delphine said, stuttering a little over her words.

'I have made coffee and I did not let Hunter maul you. I do not know what else you would expect with no warning of your arrival. You know how I feel about that, Delphine.' He glared at the older woman.

'You're right,' Orla said finally. 'We should go. This whole thing is a waste of everyone's time. Come on, Erin.'

'What?' Erin exclaimed. 'But we've only just got here. I can't go back out in the cold yet!'

'Exactly! And, Jacques, you know how my tractor is! It needs time to cool down before starting up again,' Delphine added.

'I don't care,' Orla stated, making sure the zip on her coat was fully up to her neck. 'I've never been anywhere less hospitable, and I've been to a lot of places. Thank you for the coffee. Come on, Erin.'

'Orla, what are you doing?' Delphine called.

Orla was striding towards the door with only one thing on her mind. Getting out of here as quickly as possible even if she had to walk back to the village. OK, so she knew it wasn't the shortest distance but it would be fine. She'd trekked through harsher terrain than a bit of French snow...

Suddenly there was a loud click, just as she reached the door and when she pulled on the handle it wouldn't budge. She tried again, added more force. Why wasn't this a normal door? Why wasn't there a keyhole with keys to turn? She gripped the handle again and forced it up and down and down and up, hoping for a different result.

'It won't open. It does not matter how hard you pull it.'

She turned around and faced Jacques who was standing just behind her.

'Well, that sounds like a big issue if there was ever a fire,' she replied.

'Or a plus if there is an avalanche,' Jacques answered.

'So, what do I do to get out if it's not pulling the handle?' Orla asked, frustration needling her. 'Is there a pad to take a fingerprint? Or a retinal scan?'

'Yes,' Jacques replied. 'Both. But I have deactivated them.'

She physically baulked. Was he being for real?

'I want to leave,' Orla reminded him.

'I thought you wanted to interview me.'

'No, my magazine wants me to interview you. Right now, all I want to do is completely forget you.'

The last sentence came out a lot harder and harsher than she had meant. Ordinarily, in front of someone she was meant to be working with, she would be hastily apologising right now, but the words weren't coming. And Jacques was saying nothing, those dark eyes fixed on her like whatever happened next was her move...

And then he laughed. Loud and so unexpected that Orla jumped. But the laughter kept on coming like her asking to leave was comedy gold.

'I'm sorry,' Jacques said, finally. 'It's just you go from not saying anything to exploding. It's amusing.'

Now her last nerve was rapidly unravelling. 'You think this is exploding? You obviously don't get out much.'

'*Non*,' he seemed to agree. 'You see, I have this very difficult door.'

OK, that was good. And unfortunately she couldn't help but show it on her face. She tried to stop the smile from forming.

'I apologise,' Jacques said. 'For being an ungracious host. Please, let me make better coffee than Delphine.'

His tone sounded so genuine and he was looking directly at her waiting for her response. Maybe she wouldn't say anything.

'Ah, you pretend to be mute,' he said, nodding. 'I hear it is a thing. Well, perhaps you can write down the one question I said I would answer.'

'Why do you have an expensive broken coffee machine in your kitchen?'

'Is that the one question?' He raised one eyebrow.

'You didn't say you would only answer one question,' Orla replied. 'My sister said I hadn't even asked you one question.'

He nodded. 'You are right.'

'So?' She folded her arms across her chest then felt immediately ridiculous and dropped them down again.

'So I will... make the expensive coffee machine work and we will take it from there.'

It sounded like it was as good as she was going to get and the thought of walking in icy conditions all the way back to the village hadn't been at all appealing.

'Fine,' she answered. And, he really was...

## 14

Orla Bradbee was sat at his kitchen table. Why hadn't he recognised her the second he'd set eyes on her last night? Why hadn't he even considered it was her when she had told him her first name? Maybe because the last photo he had of her was maybe eighteen months old now and that was only a small thumbnail from the by-line of her report on fish poaching in Romania. Her hair was lighter in real life and she was smaller. Granted, he remembered that in one of the pictures in her report from Zimbabwe she'd been standing next to a rhino, but she couldn't be more than five feet four. It made him feel awkward in his own space, to be a whole foot taller. And for the first time in a long time he felt nervous. How fucking crazy was that?

Just about as crazy as using the coffee machine he loathed and attempted to get rid of on a regular basis. Like some kind of weird talisman it always failed to leave or made its way back. And his morals wouldn't let him destroy something that still worked and had value, to someone at least.

'It's good coffee,' Orla remarked, sipping at the macchiato he had made. 'It should keep Erin quiet for at least ten minutes until she asks for another one.'

'I have let them go into the cinema room. It might buy us an hour perhaps?'

'There's a cinema room?' Orla asked.

He nodded. 'I don't use it.'

'Like the coffee machine?'

He smiled. 'That's many questions for someone who has not started an official interview.'

'And you're still standing up.'

'There is a law that you cannot interview someone who is standing up?'

'I'm not sure *I* said I would answer any questions.'

'OK,' he replied. 'So, it seems we need to create some ground rules.'

'Er, *I'm* the one conducting the interview.'

'In my house.'

'That was not my choice. I'm only here because my boss asked me to be here. And a crazy woman drove me on a tractor.'

'You don't want to be here?'

She shrugged. 'It's just work.'

'O-K.' He didn't like her comment at all. In fact, it was needling at him. He had read her reports on so many cultures, kingdoms, lifestyles and civilisations, and not once did he think she was someone who thought what she was doing was 'just work'. But, then again, how could interviewing him have the same appeal as interviewing the woman who lives with wild outback camels?

'Sorry,' Orla said. 'That sounded offensive and rude. I didn't mean it like that. I'm sure you're very interesting, I just usually have time to research a project and I only heard about this the day before yesterday so I'm kind of on the back foot.'

'You and me both,' he replied.

'Well, apart from the snow, I'm finding Delphine is the biggest force of nature around here.'

'And you are correct about that.'

'So, are you going to sit down or...'

He smiled, letting the silence of the ending to her sentence linger. He stayed with his back to the kitchen counter. He always liked to have something at his back.

'Ground rules,' he said.

'OK, how about I ask the questions and you answer them? Then I can take some photos and be on my way until the pregnant reindeer turns up. So... how long have you lived here?'

He smiled again. 'You know there's no reindeer, right? Pregnant or not.'

'What?' Orla said, lifting her head from where she had started to write on an electronic notepad.

'There are no reindeer in this area. And reindeer don't give birth in December. It is a nice festive story, made up by Delphine for some reason I don't know, but not possible I'm afraid.'

'Are you joking with me?' Orla asked him. 'Because it's not funny.'

Now she looked worried. *Really* worried. And he didn't know what to say next.

'Honestly, are you serious? There are *no* reindeer here? At all? And one *can't* be pregnant?' She got up from her seat and put her hands to her head. 'You're joking, right? You have to be joking because... I can't handle you not to be.'

'Yes.' It came out of his mouth before he had engaged his brain. What was he saying?

'You're joking. You mean it that there will be reindeer or at least one pregnant one?'

'I am joking,' he continued. 'Of course I am joking. I mean,

Delphine said the pregnant reindeer is coming and Delphine, as you said, is a force of nature and she does not say things that do not happen.' He swallowed. Why was he lying? All good sense told him that this whole thing was a ruse, from the reindeer to the fact Orla Bradbee was here in his home, but he could sense that she needed this to be the truth in this moment.

He watched her take a deep breath of relief and she seemed to recover slightly, picking up her electronic pen and pad and writing something on the screen.

'Listen,' he began, moving away from the countertop. 'I don't really know why *Travel in Mind* magazine would want to make me the subject of an article but—'

'You know the magazine I write for?' she interrupted.

'You told me,' he replied. 'A few seconds before you stormed towards the front door.'

'And you remembered? Amid the alleged "storming".' She made quote marks in the air.

He smiled, shaking his head. 'What can I say? I pay attention.'

He watched her looking back at him as if she was mulling this information over and trying to work out from his expression, or maybe his body language, if he was telling her the truth. He was... even if there was a bit more to it.

'To be frank,' Orla picked up. 'I think my boss is slightly more invested in a heavily pregnant reindeer this close to Christmas than you, particularly now you actually talk.' She paused. 'No offence.'

'None taken,' he answered. 'And I agree. A pregnant reindeer would be a far more interesting subject than me.'

Was that it? Had he easily managed to navigate his way out of this interview just by admitting his life wasn't report-worthy compared to that of four-legged wildlife he didn't even believe was going to turn up? Delphine had avoided every one of his questions about the absence of the reindeer at the fête the night before.

'That being said,' Orla began. 'And with the absence of said reindeer, I'd better cover all bases.'

Apparently he was still in this.

'So, what do you want to know?' he asked.

'Currently, why you won't sit down.'

He smiled. 'How long I've lived here, wasn't it? So, a little over two years now.'

'Where are you from originally?'

'You know how the reindeer is with child? Well, one night my mother—'

'Are you going to answer the questions seriously? Or is my being here a joke to you?'

'Believe me, as you and your sister are the only people except Delphine and Hunter who have been in this house in a year, this isn't a joke.' He swallowed. Even telling her that was information he didn't want to give out. His life was private. He wanted to keep it that way. The fact that Delphine had invited someone into his personal space without any thought for the consequences was eating away at him. His friend might not know the full extent of his situation but she should have known enough. Keeping his circle small was the only way to ensure his family's safety. But then there was the fact that this was a reporter he admired, someone he felt a connection with through her words in the magazine, someone who wrote stories he would look forward to in every publication... and Delphine also knew that.

'So, you're not mute, but you're a recluse?'

He shrugged. 'We could blame Covid-19 if you like. All that trauma of staying inside. Would that come over better than "he hates people"?'

'You hate people?' She was actually writing this down.

'No, Orla, *that* was a joke. I like my privacy. And, last time I checked, there was no law against that.'

'OK,' Orla said, standing up and picking up her digital pad. 'This really isn't going to work. Particularly as I was told you had developed a special bond with a reindeer that isn't here. I thought there may be something I could really get to the heart of.'

*Damn it. She was going to leave.* But wasn't that exactly what he'd wanted only moments ago? And he didn't want to do an interview. Why would he? It wasn't just wanting privacy for privacy's sake. He had good reasons. But this was Orla Bradbee... and she was packing up and about to head to his front door for the second time after he'd been almost as hostile as a battleground.

'Orla, wait,' he said as she pushed the pad into her backpack.

'Why?' Orla snapped. 'Are you going to refuse to press whatever magic button you need to press to unlock the front door? Because there is a law against keeping someone against their will.'

'I would never do that,' he stated.

'Good. So, it was nice to meet you but I'm going to collect my sister from the cinema room and—'

'Beanbags,' Jacques blurted out.

'What?'

'Sorry, you're a newcomer to Saint-Chambéry, you need context.' He sighed. 'Tonight in the village there's a contest involving beanbags. I am forced to take part every year since I arrived here because, well, I am the reigning champion but, you know, if you were to come along to that then...' He stopped talking, giving his brain a chance to catch up with what he was *actually* saying and how crazy it was, but his mouth couldn't seem to halt its progress. 'I will answer whatever questions you want.'

He couldn't believe he had said that... to someone who asked questions for a living. To someone who got to the very truth of anything she involved herself in. He held his breath, half of him hoping she would turn his offer down.

'Whatever questions I want?' Orla clarified.

He nodded. 'That is what I said.'

'OK,' Orla replied. 'But this is your last chance.'

*His last chance?* To take part in an interview he hadn't called for nor wanted? He opened his mouth to say as much but something made him think better of it.

'Understood,' he answered.

## 15

SAINT-CHAMBÉRY

'Burim says it's fourteen degrees with him and he doesn't want me to be cold. He says if I was with him I would never be cold. He says if I was with him it would be perfect.'

Orla was getting to know that Burim used the word 'perfect' a lot. Erin had sent him a photo of the crêpes she had eaten for lunch and they were 'perfect'. She had also sent him a photo of a snowmobile parked outside Gerard's bar after Burim had sent four 'wyd' messages in two minutes because she had left him on seen for ten minutes – the snowmobile had been 'perfect' too. But all the intensity was a throwback to her conversations with Henry. He'd always liked her Insta stories and commented on them. Turned a photo of the latest awful toilet she got to encounter on her travels into something much more positive... and more often than not, sexy. She missed that. She missed having someone interested in her day. It wasn't the same as your mum putting a 'love you my beautiful angel' comment on FB when the focus of your post was meant to be the jackaroo who was sheep-shearing... She needed to say something about Burim.

'Are there actually going to be beanbags at this bar or are they made up like the reindeer?'

Erin had jumped in with the comment before Orla could say anything.

'I don't know,' Orla said, putting her hands around the mug of mulled wine Gerard had insisted they both had when they'd arrived in this cosy cabin of a pub. 'Do you think the reindeer is made up?'

'Didn't you question it before you accepted the assignment?' Erin asked like she was the elder and wiser sister in this situation.

Orla swallowed, the tall stool she was sitting on which was facing a roaring fire pit where other customers were warming their hands, making her feel like a child in a highchair. She hadn't questioned anything much at all. Frances hadn't let her. Or was it more a case of there was so much drama going on with her family that this mute man/reindeer combo hadn't sounded all that bad on the face of it. But here with her sister she had no choice but to be the grown-up.

'I don't think the reindeer is made up,' Orla replied with a dash more confidence than she really felt.

'No?' Erin said. 'Because, Wolf, the really tall, really fit-looking but old dude told you? I mean he's not Ryan Gosling, but I would.'

Orla tried to pick the bones out of the sentence as her cheeks grew as warm as the coals in the fire pit looked.

'Oh shit! You *do* think he's fit!' Erin exclaimed, at a louder level than the merry Christmas music being piped around the space.

'What? No! I don't even know who you're talking about,' Orla answered rather patchily. 'But anyway, what's Delphine's reason to make something like that up?'

'Well, you might change your mind about her when I tell

you what film she wanted to choose to watch in the cinema room earlier,' Erin said, jabbing the slice of orange in her drink with the accompanying cocktail stick. 'She lets everyone see "sweet, caring, shop owner" when really she drinks coffee that must be eroding her gut lining and wants to watch *Reservoir Dogs*.'

'It's one of those films everyone's watched,' Orla replied. But something in Erin's words was spiking her journalistic instincts that perhaps something was amiss.

'She's watched it seventeen times. She told me. She knows *all* the words. It freaked me out. It's the only time I've wanted to actually say I'm not actually old enough to be watching this according to the guidance rating. So, if you're asking me if I think she's capable of making some shit up about a reindeer then yes and it's a possibility she's masterminded all the unsolved heists in France.'

Orla smiled, shook her head but made a mental note. Sometimes she did love the way her sister's mind raced away with itself. It reminded her how her own imagination had been at that age. She'd thought back then that nothing was insurmountable, that the world was hers for the enjoying. When had she stopped thinking that way? *Had* she stopped thinking that way? She swallowed. She was in a good position with her career, she just needed to move that into a *great* position. And as for relationships, well, they weren't *everything*.

'Oh, here she is,' Erin announced. 'Madame Loves-A-Big-Weapon.'

'Shh,' Orla said.

She looked to the door where Delphine was arriving, a large box in her arms.

'Pretty cruel if they've made the reindeer squash itself into that, pregnant belly and everything,' Erin said, giggling.

Now Orla was doubting that Erin's mulled wine was quite the non-alcoholic version Gerard had said it was...

'Oh yeah, I forgot, the reindeer doesn't exist.'

'Stop saying that,' Orla said, a little annoyed.

'If it doesn't exist,' Erin continued. 'Does that mean we have to go home? Because I know I said it was cold and a bit shit but home is more cold and more shit so...'

'Erin, I don't want you to worry about home, OK? I know about things now so let me work on it.'

She swallowed, she had yet to respond to her mum's text. Her dad had sold something precious. It *was* unforgiveable. Where did you start with that? But she didn't want Erin to be thinking or feeling like home was cold and shit. Home should always be warm and welcoming, somewhere you could rely on to be a safe space. Except as soon as Baby Erin had arrived Orla was planning an escape to somewhere new, out into the wider world. Not because home didn't feel safe, but because she'd always had a wanderlust and, as she'd got older, she still found it difficult to understand how her mum could be ultimately satisfied with a sedentary life on the outskirts of London. When Erin's packets of Pampers had filled every spare space, a ten-year-old Orla had started putting pins in a world map on the back of her wardrobe door. She wanted to see everything. She wanted to go everywhere. Home should be solid, there waiting, there to catch you if you fell...

'We can't go home yet,' Orla decided to say. 'Even if there's no reindeer.' What was she saying? When had she made this choice? And she kept on talking. 'Because where Orla Bradbee goes stories follow.'

'Isn't that meant to work the other way around?' Erin asked.

'Did you ever read my article on the man who only ate soup?'

'Is this a joke?'

Orla shook her head, repositioning herself on the stool. 'No. I went to South America to see what was supposed to be this phenomenon of the sky. It's called Catatumbo lightning.'

'Cata-what?'

'Catatumbo. Anyway, when I get there the locals tell me that it's not going to happen for at least three months because there has been this terrible drought. So there I am, at this restaurant in the midst of Venezuela wondering where I'm going to find a story from this expensive trip and there's this old man sitting on his own eating soup.'

'That's not that weird,' Erin said with a sniff. 'I swear Danica only eats Hula Hoops.'

'He ate five bowls. One after the other. And I couldn't keep my eyes off him. I thought, what makes someone eat five bowls of soup at a restaurant that was well-known for so many other great delicacies.'

'How did you spin that into a story?'

'I asked the waiter about him and he told me his name and that he came to eat at the same time every day. So, the next day, I came back and I watched him eat the same amount of soup as he had the day before and then I went to speak to him.' She took a sip of her drink.

'Well, what did he say?' Erin asked.

'He said he ate a bowl of soup every day for everyone he'd lost in his life. His mum, his dad, his two brothers and his wife. And he intended to do that every day for the rest of his life.'

She swallowed as she concluded. She had never forgotten Luis and what warmed her heart the most was that after her story went to print people visited the restaurant and joined him for lunch. He now had friends all over the world.

Erin was quiet until finally she spoke up. 'I don't think Dad is drinking a certain number of pints to represent people he's lost.'

'No,' Orla said with a sigh.

'But he's going to be OK, right?'

This was her sister being as transparent as it got and she needed to reassure her fully in this moment.

'Yes!' Orla said quickly. 'Of course he's going to be OK! Mum's not going to let him be anything else! You know how she is! She will decree that things must change and that's exactly what will happen. And, I told you, I've got this now, too.'

She wanted to cross her fingers. She wanted to manifest it into being but all she really had was hope...

'Beanbags!'

It was Delphine. Shattering the moment and slapping down two beanbags amid the drinks on the table. They were horseshoe shaped, like nothing Orla had seen before. And Delphine was off and away again, without explanation or further conversation, delivering more odd shapes to other tables. Orla went to pick one up.

'Wait! Don't!' Erin said, phone poised in the air. 'I want to take a photo for Burim. He'll probably make an innuendo about the shape.'

Ah, yes. She mustn't forget that as well as their parents being in crisis and there being no reindeer for her end-of-year-potentially-profit-saving story for *Travel in Mind*, her sister was in a talking stage with a Moroccan she didn't know the age of, who sent photos of himself in his underwear...

'So, Erin—'

'*Bonsoir.*'

How Orla had missed the approach of someone so tall with a chest so broad it could definitely handle a whole family-sized charcuterie sharing platter, she didn't know. But Jacques was now standing by their table looking particularly fine in a navy-blue long-sleeved top over black jeans. His beard looked newly neatly trimmed and those dark, deep brown eyes were set on her. It was then she realised her fingers had been grazing the symmetry of the beanbag.

'*Bonsoir*. Hello,' Orla said quickly.

'Ah,' he continued. 'You have the horseshoes. Not the best shape I would say but, not the worst either.'

'There's different shapes?' Erin remarked, sitting up tall and seeming to scan the rest of the tables for evidence.

'They symbolise the history of the village. There are wagon wheels, pentagons like the shape of the lake here, sausages like—'

'OK,' Orla said quickly as Erin sniggered. 'We're getting it.'

'Good,' Jacques replied. 'So, you will have to move now.'

'Move?' Orla queried.

'The beanbags are thrown at this firepit,' he told them.

# 16

Jacques watched Orla getting ready to throw their horseshoe-shaped beanbag. Despite her very firm opinion that this festive game was 'a health and safety nightmare' and 'an accident waiting to happen' she was becoming heavily invested in the outcome. She stood still, seeming to ignore the off-putting jibes coming from their competitors in the crowded bar, a horseshoe beanbag in her hands.

'That's her full-on concentrating face,' Erin whispered to him. 'Like she is not contemplating losing here, just so you know.'

'I am beginning to know,' Jacques replied.

'But how are you going to feel when she takes your crown? Like, she's not thrown beanbags before. Let alone backwards, over her shoulder and into a fiery pit.'

'Are you suggesting I could be a bad loser?'

'You're a man, aren't you?' Erin said, as if that explained everything. She went back to tapping at her phone.

Jacques tuned back in to Orla, swinging her arm and preparing to throw. Then she swung hard, the beanbag leaving her grasp, flying through the air as all eyes watched. It rotated and spun and finally slapped down on the very edge of the fire pit, tumbling to the floor. Delphine stamped on top of it on the flagstones, putting paid to any potential smouldering.

'Five points!' Delphine declared.

'Only five?' Orla exclaimed. 'It clearly hit the flames and bounced back out.'

The crowd oohed and Jacques knew Delphine wouldn't appreciate her decision being questioned. Although Orla did have a point...

'Gerard!' Delphine called. 'What is your decision as adjudicator?'

'I was not close enough to see,' the man answered.

'Oh, so now we have an adjudicator and he's not watching?' Orla stated.

There was more oohing and Jacques wondered whether he ought to step in and stop this. It really didn't matter to him if he won or not. But he knew this contest mattered to Delphine because her late husband had loved it.

'It is now the turn of Philippe!' Delphine declared.

'Wait, what?' Orla asked. 'You're moving on? But we haven't settled on how many points I have!'

He had heard enough to know now was the time to intervene. He made his way around the tables until he was standing beside Orla.

'It's not your turn,' Orla greeted him. 'Apparently it's Philippe's.'

'I am aware,' Jacques answered. 'So, we should stand out of his way. He likes to really go for it with his back swing.'

With that said, Philippe promptly arrived and began warming up for his go at tossing his pentagon-shaped beanbag.

'Did you see my throw?' Orla asked when they were a safe distance away. 'It hit the pit.'

'You are very invested,' Jacques remarked.

'What's that supposed to mean?' she replied, somewhat defensively.

'Well, before this morning you did not know that this game exists and now it is like you must be the best.'

'Says the man who told me how many beanbag crowns he has won since time began.'

'There are limited things to do in Saint-Chambéry. As you are experiencing.'

'I don't know about that,' Orla said. 'I haven't had a minute to do anything for myself since I arrived here. And I have a story to write, no mute man and no reindeer.' She looked straight at him then. 'Do you happen to have anything symbolic you do to remember a lost love or something?'

Straight away the sounds of the noisy bar diminished, and in his mind they were replaced by a hum and buzz of white noise in response to her question. *Lost love. Shattered heart. Sleepless nights. Nothingness.* It had been two and a half years now since Katie had called time on their relationship. And he knew it had all been his fault. He had given her everything he could give, but what she had wanted were the pieces he wasn't able to part with. The bits he didn't know if he was ever going to deal with himself.

'And I really want to know, do I call you Jacques or Wolf? Because that's still unclear.'

He internally shook himself, nothing showing on the outside. 'Wolf is just a name they used to call me when I first arrived.'

'Why?' Orla asked.

He shrugged. 'I do not know.'

'Come on,' she urged. 'You don't give someone a nickname for no reason.'

'I cannot answer for other people.'

'That's a nothing reply,' Orla said. 'And when I interview you, I'll be wanting more than nothing replies.'

'Has the interview not already begun?' he asked.

'In the middle of beanbag warfare? I'm a professional.'

'Wow, OK,' Jacques said with a smile. 'You really are taking this seriously.'

'Not quite as seriously as Delphine with her lax attention to the actual rules that apparently *she* makes.'

'Wolf! Wolf! Wolf!'

The chanting signified it was his turn to throw.

'You have cheerleaders it seems,' Orla remarked with a scoff. 'Oh! I didn't see how Philippe did.'

'Not as good as you,' Jacques answered.

Once he was lined up in position, he held his breath and closed his eyes. Why did it feel like it was more important this year than any other? It really didn't matter to him. He only did this because it mattered to Delphine. And, as irritating as Delphine could be, she had been like a mother to him since he had arrived here. Not just welcoming, as she was to everyone, but she hadn't judged him on anything but the here and now.

He toyed with the wagon wheel beanbag in his hand and tried to block out everything else. It was his taking part that mattered to Delphine, not the winning. Maybe it was time to give someone else a turn. He could just throw it a bit over to the left. With one quick swing, he let the beanbag leave his hand. And then...

'Ow!'

'Oh God, she's on fire! Help! Someone help!'

## 17

'Are you sure you are OK?'

It was about Jacques's fifth time of asking and Orla wasn't sure if she was more annoyed at that than she was about the large singe mark on the sleeve of her jacket. Yes, his beanbag had hit her and propelled her – or her sleeve at least – into the flames of the fire pit, but it hadn't been intentional and it had never been as serious as having to stop, drop and roll. And feeling some kind of responsibility, Delphine had brought them cognacs and made them sit at this table next to the Christmas tree and furthest away from any further potential disaster.

'I'm fine,' Orla answered. 'You're talking to someone who's had to run from lava in Italy.'

'This does not happen usually,' Jacques remarked.

'You surprise me,' Orla said. 'Seeing as how there was a lady stationed by a fire extinguisher throughout the whole contest.'

'That is Madame Voisin,' Jacques said, as if that explained it all.

'And?'

'She needs to have something to do or she will start doing things that Delphine does not want her to do.'

'Ah,' Orla said, sipping the cognac, which was pleasantly warming. 'Delphine seems to be at the very heart of everything here, doesn't she? This fiery contest, the shop-stroke-café-stroke-bed-and-very-rapid-breakfast, my being here, the non-existent reindeer...' She let the sentence linger.

'You still do not believe it is coming,' Jacques said as a statement.

'Do you? If you're really honest?'

She looked straight into his eyes, wanted to see any flicker of hesitation. She usually had a good read on whether someone was telling the truth or not.

'I believe that Delphine would not deliberately mislead me,' he answered.

'But would she mislead *me*?'

'Delphine is a good person. Why would you think otherwise?'

He had a point. What was this immediate distrust she was sending out into the world lately? Was how things had ended with Henry now making her question everything and everyone?

'I... don't know,' she admitted.

'Well, I have known her for a while now and her motive behind anything is good-natured.'

'Apart from when she's insisting I'm standing over the mark on the floor for the beanbag throw.'

'You were,' Jacques said with a smile.

'Maybe one tiny toe's worth,' she admitted.

'And you made the final so...'

Yes, that's how crazy this place was. She was in the final of a beanbag slinging contest.

'So I should probably ask you some questions before I have to spend my days practising for that. Is there a cash prize or an actual crown?'

'Is that your first question?'

It was beginning to be a running joke now but she really did have to get her journalistic head on if she was going to make anything productive out of this trip. Even if the pregnant reindeer turned out to be no more than a festive myth, she would be expected to come up with goods of some kind. And currently, in any spare second, Orla was going back over autumn conversations she'd had with Frances where her boss had definitely been budget conscious. Was *Travel in Mind* in financial difficulty? Could her job be at risk if this story didn't fly? It was one thing to want bigger and better things – like her dream of *Time* magazine – but it was quite another to have to jump ship quick if the need suddenly arose. She took a sip of her drink.

'I asked it before – why do some people call you "Wolf"?' She cradled the cognac glass in her hands.

He shrugged. 'What does it matter?'

'OK, well, I get "Wolf" is giving all manly and strong, but you're telling me if the village called you "Buttercup" or something you wouldn't want to know why?'

He shrugged again. 'Why do *you* think they call me "Wolf"?'

She looked at him again with this in mind. 'Well, it wouldn't be a name I would call you in relation to how you look.'

'No?'

'Wolves are strong, yes, but they're wiry, not tall or solid or more like... a bear.'

Why had she said that? A bear! And why when she'd said the words 'tall' and 'solid' had her eyes done an all-over body reconnaissance of him, from his dark hair, down over his broad, muscular-looking shoulders and lower to his chest in that tight-knit sweater...

'A bear,' he said with a definite look of amusement.

At least he hadn't growled. Although there were parts of her that were signalling that might have been appealing. What was wrong with her? She looked at the cognac in her glass as if it was to blame for everything.

'What is your nickname?' he asked her.

'I don't have one,' she answered straight off the bat.

He gazed at her and then swirled the liquid in his glass as if his brain was doing something similar in response to her reply. 'You lie to me.'

'What? Why would you think that?'

'I do not *think* it. I know it.'

He couldn't know. She'd only had one nickname her whole life. Given to her by her dad. Orla Orange. It had begun when she was small and she had pronounced the 'o-r' of 'orange' like the 'o-r' of Orla. It was silly. She swallowed, the cognac reminding her of some of the issues the Bradbee family were facing back home.

'So, what is it? The name?' he continued.

'I told you,' she said. 'I don't have one.'

'And I told you that I know you are not telling the truth.'

She smiled now, gaining some control back. 'And you being so confident with that leads me to thinking that you must have some kind of... psychology background.'

He smiled. It was a good smile. The kind that somehow teased.

'What?' Orla asked when no reply was instantly forthcoming.

'Now I *definitely* know you have a nickname.'

Why did she now feel like someone had dropped her out of her depth in the swimming pool? How was this man doing this to her? She never let anyone, apart from Erin get the better of her in conversation unless it was for her own benefit. It was time to stop messing around. She picked her bag up off the stone floor and took her electronic pad out, snapping the pen off its mount.

'Age?' she asked him.

'How old do you think I am?'

'I'll put thirties.'

'What?'

'Single. Obviously. Lives in the middle of nowhere in one of France's harshest mountain environments with a sole canine companion in a smart house that resembles... I think I'll put "something out of a panic-room movie".' She scribbled furiously. 'No photos of family or friends. No books. Connects with community just enough but doesn't really appear to like it. Perhaps integrates to conform to social norms or give a little to avoid questions to hide a dark back story. Smacks of only child, or maybe even orphan?'

She didn't know what was moving fastest, her pen over the notepad or her mouth firing out her thoughts.

'OK, we're done,' Jacques said, getting up.

'What?' Orla asked. 'But you said if I came here tonight you would answer any questions I had.'

'That was before.' He plucked his coat from the back of the chair and started to put it on.

'Before what? Before you scorched my favourite jacket? Before you got an attitude?'

He turned then, took a step closer to her chair, his presence filling the space. 'Before you decided to make the way I live into some kind of joke.'

She could see he was angry. There was a pulse in his neck visibly beating, his pupils were dilated, his lips were firm and, she suspected, keeping clenched teeth in check.

'I'm... not doing that. I just...' She paused, her temperature rising. 'You're not giving me anything.'

'So, what do you do, Orla?' he asked. 'When someone doesn't give you anything?'

The way he was looking at her was burning her worse than any flaming beanbag. Those dark eyes were a mix of fire and granite – alight with anger and as hard as rock. And she didn't know how to respond as the intensity hung like a perilous abseiler.

'Surprise!'

Orla jumped and watched Jacques flinch too as a pair of hands were clapped to his shoulders and someone appeared right there with them. It was a man, maybe in his late teens, dark hair fluffed on top and short and tapered everywhere else.

'Whoa, dude. You OK? You're shaking,' the newcomer said to Jacques.

'It's this cognac,' Jacques answered quickly. 'And seeing you. What are you doing here?'

'Well, you know me.'

Apparently that was all the answer this young man was going to give.

'And this beautiful person does not know me,' the man said, looking at Orla. 'But, she should. Hi, I'm Tommy.' He reached out a hand.

'Orla,' she introduced, taking his hand.

'*Enchanté*,' he said, dropping a kiss on the top of her hand.

'Orla,' Jacques said. 'Meet my brother.' He took a breath and met her eyes, sharpness still evident. 'There goes your only child theory.'

# 18

'Who's the woman?' Tommy asked, putting a beer bottle down in front of Jacques and slapping him hard on the back with the other hand.

The beanbag contest might have reached its conclusion for the night but there were still many patrons in the bar making the most of the discounted prices. Tommy's question had Jacques's eyes going across the room to where he could see Orla was being introduced to Madame Voisin. Perhaps someone who talked more than anyone would be a good new focus for her...

'What are you doing here?' Jacques said, concentrating back on his brother, taking the beer and swigging quickly.

'I asked a question first.'

'She's no one,' Jacques replied.

'Whoa. That's harsh.'

Yes, it was harsh, but he couldn't deny he still wasn't over the assumptions Orla had made about him off the cuff. How she'd rattled out her opinions didn't fit with the reporter he had thought she was. Finally he answered his brother. 'She's someone

Delphine's got to come here to... you know... write about Saint-Chambéry and all the crazy things they do at Christmas.'

'Right, so not a date,' Tommy said, sitting down.

'No,' Jacques said firmly.

'No?'

'What are you doing here, Tommy?' With no warning. Without a heads-up so he could tell him not to come.

'Why do you keep asking that? It's like you're not happy to see me or something.'

'I didn't mean it like that. I just meant I thought you were with Dad for Christmas.' And he liked to know where his family was. It gave him a tiny amount of reassurance. If he knew where they were he could act quickly should it become necessary.

'Yeah, well, Dad is heading to Hawaii.'

'What?' He had had no knowledge of that either.

'The latest girlfriend who's fallen for his online rizz and will probably fall out of lust just as quick once she sees his hairline... unless he's already shown her his bank balance.'

Jacques shook his head. Ever since their mother had left some five years ago now, their dad had plunged straight into the dating pool with, it seemed, little concern for a plan to meet someone special and much more the idea of connecting with as many people as possible in every corner of the globe. He maintained he was completely happy with his trajectory but both Jacques and Tommy had their doubts.

'And Mom and Jonathan?' Jacques asked.

'No idea,' Tommy said. 'I haven't spoken to her since the last time she tried.'

'Tommy...'

'What? So you can live your life without talking to her but I have to build a bridge or whatever? No.'

It might have been five years since their mom had announced she was leaving – when Tommy was only thirteen – but the unexpectedness of it, the hurt, the pain it had caused his younger brother more than him, was still raw like it had happened yesterday. Jacques hadn't been there. He couldn't be there. But he still blamed himself for that despite knowing his presence alone wouldn't have changed any outcome.

'And Jonathan's a dick,' Tommy added.

'We don't know that.'

'*I* know that. Anyone his age who re-posts videos of girls lip-synching to Tate McCrae needs medical attention.'

'You're still stalking his social media,' Jacques stated.

'It's part of my better life journey. I look at things to encourage me. I can't help it if I'm encouraged by other people's crazy-ass behaviour and the realisation that I may get low, but they definitely get lower.'

And it also meant that Tommy did care about their mother if he was concerned enough to keep looking at what the man their mother had married was up to on TikTok.

'So, what's the story with the woman then?' Tommy asked, sipping his beer.

'I told you,' Jacques said. 'She's writing about the village.'

'Yeah, I got that,' Tommy replied. 'Just trying to work out why that would mean you keep staring over at her. Unless you're looking over at Madame Voisin. I like what she's done with her hair. It's... pearly.'

Jacques maintained his cool and shook his head, mouth going back to his beer. He hadn't been looking over at Orla. Tommy was just trying to get him to admit something that wasn't even something. But he had taught his brother at least some of what he knew and the student rarely outperformed the master.

'There's no other story here, Tommy,' Jacques assured.

'Maybe I'll ask Delphine. She hasn't spotted me yet... wait, shit, no, I made eye-contact and she's on her way... with... OK, who is that goddess coming with her?'

Jacques looked across the bar and saw that Delphine was indeed coming their way and it was Erin who was alongside her.

'Jacques, does my hair look OK?' Tommy asked him, fingers going into the waves spiked upwards at the front.

'What?'

'Man, come on! Does it look OK? I've had my helmet on all the way from your house.'

'What? You've been to the house already? And you've taken my motorbike?'

He didn't have time to say anything else. Delphine and Erin were right there.

'Thomas!' Delphine exclaimed and then went on to ask him four different questions in French as she clapped her arms around him and immediately ruffled his hair so it was as out of place as it could get. Jacques also knew all the questions would never get an answer from his brother and that Tommy's French hadn't been fully used for five years. That's what happened when the French part of your family left...

'Is everything OK?' Jacques asked Erin as his brother tried to deflect Delphine's attention and sort out his hair.

'Apparently we have to leave,' Erin stated, indicating the cabin cases either side of her.

'What?' Jacques asked.

Was this because of what he'd said to Orla? She was really going? For a second he felt guilty.

'Yes!' Delphine announced, facing Jacques. 'It is unfortunate but finally I will get new windows in the guest suite. You know how long I have been waiting for them and tomorrow they come. So, Orla and Erin will have to move in with you. I am still not decided on how the windows should open. Do I have a tilt or a wide-opening? It is cold now but in the summer it gets very hot up there.'

Jacques's brain hurt from the speed with which Delphine was delivering the information. The women weren't leaving? There were windows? Wait, had she said they were moving in with him?

'Hi, I'm Tommy.'

'O-K,' Erin answered, looking Tommy up and down like his introduction might be some kind of trick.

'And you don't look like you should be carrying any kind of heavy bags with those perfect nails so I will take these outside and put them in my brother's truck. OK?' Tommy said as he took ownership of the cases.

What the hell was going on here? His brother was apparently staying with him and he was about to get two other house guests? He had to have alone time, just him and Hunter, and no one seemed to ever understand that. As Tommy and Erin began to leave the table with the luggage and head towards the door of the bar, Jacques turned to Delphine.

'Delphine, I can't have people stay at my house. You know that.'

He could. Theoretically. He'd been assured it was OK. But when you always trusted your gut and your gut still told you it was better to be safe and inhospitable than it was to take risks, it was hard to change that.

'Jacques, what am I supposed to do? Make them sleep between the aisles of my supermarket? Or perhaps ask Gerard if they can bed down in the cellar with his brewing equipment? You are the only one around here with the space.'

'Madame Voisin has the space. She rented out the whole top floor of her house to yoga students last summer,' Jacques reminded her quickly.

But then Delphine struck him with one of 'those' looks and before she had even said anything he knew this wasn't a situation he had a choice in.

'Jacques, I do not ask for much. It will only be for a few days and then they can come back here... maybe... if the windows are done.'

It didn't sound conclusive at all. But what was the alternative? He wasn't the creating-a-scene kind of person. Besides, Tommy was already here. A risk was a risk no matter the multiples. And he would be helping out someone who had helped him out. Except maybe there was one thing he could nail down before he agreed...

'OK,' he replied. 'But if I am to have house guests, then I need a firm date for when this pregnant reindeer will be here. You know, in case I have to also accommodate that.'

He struck Delphine with a look he hoped conveyed he was not going to take any half-truths now. He knew how she reacted under pressure. She was a rapid talker, a filler of gaps in any dead air, her expression warping and shifting as much as her lips. Except there was none of this happening. When she replied it was with confidence.

'I have been told the reindeer's transportation was delayed because of the extreme cold.'

'How far is it coming from? Because I am thinking the vet in Grenoble would be better—'

'Should I send Orla and Erin to the vet in Grenoble too?' Delphine interrupted. 'Because I always thought Saint-Chambéry was a place where people... or animals... were welcomed without question.'

What could he possibly say to that?

He nodded. 'OK.'

'Good,' Delphine answered. 'But I would make sure you keep Tommy and Erin at separate ends of the house. The way the boy was looking at her was the way Hunter looks when he sees a wild rabbit.'

## 19

'Hello, Mum.'

Orla was in Jacques's kitchen being watched by Hunter while the others were in the living room. She could hear Erin and Jacques's brother all making loud comments about the wood burner Jacques was trying to relight. How was she in this weird domestic situation all of a sudden?

'Oh, hello, Orla love. I know I said don't worry about me, but I was starting to worry about you. There's no storm front is there?'

Orla swallowed. Her mum sounded so far away and coming from someone who had spoken to her mum from places much further from the UK than France, Orla knew it was completely to do with the family predicament.

'No,' she said. 'Just Hurricane Erin.'

'Oh, Jesus, what's she got herself into?'

'Not the size-eight dress yet, apparently,' Orla replied. 'But that's probably a good thing with this weather.' She looked to the window. The sky was black outside but the bright white snow illuminated everything from Jacques's truck that had brought them back here to the craggy mountain backdrop. 'No storms, but it's pretty cold.'

'You need candles,' Dana answered. 'Warm you up a treat when the heating's on the blink.'

'Your heating's not working now?' Orla exclaimed.

'Temporarily. Your dad's getting Terry to look at it when he can. I told him if we don't have the cash I'm selling his golf clubs the way he sold my mother's jewellery. The liar can't even admit to selling it. Says I've misplaced it like I'm an eejit or something!'

Orla could hear the emotion in her mum's tone now. 'Mum, don't cry.'

'Catch yourself on, I'm not crying. I have no tears left for that man right now.'

Orla leaned against the countertop, adjusting the phone at her ear and Hunter raised his head, watching. 'Oh, Mum.'

'Don't you worry. Everything will be grand. Well, you know, not grand perhaps, but OK.'

'Did you manage to speak to the doctor?'

'Yes, love, I did.'

'And what did he say?'

'He said I could have some anti-depressants if I wanted.'

'What?' Orla exclaimed.

'I said no. For now. But, you know, it mightn't be a bad thing.'

'Mum, no! What did he say about seeing Dad? About the drinking.'

'He said that unless Dad wants help there's no help to be had.'

Orla closed her eyes and took a breath. This was a nightmare and it wasn't good enough. She opened her eyes again. 'Is Dad there now?'

'In spirit. Full of spirits actually. Fell asleep before the end of *Would I Lie To You*.'

'Wake him up,' Orla said. 'I want to speak to him.'

'Orla, no. I can't wake him up. In fact, the local brass band couldn't wake him up.'

'Well, someone needs to speak to him. Things can't go on like this! He's not well and he's making you unwell and... I don't want Erin to come back to this.' She swallowed as she heard Erin's laugh filter through from the living room.

'That girl barely spends any time with either of us. She wouldn't know if your father turned into Jeremy Clarkson.'

'I disagree,' Orla said. 'I think she notices much more than you think.'

'How can she? She's permanently on the phone to that man in Morocco! And what have you found out about him?'

'I haven't had much of an opportunity to ask her about Burim. I'm working here, Mum.'

And her mother had expertly pulled the subject of the conversation away from her dad. What was she going to do? From this far away?

'Mum, I want to talk to Dad. I want you to tell him that I will call him tomorrow and I want him sober when he answers.'

'He's not going to like that I've told you half of what I've told you,' Dana said, sighing.

'I don't care,' Orla stated. 'That's what's going to happen.'

Hunter made a noise and got up, starting to pant, mouth opening and tongue hanging out. It was then she realised Jacques was entering the kitchen as, on the phone, her Mum began to protest again.

'Mum, I have to go. I'll call Dad tomorrow. Don't forget to tell him. And... don't worry, OK? Everything will be all right.'

As a lump arrived in her throat, she rushed a goodbye and ended the call. She forced an overenthusiastic smile and petted Hunter on the head.

'Parents!' She gave a dramatic sigh and hoped that explained everything she definitely wasn't going to say.

Jacques pulled the large coffee machine forward and opened a cupboard above.

'Did you manage to get the wood burner going again?' Orla asked him.

'You really think I would not?'

'No, I just... I don't know... I guess I was just thinking... I...' She stopped talking as the lump in her throat had somehow managed to grow in size and become a boulder lodged in her chest.

'Listen, Orla, I want to apologise for earlier. The way I reacted was... not how I should have reacted.'

She shook her head as she tried to maintain some equilibrium with her emotions. 'No, I was to blame too. I was unprofessional and those things I said were, I don't know, ridiculous.'

'Is everything OK?' Jacques asked her. 'With your parents?'

'Yes,' she said quickly. Too quickly. 'No, actually... they are... going through something right now and it's difficult, you know?'

'They are separating?' he asked, pressing buttons on the machine.

'No!' she said immediately. But then she thought over his question. Would they? Because this was no good for either of them. Except when you had been married for as long as they had surely you worked through every kind of problem without deciding there was no hope? And she still hadn't given him an answer.

'My parents,' Jacques said. 'They separated.'

'Oh, I'm sorry,' Orla replied.

'No, don't be sorry,' Jacques answered. 'Sometimes people just aren't meant to be together forever. No matter what promises they've made.'

'Do they still both live in France?' Orla asked him.

He shook his head. 'No, we are originally from Canada. The French part. My mother's parents were both French. My father's parents, Canadian. Tommy and I are a mix of the two.'

'So, that's where he's come from now? Canada? All that way?'

Jacques smiled. 'Yes, but knowing my brother he probably began this trip a week ago. He has never been one to shy away from exploration. It would not surprise me if our father hadn't even realised he had left the country.'

'And now here you are, going from a recluse with only his trusty canine companion to having a house full of people,' she remarked.

'And two teenagers who demand I must try to use this fucking coffee machine I've never been able to get to work the same way twice.'

She smiled, enjoying the slip in Jacques's usual aloof demeanour and a sliver of humour.

'Do you want me to look at it?' she asked him.

'Please! I thought you would never ask,' he said with another smile.

'OK,' Orla said, sizing it up like it was an opponent in a wrestling ring. 'How hard can it be?'

'Well, it was not originally mine and I have never established a working relationship with it.'

'So do we go through it methodically? Or shall I just press each button in turn and see what happens?'

'That is really what you are going to do?' Jacques asked, sounding a bit shocked.

'You haven't had a better idea in years so...'

She started to hit buttons one after another and suddenly the machine burst into life, whirring and whizzing and spurting until steam started shooting out of places that it didn't look like steam should come from. Orla screamed.

'I don't want to be burned again! Make it stop!' She pressed more buttons, trying to halt what she had started.

'*You* did this!' Jacques exclaimed, pulling the handle.

The machine started vibrating so much it was almost walking itself across the counter. Instinctively they both rushed forward to pull the plug and Orla slammed into Jacques's shoulder. It was like running into a brick wall.

'Orla, are you OK? I am so sorry!'

'It's OK,' she answered, holding her arm but laughing. 'Stop the machine!'

He pulled the plug out and the machine gave one last spurt and Jacques ended up with foam on the end of his nose.

'You look like one of the snowman faces Delphine drew on those cookies she was serving tonight!' Orla said, laughing even more.

'Really?' he replied. He put a finger to the foam, scooped it off and, in one quick move, wiped it on her cheek.

'What? That's disgusting!' Orla exclaimed, immediately putting her fingers to the cream and getting it off her face.

'Don't do it,' Jacques warned her, taking a step back from her.

'Do what?' she asked, advancing.

'I'm warning you, Orla. Don't do it.'

There was nothing she loved more than a challenge. And being told *not* to do something was one of her personal favourites. She went for him, intending to wipe her foamy fingers all over his beard... except, somehow, in a split second, she was on her back on the table, her foamy hand up above her head, pinned into a position where she couldn't strike. How had she got here? And how was this man managing to keep her in place with one hand on her wrist and one hand... where was his other hand? She could kind of feel it, but she also couldn't and she was sort of temporarily immobilised.

'How did you do that?'

'I can't tell you,' he answered.

His body was close, nothing touching her apart from that hand on her wrist, but she could feel the sensation of him. Her stomach did a deep dive.

'O-K,' she managed to say. 'So... what happens next?' Her mind was already conjuring up images of how this might play out and most of them involved fewer clothes. What was she thinking? All this man had done since she had met him was wind her up!

'That is up to you,' Jacques answered, a wry smile on his face that was somehow peppering her vagina.

'Is this like the locked-door scenario?' she asked, her throat becoming drier. 'Because I thought we as good as agreed that was weird.'

'I'm going to stop pressing on your ear if you promise not to wipe that foam on me.'

He was pressing on her ear? Why couldn't she feel it? And now she was focussing on why she couldn't feel his touch on her ear more so than anything else...

'Whoa! OK! I am closing my eyes and wishing I hadn't witnessed this!'

It was Tommy's voice and suddenly Jacques had rebounded from the table like someone had thrown a grenade into the room... or tried to wipe his face with foam.

'Tommy,' Jacques said. 'We were just—'

'Yeah,' Tommy said. 'I get it! I'm eighteen now, bro. But, seriously, in front of Hunter?'

It took the dog to whine for Orla to realise she was still lying on her back on the table. She propelled herself upwards, her hand still covered in foam.

'Yeah,' Tommy said, nodding at Orla, hand held out awkwardly. 'I don't even want to know what that is.'

## 20

'Oh my God,' Erin said, star-fishing across a king-size bed in another clean-lined, non-personalised room. 'This is so much nicer than Delphine's.'

'Delphine's room had character,' Orla remarked, putting her case into one of the large wardrobes that spanned the whole of one wall.

'It was full of crap you mean. I found a puppet under the bed. A puppet. Let it sink in how creepy that is. I took a photo and showed Burim. He said it looked like a dead baby.'

Orla rubbed at her eyes as she sat down on what little of the bed there was left for her to currently occupy. She was suddenly utterly exhausted.

'I don't believe the window story by the way,' Erin remarked, scrolling on her phone.

'What?'

'Delphine's double-glazing situation,' Erin said like she was explaining to a toddler. 'It's all bullshit. Like the reindeer.'

Orla was getting to the point where the word 'reindeer' was feeling like a code word for an ex or a new Class A drug.

'I need to come up with a plan,' she said, a yawn escaping her lips.

'What sort of plan?' Erin asked, curling up her legs and doing a body roll towards Orla.

'One that's going to get me a proper story to give to my boss whether it involves reindeer or not. Because as soon as I do that, the sooner we can get out of here.'

'But... we've only really just got here,' Erin said. 'And now we're at this much better place with Wi-Fi that actually works and this much bigger, better bed and—'

'And you know this isn't a holiday, Erin,' Orla interrupted. 'It's my work. And you aren't actually meant to be here.'

'Wow, OK.'

Orla hadn't meant it to come out so harsh. Her little sister had enough going on in her life without her being snappy with her. Even if this wasn't a holiday, what she had waiting for her when she got back to England was their parents in crisis.

'Sorry,' Orla apologised. 'I didn't mean that. I told you, I'm just tired, that's all.' She tipped herself backwards, aligned her head so she was face to face with Erin. 'What do you think to Jacques's brother?'

'Tommy?' Erin said, as if there were a line-up of brothers to choose from.

'Yes, I mean, he's your type, isn't he?'

'No.'

'But he has, you know, the fluffy hair you like.'

'Used to like. When I was like thirteen. Anyway, I have Burim now.'

'But, Burim, he's in Morocco.'

'What?'

'Burim lives in Morocco, right?'

Erin suddenly sat up. 'Why do you think that?'

'Because Mum said he's Moroccan.'

'I knew she didn't listen to me,' Erin said, sounding annoyed. 'I told her about Burim once. I didn't want to, not really, but I thought, I don't know, share something with my family. And she doesn't even remember anything I said!'

Orla sat up too. 'But, if he isn't Moroccan then—'

'Is that all you've got to say?' Erin thumped the pillow. 'I don't know why it matters what nationality he is. He likes me. That should be enough. Unless I'm so utterly unlovable that my family can't comprehend that someone fit like him would be into me.'

'No, Erin, it's not that! Of course it's not that! You're so beautiful, inside and out. Mum's just Mum and she worries and wherever Burim is in the world he's so far away and—'

'So she would rather I smashed one of the local goblins who hang outside H&M vaping and sending a constant mist of tropical fruits into the air?'

'I don't think anyone said anything about smashing.'

She swallowed. Was Erin thinking about sex? She was sixteen. Of course she was thinking about that. And suddenly Orla felt completely out of her depth. What advice could she impart when her last in-person intimate encounter was with someone dressed as a convict at a Halloween party in Berlin whose name she hadn't even asked...

'Well, Burim and I have talked about it and we both want to do it. We talk about it all the time actually.'

'Of course you do,' Orla said sighing. 'But, Erin, it might not be that...' She stopped herself continuing.

'What?'

'I just worry that, you know, with internet relationships, there's usually one person who is more invested than the other.'

'And you think that's me?'

'Well, I know how enthusiastic you get with things.'

Erin's mouth turned into a firm line before she said the next words. 'You just called me obsessive.'

'No,' Orla said. 'Not at all. But guys can be very... expressive. And they can paint a lovely picture of all the things you'd like to see in your future and, you know, you might not be the only girl they're painting the picture for. When you meet someone in real life it's different.' She swallowed. If that's how she *really* felt why did she always fall into these Instagram situationships where she never met anyone in person? And the sad fact was, the people she had so far met in real life and had relations with had lasted less time than any of the online-based guys. She had known a lot less about someone she'd actually swapped bodily fluids with than the men in her DMs.

'Oh!' Erin said, almost vaulting off the bed to stand. 'Oh, it's different, is it? You don't think a liar can lie as well when he's looking at you over a box of Chicken Selects as he can when he's talking with his thumbs?'

'Well, I wouldn't say—'

'I know more about Burim than I know about anyone. I know what brand of toothpaste he likes, I know how many cousins he has and all their names, I know that on Tuesdays he always eats pizza and on Thursday nights he does boxing. I know that because he tells me everything and he asks everything about me too. Why isn't that real just because we haven't met in person yet?'

'Erin, I wasn't saying that—'

'I don't want to talk any more,' Erin said firmly. 'And I'm going to get changed in the bathroom.'

'Erin.'

Orla's last attempt to not end the conversation was met with the slamming of the door of the en suite. It seemed that she was getting everything wrong in all aspects of her life at the moment. Rolling towards the edge of the bed, she got up too and made her way to the window. Looking out at the snow scene, so soft and pristine, yet also so incredibly hard and stark, it was a bit like a reminder of life and all its layers. And it seemed like she was the one always in charge of peeling them away or sticking them back into place...

Suddenly a light went on and Orla could see the other 'wing' of the wooden house. It was a bedroom, not unlike this one, large bed, neutral furnishings, and... then Hunter appeared. Was this Jacques's bedroom? Before Orla could make a decision to step away or close the curtains, Jacques was there in the room... wearing only a pair of low-rise trunks. She swallowed, watching him put on a pair of glasses, stroke Hunter before the dog curled up on a pet bed in the corner of the room and then pluck a book from a stack on the nightstand... He *did* have books. He was a reader. There was something about a man who read that she had always found attractive. She watched him sit on the edge of the bed, honed abs on full display, already apparently fully invested in his reading as she did a further reconnaissance of his body. She swallowed as she remembered what had happened in the kitchen. He'd apologised, she had got upset about her parents and then suddenly she was spread out on the kitchen table while he performed some ear voodoo. Except the overwhelming recollection was the way it had felt to have someone that close to her again. Someone appealing, in a physical sense at least, because his stubbornness was not attractive in the slightest and he wasn't making her assignment here super easy. Someone so close in her personal space that she had been able to feel his breath on her chest...

And then she bolted from her position and grabbed at the curtains, pulling them closed. Because while she had been letting her mind wander, Jacques had looked up from his book and stared straight at her.

## 21

'Tommy, don't touch it. It's broken. You know it's broken.'

'Right, so that's what you and Orla were doing last night in the kitchen? Trying to make it work?'

Jacques appreciated his brother's eyebrow raise less than he appreciated the fact Tommy was preparing to start the coffee machine again. He was really going to have to get it out of the kitchen once and for all. Why was he holding on to it? Yes, he might have told Orla one reason but the truth was because it had been Katie's.

'You have the wrong idea,' Jacques said, getting two mugs out of the cupboard and setting them aside.

'About the machine? Or about Orla?'

'Both.'

'Yeah,' Tommy said. 'Not sure I believe you on either count. You were up at 5 a.m. and you've already chopped logs this morning.'

'It's called a routine,' Jacques answered. 'Some of us have them.'

'Is that right, Hunter? Or is he lying to us both? Hey?'

Jacques shook his head as Tommy began to fuss over Hunter until the dog was whipped up into a frenzy and began spinning around in a circle chasing the tea towel Tommy was swinging in front of him. He hadn't slept particularly well and as soon as the smart home monitor told him the outside temperature was warmer than it had been in the past couple of weeks, he had gone out for a run.

'Good morning. *Bonjour* and all that,' Erin greeted, sashaying into the kitchen and heading straight for the coffee machine.

'*Bonjour, ma chérie,*' Tommy replied, standing up straight and putting the tea towel down on the worktop.

'Did you call me a cherry?' Erin exclaimed. 'Because that's pretty presumptuous and also none of your business.'

'What?' Tommy asked.

'Tommy said "good morning, my dear",' Jacques translated.

'Huh,' Erin said. 'Bad joke seeing as we have issues with a deer that hasn't turned up.'

She side-stepped Tommy, took one of the mugs Jacques had got down, slipped it on to the machine, pressed two buttons and the machine set to work.

'What the hell!' Tommy exclaimed in awe. 'How did you do that?'

'Do what?' Erin asked.

'Get that thing to spurt actual stuff that looks like coffee into a cup without it showering everyone or doing nothing at all. Never really knew which one was worse but none of them got me coffee where it should be.'

Erin shrugged. 'Life skills I guess.' Her phone made a noise and she tipped it over so it was screen down on the countertop.

'OK, Jacques, I put Erin in charge of making all coffee from now on,' Tommy announced. 'I drink a lot of coffee by the way.'

'I can tell,' Erin replied.

'Yeah? Well, what do you think my go-to is?'

'Judging by your constant high energy, I'd say triple espresso.'

Jacques couldn't help but laugh and straight away both of them looked at him as he began to cut bread into slices at the table.

'Wow, you bossed the coffee machine *and* you got my brother to laugh this early in the morning. Grand feats,' Tommy said.

Erin's phone made another noise.

'Sounds like you're in high demand,' Tommy remarked. 'Maybe it's the universe calling, asking you to fix global warming.'

The phone dinged again.

'Wow,' Tommy said. 'Either you're going viral, or you have a stalker.'

'I'm in a talking stage with someone. It's three months now.'

'Sounds like he's the one doing all the talking. Jacques, where's the eggs?'

'Damn it!' Jacques remarked. 'I meant to get some from Delphine yesterday.'

'What happened to your chickens?' Tommy asked.

'It's cold, Tommy. They are in the barn. They do not lay in the winter.'

'You have chickens?' Erin said.

'I do,' Jacques answered as he put bread into a small basket.

'Orla loves chickens.'

'Really?' Jacques said. This was interesting. Someone who had seen many different animals from every part of the globe loved common farmyard poultry?

'Our mum used to joke that if Orla never got married she would be a chicken lady rather than a cat lady.'

Erin's phone dinged again.

'Make it stop! It's distracting,' Tommy said.

'A bit like your voice,' Erin snapped back.

'Morning.'

Hunter barked good-naturedly at Orla entering the kitchen.

'Good morning,' Jacques replied.

She was wearing jeans and a cream-coloured jumper, her hair down today, sitting just past her shoulders. It was a different look to the one he'd seen her in last night – dressed in pyjamas, staring out of the window. He'd thought, for a moment, that she'd been looking at him but it was more likely that she had been gazing at the moon.

'If you want coffee,' Tommy began. 'Erin will make you one. If she doesn't have to message Kim Jong Un and get him to stand down on whatever button he's threatening to press.'

Erin's phone erupted twice in quick succession.

'See!' Tommy said, as if his point was proven.

'Don't listen to him,' Erin replied. 'He talks more crap than Barney Walsh on *Gladiators*.'

'I have no idea who that is.'

'Do you have any headache tablets?' Orla asked. She had gravitated towards Jacques at the table.

'You have a headache?'

'That's why I asked for the pills.'

'OK,' Jacques said. 'Come with me.'

'I have to not take them in the kitchen?' she asked, looking confused.

He smiled and beckoned her away from the noise of the coffee machine, Erin's phone and Tommy and Erin's bickering. He led the way down the hall until he was pushing open the door to his gym.

'O-K,' Orla said, following him inside. 'I was not expecting something like this. It looks like a fitness suite just... without the weights. Are those gymnastic rings?' He watched her checking out the punch bags, and the martial arts equipment on the walls.

But it wasn't all fight club in here. There were yoga mats and exercise balls he used to get mindful.

'Welcome to my dojo,' Jacques said, bowing towards her.

'OK, so you do karate?'

He shook his head. 'No.'

'Taekwondo?'

'No.'

'Judo?'

'No.'

'OK, I am running out of martial arts names now.'

'What I practice doesn't really have a name,' Jacques informed her. 'But this is where I come when I need to get away from noise. Or if I have a headache.' He pointed to the floor which was soft matting. 'Take a seat.'

'This isn't my first rodeo at a dojo, you know,' Orla said, dropping down onto the floor. He watched her cross her legs and appear to get comfortable.

'No?' He knew. She had interviewed sumo wrestlers.

'I interviewed some sumo wrestlers last year. It is one of the craziest professions ever. Did you know they aren't allowed to drive? One wrestler had a bad accident and after that they were all banned from driving.'

'I did not know that.' He did know that. From her article. He sat down behind her.

'What are you doing?'

'I am going to cure your headache.'

'Honestly, just some Nurofen will be good.'

'Close your eyes.'

'You're not going to touch my ear again, are you?'

He smiled to himself and then he placed his fingertips at either side of her neck. OK, he hadn't really thought this through. Touching the curve below her jaw, how soft her skin was, how that was sending prickles across the back of his own neck. He steeled himself. 'Are your eyes closed?'

'Is it a pre-requisite?'

'Well, you should know that I was able to get you across a table last night, so I can also make you close your eyes if you'd like to do it that way.'

'Wow,' Orla said. 'Is that what they call a slightly veiled threat? OK, I'll close them.'

He inhaled slowly and then pressed his index finger and thumb lightly on her trapezius muscles. He focussed, keeping his breathing even and then gradually applied a little more pressure.

'Ow,' Orla said.

'Shh.'

'Did you shush me?'

'Does it really hurt?' Jacques asked. 'Or does it just feel different?'

\* \* \*

Who was this man? And how was he managing to do all these weird things with her? Weird and ever so *sensual*. Sensual had been out of her dictionary for so long she'd started to wonder if Susie Dent had banished it. Did his touch really hurt? No. It was intense, but oh-so tingly and pleasurable in all the right ways. And the tension in the base of her skull was definitely lessening.

'This room is the most personal room in your house,' she remarked.

'Orla, you're meant to have your eyes closed.'

'They are. I can recall things I've seen no more than three minutes ago.'

'What do you mean "personal"?'

'There are things in here. Things you use.'

'There are things I use in the rest of the house.'

'That everybody has. A table. Chairs. That bloody coffee machine.' She carried on. 'You made this room what it is. With things you use because of what you like to do when you're not doing whatever everyone else does. Still no photos though.'

'Are photos important to you?'

She hadn't expected that question but she was ready. 'They obviously aren't important to you.'

'Photos are just memories on paper,' he answered.

'And what? You don't like to look at them?'

'Perhaps I don't need images hanging behind glass to remember.'

She had never thought of it that way.

'Let me ask you something,' Jacques continued. 'When you interview someone for your magazine, do you always need all your notes to make the article?'

'What do you mean?'

'Well, I think some things you do and some things that people say, they stick with you so hard that you don't need to write them down to recall them.'

She thought about Luis eating his bowls of soup for his lost loved ones. She hadn't needed to refer to any notes to remember the look on his face, to recall the sadness in his voice, to smell the humidity in the air of that restaurant. And it was those things that had made her story stand out. Sounds, smells and sensations sold stories, not the hard facts. She needed to remember that.

'I bet you have many photos where you live,' Jacques continued.

'The pictures of people I care about make me happy.'

'Disagree.' She felt his fingers move gently up her neck.

'It's true.'

'And in these pictures of the people you care about, are they smiling?'

'Of course!'

'So it's their smiles that make you happy. You don't need physical paper evidence of what their smiles look like. You feel it. You know it by heart.'

And as his fingers traced her hairline at the back of her neck, it was no longer her head that was aching. His words, spoken in that deep, slightly husky tone, were suddenly sliding up to the locked gates of her heart and demanding the key. He was right. Everything he'd just said was so absolutely true.

Then, suddenly his touch left her and she snapped her eyes open. He had stood up, was pacing towards the window. She watched him, hands on his hips, lengthening his torso. But it was his mind she wanted more of an insight into. There was a depth to Jacques Barbier, an emotional intelligence he kept hidden for some reason. Article or no article, while she was here she needed to know what made this man who he was.

'It's warmer today,' he commented, looking outside. 'Still minus figures, but we could go out.'

'Is there anywhere to go except Saint-Chambéry that doesn't involve a full-on road trip?' She got to her feet.

'You need a story, right? In case the reindeer does not arrive.'

'I do,' she agreed.

'I might have something,' he said. 'If you have boots.'

'I have boots,' she confirmed.

'Good,' he answered, nodding. 'Then we shall go.'

## 22

---

'Tommy won't take Erin on that motorbike, will he?'

Orla had wanted to make it clear to Tommy and her sister before they'd left the two alone in the house that there would be no riding of any kind. However, as she'd had to change twice, adding more layers, when Jacques had told her it was still minus four degrees, she had missed her opportunity before the two of them had disappeared off to the cinema room. Now they were out in the elements, already a long way from the cabin, hiking through the snow, upwards, towards sheer mountain faces that Orla very much hoped they would not be traversing.

'He definitely would,' Jacques answered.

'What? No. We have to go back. Or call him.' She had already turned around in a circle, mentally deliberating what to do.

'Relax, Orla,' Jacques said. 'This is why you have a headache. The motorbike is now locked up. Tommy does not have the combination.'

'OK,' Orla said, taking a deep breath. That was one of the riding options dealt with. The other she really didn't want to discuss with Jacques.

'And Tommy, he is... respectful. Despite the smart mouth.'

'Oh, OK.' Why her cheeks were responding like they had been placed in a griddle pan she didn't know.

'You did not think about that? Two teenagers alone in a house?'

'No, I mean, yes, I did. I just wondered if they might fight or shave each other's eyebrows off before they, you know, thought about anything else.' She sighed as they continued to walk. 'And Erin has this situationship online she seems very invested in.'

'O-K.'

'Our mum is a bit worried about it actually and she's asked me to find out more and I don't quite know how best to handle it.'

'Because you don't have any experience in... what did you call it? A "situation"?'

'Situationship.'

'What is that exactly?'

'You don't know?'

'Is it a social media thing?' Jacques asked. 'Because I don't have that.'

'You don't have social media?'

'No.'

Orla couldn't believe it. She had never met anyone who didn't have some form of account even if they no longer used it. If she made a connection online she automatically made sure to check the person out in other places to see if things matched up. It was common sense to be safe.

'Not even Facebook?'

'Why is that hard to believe?'

'Because it's 2024. Because how do you communicate with people?'

'I call them. I send them a text message. Sometimes I write a letter.'

'You write a letter?!'

She was in shock. And now she could not get Noah from *The Notebook* out of her head...

'So a "situationship" is what? A romantic connection?'

'Um, well, yes, it's like an online relationship where you talk a lot, like every day, and then you might move it on to meeting the person in real life.'

'So like having a partner.'

'Well, yes... but no... because, you know, you haven't established that yet.'

He stopped walking and looked at her, his expression suggesting that he didn't really understand what she was saying. 'Messaging someone a lot, every day, meeting up with them but you're not boyfriend or girlfriend.'

Orla nodded. 'Yes.'

'Because no one has asked that question?'

'Mainly.'

'But why does no one ask the question?'

'Because they're too scared to ruin what they have.'

Perhaps she had answered too quickly. She had to remember she was talking about this from the perspective of Erin not herself. She had never asked Henry any of those questions. *What is this? Are we exclusive? Do you talk to other girls too?* But, then, he had never asked her either.

'I wish to go back in this conversation and not know what this thing is.' He started to walk again.

'Well, that's just how dating is these days,' Orla said, following.

'But how can you say it is dating when it's only talking via social media most of the time?'

'I... don't know.'

'Do you have someone you do this situationship with?'

She swallowed. 'No. Not any more.'

'But you have done this interaction before?'

'It was a while ago.'

'And how long do you do this messaging and not meeting for?'

'Well, sometimes a few weeks.' She swallowed. 'Other times... a few months.' She had talked to Henry for just short of five months.

'Months! Of just typing? I do not understand this.'

'Well, I don't know what it's like here in the wilderness of France, but in the UK it's about the only thing people do when they want to find a connection.' And sometimes she really missed it. Just having someone checking in on her every day, seeming to care, saying nice things, being part of her day. But now she had said it out loud to Jacques, it sounded all kinds of ludicrous. Perhaps it was time to change the subject. She didn't even know where they were headed.

'So, what are you taking me to see?'

'It is a cave,' he answered, upping his pace.

'Oh,' Orla said.

'You do not like caves?'

'I don't dislike them. The last time I went in one was in Hungary with a colony of Alcathoe bats.'

'Were they in a long-standing relationship or situationships?'

She smiled. 'Very funny.'

'Come on,' Jacques encouraged. 'It's not far.'

## 23

By the time they had reached the cave, Orla wasn't cold any more and she was slightly out of breath. As much as she thought she was quite fit in a cardiovascular kind of way, nothing prepared you for snowy mountainous terrain. The cave was nothing much more than a small fissure in the grey rock and she couldn't help feeling a bit disappointed. On the plus side, there was sunlight coming through the clouds now, taking away the chill and making their surroundings look a tiny bit less barren and bleak.

'Orla, come and sit here,' Jacques called, beckoning her over.

'Sit?' she queried. It might be a few degrees less hostile out here but it wasn't camping chairs and picnic blanket weather just yet.

'Come on,' he encouraged. 'I have brought cheese.'

The moment the 'c' word was said, her stomach flexed in appreciation. She stepped towards where he had positioned himself, sitting on a rock that was free of snow. She lowered herself down next to him and looked out at the incredible view down the valley. She could just about see the top of Jacques's house and then flowing down, through the forest, were the first signs of habitation and the spire of the Saint-Chambéry church.

'OK,' Jacques said. 'So, when I pass this to you, you have to sit very still and quiet.'

'You have to eat cheese in silence?' Orla asked. 'Is that a Saint-Chambéry tradition?'

'Please, Orla, it is for your own safety.'

'My own *safety*?' She said it rather loudly and it echoed. She repeated it in a whisper. 'My own *safety*?'

'You are a reporter. You have travelled across the world and been in many situations. There is always some level of danger when you go to different places, right?'

'And I usually always know what I'm going to be faced with before it happens.'

'Still and quiet,' Jacques repeated. He passed her a foil-wrapped parcel. 'Take one piece out, hold it out away from you, and keep the rest covered.'

'Hold it out how? At arm's length?'

She suddenly had visions of a falconry display, this cheese being the bait for a wild French eagle that was going to come soaring down from the sky and take the food and possibly her whole hand with it.

'Quiet and still,' he repeated. He already had a lump of gooey Brie in his fingers that smelled so delicious she really wanted to eat it, not hold out for whatever was coming.

She removed a wedge of... was it Camembert?... and held it between her thumb and forefinger, out to her left. How long did she have to wait? She was too scared to ask Jacques for a timescale when she was meant to be being still and quiet...

Then she heard it. Rustling. Scratching? Something was definitely happening and the sound was getting closer. She wanted to turn her head in the direction of the noise but something was telling her not to. She stayed still and then... something brushed her hand. The urge to move was so strong but she held it together, only her eyes darting. As the 'something' snatched at her hand she saw it. A silver fox. It was right there next to her, the cheese hunk hanging from its lips. She wanted to gasp, to say something to Jacques, but she also didn't want to shock the animal away. Except now her bottom felt numb from the rock-sitting and the more she was mentally telling herself not to move the more she wanted to move...

And then another fox walked right in front of her and nudged at the foil-wrapped parcel in her lap.

'Oh... hello,' she whispered.

'Don't let it take the foil,' Jacques instructed.

It was then she saw he had cheese in each hand and there were two foxes feasting from his fingers. It was one of the most ridiculous yet enchanting scenes she had ever been lucky enough to see. She took the parcel and peeled the wrapping back, taking out another piece of cheese.

'Here you go,' she said softly, stretching her arm towards the fox.

The fox looked suspicious at first, took a few tentative steps backwards, making indents in the snow. But Orla kept her hand steady, as well as her nerve and after a minute or so, the fox came back to her, not grabbing and running, but putting its snout to her hand, then a tongue and finally taking a nibble of the cheese.

'OK, now we can talk,' Jacques said, giving 'his' foxes more food.

'Have you tamed them?' Orla asked him.

'They are not tame,' Jacques answered. 'No wild animal is tame unless it has been made that way and does not really know anything else.'

'But you feed them regularly?'

He shook his head. 'I feed them sometimes. When I check on them. When I know the weather is bad and they will be struggling to find food in their habitat.'

'And you know they like cheese.'

'It is not all I give them, but the scent of it always brings them out of the cave.'

'So that's why we're at the cave,' Orla said, the fox taking the remainder of her chunk of Camembert. 'Is that where they live?'

'When the weather is as bad as it has been,' he answered.

'I've not seen foxes this colour before.'

'These ones are not quite silver, not quite black, not quite blue. A mix of all the colours.'

'They are really beautiful.' And she should really take a photo for her article. Except one of her hands was covered in creamy cheese... She reached into her coat pocket anyway and extracted her phone.

'What are you doing?'

'Taking a photo. If you move your cheese that way then that one will turn around and I can get his face more with the other two.'

'No,' Jacques replied.

'They're quite settled so now would be a good time. Before all the cheese runs out.'

'You're not taking a photograph,' Jacques said again.

'But you brought me here to give me something for a story, right?' she asked. 'And everyone knows that most people look at the photos before they read the story. The story won't be as well-clicked if there are no photos.'

Jacques was just staring at her now, those intense dark eyes meeting hers and not letting go. Well, neither was she. She made no further comment and let the looking carry on. She would break him. She always won a staring contest. Except... this was hard. He was not letting up. In fact, as the seconds ticked by, his gaze seemed to be getting all the more intense and she was starting to feel the need to blink. She hated this. She felt so out of control. Finally, she couldn't stand it any more. She let out a dissatisfied grunt as she dropped her eyes from his and the foxes scattered.

'Oh my God,' Orla said, getting to her feet. 'That was your fault and now they're gone.'

'*My* fault,' he said, shaking his head. 'You just told me that people are more interested in photos than words. And *you* are a writer.'

'I didn't say *more* interested. I definitely did not say that. I said that people look at the photos first, particularly online. And online is really important. If the magazine doesn't have a great digital presence and make the advertising revenue work then there won't be a budget for the print edition and I will start getting sent to locations much nearer to home and there won't be any more remote and undiscovered reports.' And with the way Frances was pushing this reindeer article was there a chance the print edition may be in trouble?

'But, we talked about it; it's the feelings, the sounds, the scents, the moments that you describe that hit harder than pictures.'

'Most people need a visual to accompany those things. Like a prompt to open their understanding of what comes next.'

'Like with these situationships?'

'Maybe.'

'But no in-person moments. No stopping to look and sense and enjoy. Just a photo and on to the next topic.'

She watched him put a finger in mouth and suck off the cheese like it was sexy fondue.

'I don't think you get it,' Orla said.

'Your magazine? Or this way of interacting with people?'

'Both,' she answered, putting her hands in the pockets of her coat.

'So, tell me.'

His answer took her by surprise and she didn't immediately know what to say.

'Tell you what?' she said.

'Tell me what you think.'

She swallowed. Now she really didn't know what to say. Why didn't she know what to say? Because no one ever asked her to tell them things. It was her job to ask others. That's what she did in her profession. That's what she did with her parents and Erin. That's what she had done with Henry...

'I think we shouldn't be out too long, no matter how respectful you think your brother is,' Orla replied. 'And I've scared away the foxes now and there's no photographic evidence they were even here so...'

'Orla—'

'Is it me or is it starting to snow again?'

'You like to change the subject when you are scared you will be the one *answering* the questions instead of asking them.'

'That's just being a journalist.'

'But I was not asking you as a journalist.'

He was looking at her with those dark, soulful eyes that seemed to speak a whole language of their own and one that apparently her whole body was desperate to interpret. And he was challenging her. To look inside herself. To talk from the heart. It was terrifying.

'Well, then maybe I... just don't have any answers,' Orla said, her voice a little weak.

Then she turned away from Jacques and began walking back the way they'd come.

## 24

Orla had made small talk the whole walk back to his cabin and Jacques didn't get it at all. This woman made her stories about habitats and humanity come to life with her words, yet when he'd asked her to tell him her thoughts and feelings on things she had seemed *terrified*. It didn't fit with the type of person he'd assumed she was. Coupling that with the knots of stress he'd felt across her shoulders earlier, it didn't make for a healthy mix. When they had arrived back she had greeted Erin and Tommy with smiles and a very basic version of seeing the foxes and then she had gone to the guest bedroom and closed the door. That was over an hour ago now and while Erin and Tommy were sat on opposite ends of the sofa slating YouTube videos and teasing Hunter, he had washed up the breakfast things and wondered what he was going to do to entertain his house guests for the rest of the day, let alone any longer. He wiped a plate with a tea cloth and put it back in the kitchen cupboard.

'Could I borrow your truck?'

It was Orla in the kitchen now, her coat on.

'To drive?' he asked.

'What else can you do with it?'

'*You* want to drive it?'

'Why is it so difficult to do anything around here? Why are there always so many questions?'

'I think I have asked you something similar,' Jacques answered.

'Well, can I borrow it or not?'

'No.'

'Why not?'

'Because you have not driven in this area before.'

'Well, I've been in the back of a car with Gerard who must have spent his whole life driving here and he didn't seem that accomplished, so how hard can it be?'

'Hard enough that I have to say no for your own safety.'

She was angry. He could see it written on her face and through her body. It was like she didn't know what to do with her arms. They looked almost like a scarecrow, awkward.

'You seem very safety conscious for some reason. The foxes. Your car. This fortress of a smart home you seem to love and hate in equal measure.'

OK, she had pretty much nailed how he felt about this house. He kept his expression blank. 'Who doesn't want to be safe?'

'Me, right now,' Orla answered. 'Because "safe" doesn't sell magazines and I need photos and videos and *something* I can make an article out of until either this reindeer turns up or I get sick of waiting and get on the next flight out of here.'

Her breathing had quickened. There was a whole mix of anxiety, frustration and irritation pooling in her eyes.

'OK then,' Jacques said. 'Let me get my coat.'

'What? I can take the truck?'

'No,' Jacques answered, heading to the hallway. 'But I can drive you wherever you need to go.'

'That wasn't what I meant,' Orla began. 'Because I don't know where I want to go and having someone with me will... make me lose focus. And I'm sure you have lots of things to do other than take me out.'

'Did someone say we're going out?'

It was Tommy speaking and he and Erin were suddenly in the space too.

'Orla needs to get some photos,' Jacques began. 'And I want to see Delphine's window project for myself.'

'Does Delphine still make those hot Christmas milkshakes?' Tommy asked.

'If they are not already on the menu for the tourists I am sure she will make one for you,' Jacques said.

'She never offered *me* a hot milkshake,' Erin answered glumly.

'Want me to teach you how to charm Delphine?' Tommy asked her.

'I'm not sure I could stand to watch bad rizz used on someone old enough to be your grandma,' Erin replied.

'No deliciously, melt-in-your-mouthy, chocolately, caramelly, brown-sugarly, honeyly, creamy, hot milkshake for you then. Did I say melt-in-your-mouthy?'

'Oh God!' Erin exclaimed. 'I swear if it's not as good as you just made that sound then I am going to shave your eyebrows off later.'

'Well, I haven't had her make one since last year so she's another twelve months older.'

'Ready with your excuses?'

'No, I have faith in Delphine. She won't let me down. And I really want to keep my eyebrows.'

'Right,' Orla said. 'So, we're all going. Fantastic. I'll get my laptop.'

And with those words said with a deep sarcasm no one could possibly have missed, Jacques watched her leave the kitchen.

## 25

Orla stood in front of the *brouette* and took another photo. How did you make a wheelbarrow look a little bit extra? To be fair it was looking more festive now since the last time she had seen it. There was tinsel wrapped around its handles and there were more gifts piled into its basin; there was also now a fir tree either side of it, teeming with golden stars, bright icicles and effigies of Santa Claus. It was a reminder that Christmas was fast approaching.

She put her fingers to one of the more rustic ornaments on the slightly bigger tree – a carved stable with the nativity tableau depicted on it. It reminded her of something she had made at school, something her dad had helped her with. He had always been a hands-on kind of father. A doer rather than a talker. Actions speaking louder than words. Was that one of the reasons why he was struggling now? Because he didn't have a job any more, no real hobbies or purpose?

She let go of the ornament and slipped her phone out of her bag. Pressing on the screen, she put it to her ear and waited for the call to connect. While the dial tone sounded she looked around at the village. There were definitely more Yuletide offerings on the outside of the homes and businesses. Bright garlands were draped from the eaves of overhangs, lights were stuck around the edges of windows and there seemed to be the scent of pine, peppermint and pumpkin spice infusing with the winter air.

'Hello.'

Her dad's voice on the other end of the phone threw her for a second and she rapidly regrouped.

'Hi, Dad. It's... Orla.' She didn't know why she'd felt the need to tell him who it was but it was done now. Had her mum told him she was going to call?

'Hello, love. I thought you were in Spain.'

She frowned. 'I'm in France, Dad.'

'Oh, perhaps that was it. I knew it was some place I haven't been. Well, you've been to all the places I haven't been. Is everything OK?'

*No,* she wanted to say. *Because I'm worried about you.* She just had to say it. But that would involve admitting her feelings.

'Yes, everything's fine here.' *No pregnant reindeer. Staying with a crazy guy who lets foxes eat cheese. Erin probably one Insta message away from 'doing bits' on video call.*

'Weather all right?' her dad asked.

'Yes. I mean, it's been very cold. But it's a few degrees warmer today so, you know, better.'

'That's good, love.'

'So, how are you?' Orla asked. 'Everything OK?'

Why couldn't she get this right? She had given her mum the air of someone who was going to problem-solve the shit out of the situation yet here she was talking around it as much as anyone else.

'All good here. Was it your Mum you wanted to speak to? Because you phoned my mobile.'

'No, I wanted to speak to you, Dad.' She took a deep breath, kicked at the snow on the ground. 'I'm… worried about you.'

As her stomach coiled itself up like it was a spring that needed restricting there was a deafening silence from the other end of the line.

'Dad? Are you there?'

'Yes, I'm here. Your mum's been talking to you, hasn't she?'

'Mum's worried about you too.'

'Is she? Or is she more worried about not having enough money to buy candles that make the house smell like an over-priced brothel?'

Orla was taken aback. She had never heard her dad talk like that before. She wasn't quite sure how to react.

'It's nag, nag, nag whenever I'm home. Don't do this, Dalton. Don't do that, Dalton. If you're doing this then you shouldn't be doing that as well. If I fart she would tell me it's in the wrong octave. And, did you know she accused me of selling her mother's jewellery? I don't know what *she's* done with it, but I've done nothing with it!'

'She's worried that you're drinking too much, Dad.'

'She told you that, did she? Knew I was fed up with the nagging and thought she'd get you to do the work for her now?'

'Dad—'

'I am fine, Orla. I'm grand. The one who isn't fine is your mother. She doesn't leave the house and she keeps track of Erin like she's starring in an episode of *FBI*. That poor girl can't take a crap without your mother wanting to know the consistency of it.'

Now Orla was confused. Was this turning-the-tables talk because he was a proud man who knew he was struggling and didn't want to admit it? Or was there some truth to his comments about her mum? She was very invested in finding out everything about Erin and Burim and being concerned about Erin's coursework but surely that was just being a good mother. While she was thinking she tuned into the background noise across the line.

'Dad, where are you?'

'Why? Are you going to tell your mother?'

She sighed. 'No, I'm just... wondering.'

'I'm on the bus with Greta.'

Who was Greta? It wasn't someone Orla was familiar with. And it was a woman's name...

'And before you go reporting back to FBI Agent Dana,' her dad carried on. 'Greta is an Irish Wolfhound who's having a diabetes check at the vets.'

She didn't really know what to take from that sentence. Why was her dad with a dog that wasn't his on public transport going to the vets?

'I don't—'

'The person you should be talking to is your mum,' her dad carried on. 'She's the one who's fallen out with all of her friends except Helen. She's the one who's doing nothing all day except finding fault with everyone else. She's the one who barely leaves the house and accuses people of doing things they haven't done.'

Orla didn't know what to say to this. Who was telling the truth? And why would whichever one it was be lying to her anyway?

'Listen, love, I've got to go. The vets is the next stop. But, don't be a stranger, will you? Call me again if you need to. Bye, love.'

There wasn't a chance to say anything else before her dad ended the call and she was left even more confused.

## 26

'Delphine, we need to talk.'

Jacques had bided his time while Delphine had *very slowly* served customers at the checkout of the store, then attended to service in the café despite all her staff being there, then made a fuss of Tommy and Erin and made their hot milkshakes. But now there was no reason for her to be able to avoid this conversation he needed to have.

'I know what you are going to say,' Delphine replied, adjusting her glasses and plucking some festive chocolates from the shelf.

'Oh, really?'

'Yes,' she answered. 'You are going to ask to see the progress of the installation of my new windows in the guest bedroom.'

'Yes, I am,' he agreed.

'And I am not going to show you,' Delphine said. 'Because I already know that you will have been around the building outside and seen for yourself.'

'Delphine, there is a black sheet over that entire section.'

'I wonder why!' Delphine said, putting the chocolates into a different section. 'Because I am having the windows replaced.'

Jacques shook his head. 'In the winter. When it has been the coldest spell for years.'

'And now it is thawing so they come.' She picked up some cinnamon rolls. 'Anyway, who is to say when the right time really is? Also, everybody knows if you have your windows replaced in the winter it is cheaper.'

'This is sounding like the reindeer being pregnant when it cannot be,' Jacques said.

'Was that what you wanted to talk about?' Delphine asked. 'Before you climb the outside of the building and look under my black curtain?'

He had thought about it. Briefly.

'No,' he answered. 'I want to know what Orla Bradbee is doing here, Delphine.'

The cinnamon rolls were returned to the shelf and Delphine continued down the aisle. 'These shelves are so disorganised. Remind me not to let Gerard mess with my biscuits again.'

'Delphine, you cannot avoid talking to me about this. She is currently staying in my home!'

'I do not know what you want me to say,' Delphine hissed. 'She is here to write about the reindeer and, you know, Saint-Chambéry.'

'And a mute man?'

'Sometimes you have to embellish things a little to catch media attention.'

'And what do you need media attention for, Delphine?' he asked. 'You have a love/hate relationship with tourists as it is. You wish for many more to come here? You know there are reasons I live a distance away from the village, a reason that *I* do not want media attention.'

'I know that if you do not step out now you will never step out.'

'That is my decision to make, Delphine. Not yours.'

And now there was anger brewing in his gut. He needed to remember that whatever this was, Delphine *did* care about him, had kept his secrets. He swallowed down the feelings, focussed on facts not the potential consequences.

'But, you know, if I am to believe your need to promote the village in this way, tell me, why does the reporter have to be Orla Bradbee?'

'Oh, Jacques,' Delphine said, shaking her head, a smile on her lips. 'Why are you asking me that question?'

'The same reason everyone asks questions. Because I want to know the answer.'

She pressed a packet of Christmas chocolates to his chest. 'You already know the answer. You knew why the moment you realised it was her.'

His mouth was suddenly dry and the weight of the chocolate box felt constricting.

'But, for the purpose of clarity, I will spell it out,' Delphine began. 'She is the only person you have shown an interest in in all the time I have known you. Not one sharing platter night I arranged, not one bowling trip, not any of the single women I have found and put in your path has sparked the slightest change in your demeanour. But Orla. Every month when you come to collect the magazine. The following days when you tell me about the latest place she has been and the things she has written about... the transformation in you!'

'Stop,' Jacques said, taking a grip of the chocolate box and poking it back on the shelf. 'This is craziness.' But he couldn't deny it.

'What is crazy about it? You come to life when you talk about her and her adventures! That is what I want for you, Jacques. For you to come out of that house and live again. Meet someone with similar interests. Reconnect.'

He was shaking his head on instinct now as the realisation dawned. Delphine had got Orla here on false pretences because she had some mad idea that they should what? Date? He wasn't stupid. He knew Delphine had put women in his path, organised Saint-Chambéry events and teamed him up with the latest divorcée, but she had never really been *that* forceful with it. Not in the realm of getting someone on a plane to travel here on the basis of some mad story. And what she had said about reconnecting, it wasn't as easy as flicking a switch.

'I enjoy her writing,' Jacques finally said. 'That's all.'

Delphine made a noise she always used when she was frustrated. It was part snort, part whistle. 'I enjoy playing cards with Madame Voisin but my entire demeanour does not morph into a deliriously happy Disney Princess whenever she suggests a game of bridge.' She began to walk up the aisle towards the café area.

'I do not do that,' Jacques told her as he followed.

'For someone who is the most observant person I know, you are pretty clueless when it comes to yourself. Gerard and I decided you should have some help.'

'Gerard is in on this too? I should have guessed.'

'Well, now you know,' Delphine said, as if the conversation was over. She began busying herself with wiping down the countertops.

'And what do you suggest I do with that information?' Jacques asked.

'I do not know, Jacques! That is the thing about people. You can assist but you cannot *insist*. I have brought Orla here. She will hopefully write a wonderful piece for her magazine about the reindeer and the village. What else happens is up to you.' She looked at him directly. 'But do not close down an opportunity because you are too proud or too scared to take a chance.'

Before he could make any reply, Delphine was rushing into the café, taking issue with something one of her staff was doing. He took a breath, his gaze going to the window of the store, part misted with condensation. He could see Orla by the *brouette*, taking photos, most of her hair tamed by a woollen beanie. She had always intrigued him. Somehow, through her stories, the richness of her words, she had taken him places he hadn't been, yet after he had read each article he had found himself wondering how someone did the job she did. What sort of person travelled around the world to give a voice to endangered species, outlying communities, ordinary people with extraordinary ways. Who was Orla Bradbee? What did she do when she wasn't writing? He shook his head. He wasn't a weirdo. He didn't have her stories pinned up in a closet like a shrine to someone he was crazy about but Delphine was right. Her magazine was a highlight each month. She was someone he found attractive. It had been safe to feel that way because she was out of reach, a never-going-to-come-into-his-life fantasy. Except now she was here. And, no matter what he told himself, the desire to find out more about her was stronger than ever.

'Hey, Jacques!' Tommy called from across the café. 'You'll pay for these milkshakes, right?'

'Yes,' he called back. 'Just ask Delphine to put it on my tab.' He looked to the door. Was he really going to do this? He took a breath and took a step forward.

## 27

'How is the photo shoot going?'

Orla jumped at the sound of Jacques's voice. Her mind had been wandering, still going back and forth on what on earth was going on with her parents. She hadn't really realised she was still snapping photos of the symbolic wheelbarrow. How many pictures did she really need?

'OK,' she answered. 'You know, trying to envisage a colour spread in the magazine. Don't think I've covered a wheelbarrow before.'

'No?'

'I think the nearest I've come is doing an interview in a rickshaw.'

'Well, don't even think about moving this wheelbarrow. I think the punishment is public flogging.'

'Who says the French aren't still suckers for tradition?' She forced a smile she didn't really feel.

'Listen,' Jacques said, moving next to her and putting his hands in his pockets. 'I wanted to apologise for earlier. With the foxes. I shouldn't have tried to push my opinions on to you.'

'Oh, well, that's OK,' she said. 'I probably shouldn't have got so angry about it. Or demanded you give me your truck when I really wouldn't be able to drive here. I mean, it's like an extreme sport.'

He laughed. 'Something for the next winter Olympics maybe.' He paused before carrying on. 'But, seriously, the photos thing. That's a me thing, and I shouldn't have tried to make it a you thing when you're here to do a job.'

He had said sorry. That was unexpected from someone who never minced his words when it came to expressing his opinions. Another unforeseen quality, to admit when he had overstepped the mark.

'I appreciate the apology,' she said. 'And I apologise if I made you feel like I didn't understand your point of view, because I really do.'

'Yeah?'

'Yes, of course,' she said. 'Sometimes even telling people's stories feels like a violation and I know how that sounds when my whole job is to put this news into the public domain. But I don't do it without thought. It's not always about the bottom line and, for me, it's not at all about sensationalism.' She sighed. 'Although, sometimes, I don't get a final say in the headline and my bosses do usually come down on the side of dramatic.' She took a breath. 'I think what I'm trying to say is... I don't want you to think that I don't care.'

Why was she telling him this? She didn't tell people anything unless she had to. She was definitely the narrator of other people's stories not her own. And why wasn't Jacques saying anything in response? But then, he did speak.

'Perhaps we can separate professional from personal and make that work.'

'O-K,' she said, a little confused.

'I know the perfect place. Come on.' He nudged her shoulder with his.

'There's somewhere else other than this village that isn't all the way back to Grenoble?' Orla asked.

'There is.'

'But what about Erin and Tommy?' She looked back over at Delphine's.

'Have you not experienced one of Delphine's hot milkshakes yet?' he asked her. 'They take at least half an hour to get through and once you are halfway down the glass the only thing you can do is finish the rest with a spoon. And...'

He'd let the 'and' trail. 'And what?' she asked.

'And I kind of agreed Erin and Tommy could have a second one. And *pommes frites*. And then there is certain to be *bûche de Noël* if Delphine has made some.'

'What's that?'

'It looks like wood. It is made of chocolate.'

'Ah,' Orla said, nodding. 'Yule log.'

'So, they will be a while, and, when they have finished eating, they will not be able to move for even longer.'

'OK,' Orla replied. 'So where are we going?'

'Somewhere you can take photos.'

## 28

They had got in Jacques's truck and he had driven away from the village in the opposite direction to his home, a route Orla hadn't travelled before. Not that the scenery was immediately any different to the area around Saint-Chambéry but, as the minutes ticked by, there were slight changes. It was like they were leaving the harsh ruggedness of the mountainous backdrop and making way for subtler terrain – flatter ground, trees that didn't look like they reached up to the clouds, a hint of a valley to come. Yet it was still such a winter wonderland, no hint of greenery on the ground, just more ice and snow, as beautiful as it was slightly hostile.

Within fifteen minutes Jacques was pulling off the road and coming to a stop next to a wide-open space, like a forest clearing. There was literally nothing around and, as she reached to undo her seat belt, Orla wondered what exactly she was going to be taking photos of.

'We are here!' Jacques announced as though he had brought her to the greatest show on earth. He had spread has arms wide, as much as the confines of his cab would allow and it only high-lighted how little there was.

'Is it an event?' Orla asked. 'Is a marching band going to appear every hour on the hour?'

'That would impress you?' he asked, opening the door of the truck.

'It depends on the horn section.'

Why had she said that? Immediately her cheeks flooded with colour as she rooted around in her brain for something else to say to fill the quiet.

'Make sure your coat is fastened,' Jacques said, jumping down. 'It is usually five degrees cooler here than near Saint-Chambéry.'

'What? You've brought me somewhere colder?'

He slammed the door shut and Orla was left tugging at the zip of her coat and making sure the overlapping poppers were also done up before she got out.

Her feet touched down onto snow that was hard, a layer of crunchiness rather than soft and powdery. She had been to many snowy landscapes but the terrain around this French mountain village seemed to have a whole micro-climate all of its own.

Jacques was getting equipment out of the back of his truck. Was that a spear? A memory washed over her the second he pulled a long metal device that looked like a giant screw from under the tarpaulin. Then he began pacing, deliberately, like he was counting, spear in one hand, screw implement in the other. She rushed to catch up.

'Ice fishing,' she said, finally reaching him.

'Gerard and I take it in turns to set traps,' he answered.

'You're counting to find them?'

'Yes... forty-eight, forty-nine...'

'What kind of fish do you get here?' she continued.

'Fifty, fifty-one… all kinds.'

'Yes, but what kinds?'

'Orla,' Jacques said, stopping. 'I will answer your questions, but if you keep talking to me when I am trying to count, I will not be able to find the traps.'

'Sorry.'

She walked bedside him, silently, wondering just how far away these traps were and how different the paces of Gerard and longer-limbed Jacques had to be and, if that was the case, did they have a different method of counting?

'OK,' Jacques said. 'We are here.' He stuck the spear into the snow. 'Now we drill.'

'I know how it works,' Orla told him. 'And I also know it's hard to work that drill.'

'It is all about the technique.'

'It's a two-person job.'

He laughed. 'You cannot work this thing with two people.'

'I didn't mean at the same time,' Orla replied. 'I meant, when one person gets tired the other person can have a turn.'

'I will not get tired,' he answered.

'O-K,' she said. 'We will see.'

'Trust me,' Jacques said. 'I have done this more times than you have.'

'OK,' Orla said. 'Then I will just stand and watch.'

'No,' Jacques said. 'You will take photographs when we see what we have caught.'

It took a while for Jacques to make any real headway with the turning device. It was like watching someone really have to go to town in a bid to open a giant bottle of wine, or corkscrewing like he was boring for oil. She had taken photos, although unfortunately, due to the layers and thick coat he was wearing, she could only imagine the work his muscles were having to do rather than seeing them in the flesh, but she *had* imagined...

'Orla, come here. I am through the ice and now we will find the rope and pull it up and see what we have caught.' His enthusiasm was evident in his tone and she stepped up to the hole and looked down into it. It currently looked like a wishy-washy Slush Puppie, a grey-blue mash.

He had thick gloves on now and he plunged his hands into the ice. Orla waited, camera phone poised in hope. As the seconds ticked by, she worried for her phone's battery.

'There is something,' Jacques declared. 'But I think it is stuck.'

'How annoying,' Orla replied. 'Looks like you and Gerard will have to rely on Delphine's store for tonight's food.'

'No,' Jacques said, on his belly now, one hand still down the hole. 'This is where you can help. Take hold of the spear.'

With a euphemism ringing around in her head, she grabbed the wood with a metal spike, pulling it out of the snow.

'Do I need to jab the fish?' she asked.

'No,' he said. 'You just need to make the hole bigger with it. If the fish we have caught is too big it will not come out of the hole I have made.'

'OK so I need to jab at that instead?'

'Not *at* the hole, just around it, very carefully.'

With Jacques's warning about 'carefully' weighing on her mind, she began to probe the ice, silently wondering if she was going to permeate the whole layer underneath them and lead to a full-on icequake.

'It is OK,' Jacques said. 'Do not worry about the ice.'

'I'm British, Jacques. We are brought up with tales of ice breaking the second you set a toe on it and about swans attacking and breaking arms.'

'You have swans that live on the ice?'

'No,' she replied with a laugh. 'Just over-anxious parents worried about everything.' She poked at the ice a little harder. 'Like this?'

'Yes, that is good. A bit more. OK, let me try and move the rope.' He stretched down into the water again and put more of an effort into it. 'OK, it is coming, one more press with the spear to make this open up.'

Orla swallowed as her mind went other places again. *Concentrate.* 'I hope this is going to be worth it.'

'I think it will be worth it. Trust me.'

She pressed at the ice which *was* getting easier to manipulate and Jacques got up on his knees, dragging at the string.

'OK, here it comes,' he said.

'Really?'

'Yes, and I think it is big.'

Now she was getting excited. She put the spear down and got her phone to take pictures.

'Orla! Be ready!' Jacques said, still pulling.

'I'm ready!' If slightly distracted at the sheer admirable physicality of this man-mountain, heaving a weight from the icy depths. If it wasn't so cold she would be close to boiling point.

'It's coming!' he yelled.

*Concentrate, Orla.* 'Oh my God, what is it?'

With one last tug, Jacques fell back onto the snow and landing on top of him was a slithering, thick, brown fish.

'Argh!' Orla exclaimed, caught between photo-taking, videoing, being jealous of the fish lying across his abs, or doing something to help. 'What should I do?'

'Take photos! I told you that!' Jacques said, laughing as he put two hands around the fish and tried to hold it still.

Orla did as he said, capturing video and pictures of the writhing fish and Jacques trying to steady it and do something with the line it was attached to. How could someone look so sexy wrestling with an aquatic animal?

'What type is it? It looks like a giant pike,' Orla said.

'It is! I have never seen one this large before!'

'Careful!' she exclaimed. 'It looks like it might be able to eat you!'

'Help me now, Orla! I cannot get to my feet holding it.'

She stopped her camera work and headed forward to assist him. It almost looked like something prehistoric. 'What do you want me to do? Which bit do I hold? Of the fish?' She felt her cheeks pink.

'Just grab him around the middle for a second and I will try to get up.'

'Ugh,' Orla said, putting her hands on the fish. It jerked wildly and she had to grab on tighter for fear it was going to escape and somehow manage to get itself back down the hole. 'Ow! Quick! I can't hold it!'

Jacques got to his feet and took over. 'OK, grab the spear.'

'What are you going to do?'

'I am going to put it out of its misery quickly.'

She didn't need to ask any more questions about that. She reached toward the spear.

'OK,' Jacques said. 'You hold the fish but... look the other way.'

'Jacques, I'm a reporter,' she said, meeting his eyes. 'There isn't a lot I haven't seen on my travels, believe me.'

He matched her gaze. 'You haven't seen me kill something before.'

She swallowed as the atmosphere heightened ten-fold. She turned her head almost subconsciously, fingers holding the fish as firmly as she could. She held her breath as she felt the thud of the spear make contact and then it was over. She still had her eyes closed when she felt the fish leave her hands.

'It is done,' Jacques said. And then, in more upbeat tones, 'Gerard is not going to believe it.'

She opened her eyes. 'It looks like it could feed a family of ten.'

'We should cook it. At the village. Let everyone see.'

*Let everyone see*. This was new from the man who seemed to want to hide himself away in his digitally controlled smart home…

'I can imagine Delphine now,' Orla said. 'Setting up a spit by the fountain, opposite that wheelbarrow.'

'Whoa, let us not go too close to the *brouette*. The ancestors of Saint-Chambéry will not like it.'

'But it is not the original one,' Orla reminded him.

'You think the one in the square has not been blessed by the priest? That there is not a big ceremony whenever a new one has to be put there?'

'I need to hear more about this. With foxes and fish and wheelbarrows I might be able to get away with there being no pregnant reindeer.'

Jacques smiled. 'Good.' He gestured to the fish. 'And I know this ice fishing is not the same as Oymyakon, but it was a good catch.'

Now the breath caught in Orla's throat at the mention of Oymyakon but she managed to smile and nod.

'Shall we take it back to the truck?' Jacques asked.

She nodded again. 'Yes.'

And as he went about collecting the equipment together, Orla was left wondering how he knew she had been to the coldest inhabited village on earth.

# 29

## SAINT-CHAMBÉRY

'It really is a monster!' Tommy exclaimed later that night when the fish had been introduced to the whole village and skewered onto a spit that was rotating in the square above hot embers. Its reception had been something like a king returning from battle. All the residents had appeared from their homes when word had got out; Delphine had made sure everyone knew this was a blessing sent from the ancestors and somehow another Saint-Chambéry event night was born.

'Gerard says he has never seen a fish this big in his whole life,' Jacques answered.

'I believe him,' Tommy said. 'This guy has to have whale ancestry somewhere in its backstory.' He nudged Jacques with his arm. 'So, you were trying to impress Orla with your ice fishing skills.'

'Did you impress Erin with your ability to finish two of Delphine's hot milkshakes?'

'I asked first.'

Jacques shook his head. 'I am not out to impress anyone.'

'Neither am I,' Tommy agreed. 'Especially someone who is attached to their cell phone like it's a baby they're taking care of.'

'OK then,' Jacques said, taking a sip of his beer.

'But seriously, you were trying to impress Orla with your ice fishing?'

Jacques smiled. 'I was giving her something for her magazine article.'

'Is that what the old people call it now?' Tommy said, winking.

'You are not funny.'

'I'm not kidding, bro. It's good to see you interested in someone, you know.'

*Interested in someone.* Was he really? Or was this because of Delphine's forced proximity? He shook his head, on instinct maybe.

'Come on, this is the first woman you've let within a mile of you since Katie.'

He was shaking his head again but this time he had a smile on his face. 'That's not true. I have been on dates.'

'I know,' Tommy said, kicking a little at the snow on the ground. 'You think I don't speak to Delphine? I heard all about the girl you *almost* met at the restaurant in Grenoble. And the other girl you *nearly* went skiing with.'

'You are behind the times,' Jacques said. 'There was a hiker I had to stop from getting hypothermia.'

'Ah yes,' Tommy answered, nodding. 'You brought blankets and hot coffee and did not ask her to come to the house.'

'Tommy, we were five miles away from the house. She did not have the strength to stand, or get up onto my back. The sensible thing was to call for mountain rescue.'

'The sensible thing,' Tommy said. 'Always the sensible thing. You are sounding like Dad.'

'Ha!' Jacques replied. 'You think Dad going to Hawaii is sensible?'

'No,' Tommy agreed. 'But I think Dad being like he is being now with other women is kinda how he should have been with Mom and then she wouldn't have left like she did.'

It was a big statement from his brother and an impassioned one too. And now the only sound apart from a little light revelry from Gerard's bar was the licking of the flames around the hot coals and the slight sizzling of the fish. Tommy sharing his feelings was almost as rare as Jacques sharing his. It wasn't how the Barbier family did things. Ignorance and quiet was chosen over confrontation and noise.

'Mom is Mom,' Jacques finally replied.

'What does that even mean?' Tommy asked, swigging from his beer bottle.

'It means that no matter what anyone did differently it would still not be enough.' He sighed. 'She still would have left.'

'You don't know that.'

'I know that you cannot blame Dad for what Mom decided to do.' He was gritting his teeth now. Because this wasn't just a conversation about how things had ended with his parents, it was also a conversation about how things had ended with him and Katie.

'You always take his side,' Tommy stated.

'Tommy, don't do this.'

'Do what? *Talk* about it? Actually get things out into the open?'

'You want to talk?' Jacques scoffed and instantly regretted it.

'Yeah, you know, maybe I do wanna talk. Because we don't, do we? None of us. And my therapist says that our behaviours are learnt, often subconsciously, from when we are very young.'

'You're in therapy?' This was something else he didn't know

about his brother and something their father had made no mention of.

'Wow, Jacques, you don't need to whisper it. It's not something to be ashamed of.'

'I know. I just... it's not...' He didn't really know where he was going with the sentence.

'I find it good,' Tommy cut in. 'Having someone to check in with who isn't gonna treat me like a kid and is actually gonna listen to the things I wanna talk about.'

Jacques didn't know what to say. *Why* didn't he know what to say?

'It's made me look at things differently, you know. See life from an alternate perspective. Realise that I can make my own decisions about how *I* feel and think and not rely on someone else to tell me how to be.'

He looked at Tommy now and realised exactly how much he had grown. Not just in stature and build but on the inside too. He did always still think of him as his baby brother, but even baby brothers grew.

'I think that is a good thing,' Jacques told him, putting a hand on his shoulder.

'I *know* it's a good thing. And that's why I wanna share how great it makes you feel to be in control of your life like that.'

'I get it,' Jacques said. 'I have a whole room in the house to help me with control and grounding.'

'Yeah,' Tommy said, sounding less than convinced. 'But you leave it all in that room. Let out as far as the four walls and not dealt with.'

'Is that not what you do in the therapy room?' Jacques asked.

'No,' Tommy said. 'I only leave the bad stuff in the room and I take away new, clean positive thoughts and feelings. All you take out of your *dojo* is a renewed focus to keep hiding everything away. A bit like the family photos.'

And now Jacques definitely wanted this conversation to end. He picked up the basting brush from the wall and placed the bristles on the skin of the fish, slicking it with oil.

'I know Mom hurt you too,' Tommy continued. 'And I know Katie hurt you more. But we can only take responsibility for how we react to what life serves us. We can't make other people act a certain way. And yeah, even if I think Dad made mistakes with Mom, I can't change it. I can only decide to do better for me.'

Eighteen years old and he was wiser than Jacques had been at that age. Yet, still he couldn't respond.

'But, you know, I get it's not for everyone. Just... think about not holding back with Orla. If you want.'

'Can you keep a check on the fish?' Jacques asked Tommy. 'I need to see Gerard for plates and other things.'

'Yeah, sure,' Tommy agreed.

And Jacques couldn't leave the conversation fast enough.

## 30

'Burim says he's caught a fish bigger than that before,' Erin said, nudging Orla as they gathered around a communal trestle table filled with an assortment of different accompaniments to the fish barbecue. There were baguettes, cheeses, Delphine's cookies, pots of vegetables in sauces, creamy potatoes and salads. Everyone had rustled up something to share with the village in literally no time at all.

'Of course there are bigger fish in the world,' Orla replied. 'But I don't think you'd get bigger in ice fishing.'

'Well, Burim says he caught one under the ice in Kosovo.'

Did they even have ice in Kosovo? Why was she even questioning it? Was Burim Kosovan?

'Erin, do you think perhaps Burim might be... I don't know... stretching the truth a little sometimes?'

'You mean lying to me?'

'Well, I don't think I actually said it quite like that but—'

'Why would he lie about a fish?' Erin asked, spooning vegetables onto a paper plate. 'I mean, what would be the point?'

'I don't know. I guess to make himself sound more important? Bigger?'

'You saw the photo of him in his grey sweatpants. Could he get bigger?'

'OK, OK, that's too much.'

'I think that's what I might be saying when we meet.'

'Erin!'

'What? We *are* going to meet, you know. We've been planning it for ages now.'

'Erin.'

'What?'

'I just...'

'What?'

'It's a lot isn't it?'

'Are we still talking about his sweatpants pic?'

'No!' She sighed. 'But, you know, a guy from another country.' She still didn't know what country. 'One of you travelling to a place you haven't been to before.'

'He wants to come to England but he needs to get a visa and it's really hard. I think it's prejudice actually.'

'Where is he from, Erin? Because you've done quite a lot of telling me where he isn't from, but you haven't said where he *is* from.'

'Because you'll judge,' Erin said. 'Burim says everyone judges him based on his nationality.'

'Narrow-minded people might,' Orla stated. 'But I'm not narrow-minded, am I?'

Erin shook her head. 'You haven't given him a chance yet.'

'How am I supposed to do that when I can't meet him because he lives somewhere the UK officials need to vet people from.'

'See!' Erin exclaimed. 'Judgement!' She put down her plate of food and stomped off towards Gerard's bar.

'Erin! Wait!'

She sighed. What was it with their family? They wanted this persona of being this happy nucleus to the outside world but, in reality, nobody spoke to one another and, if they did, it was miscommunication and half-truths.

'Is everything OK?'

It was Jacques beside her now, the guy who was being hailed as some kind of superhero for bringing the fish back to Saint-Chambéry like the village was in a dire famine situation. The rest of the non-fish spread would definitely suggest a shortage of food could never happen here.

'Yes, good. Erin just being a teenager and me being an inadequate older sibling who knows nothing about anything. Her thoughts not mine.'

'Is that all?' Jacques answered with a small smile.

'Yes,' Orla answered. 'That is all. I mean it's completely nothing when you put it into context and align it next to the commissioning of a statue of you next to the wheelbarrow to commemorate the day you brought a rare and gigantic fish back to the village.'

'No one has mentioned a statue yet,' Jacques told her.

'"Yet" being the operative word.'

He smiled. 'Do you think it should be bronze or something else?'

'Not pure gold?'

'We are a very humble village,' Jacques reminded her.

'I can see that from this banquet fit for fish-catching royalty.'

'What can I say? We are a humble village that likes to share good fortune.'

Community. Old-fashioned values. She saw it so much in the

tiny places she visited all around the world. How the UK once was but seemed to be drifting further and further away from.

'You are thinking,' Jacques stated.

'Oh, well, yes, you know, a journalist's brain never really goes to sleep. If it did then I might miss out on a scoop.'

'Here,' Jacques said, a spoon dolloping something that looked like black shiny paste on the side of Orla's plate.

'What's that?'

'A scoop,' he answered. 'Of Madame Voisin's famous sloe and blackberry jam.'

'O-K. It looks very dark.'

'Doesn't every scoop have to have an undercurrent of mystery?' he asked with a raise of his eyebrows.

'These days I prefer mine with fewer surprises and a whole lot more planning.'

'Ah, but then we would not have gone ice fishing and we would not be having this beautiful night with the village.'

She looked at him, remembering the first time she had set eyes on him. There was something different about his features now. He was still incredibly good-looking, still had that sharp jaw covered in a smattering of short beard, but there was somehow *softness* there now, *warmth* in the depths of his eyes...

'Now you are thinking *and* staring,' he said.

'Oh, sorry, I didn't realise I was doing that. The staring I mean.' She stuck her finger in the mound of jam and inspected the consistency like she was a food aficionado. Desperate to distract him from the fact she had been staring, she put her finger in her mouth. And sharp sourness took over everything.

'Oh my God!' Orla exclaimed, her mouth hanging open, her finger now also feeling like someone had set light to it.

Jacques began to laugh. 'Are you crazy?! Why would you eat it like that?'

'This... isn't... just... blackberry and sloe... this is... chilli and... it's burning!'

Her cheeks were getting hot now and she put her tongue out into the freezing air in the hope of some relief.

'I was going to tell you to only have the smallest of bits. You are insane. Here.'

He was holding out a glass of something creamy looking.

'What's that?' Orla asked, tongue still not very much involved in helping with speech.

'It's a honey and milk mead. Gerard's speciality.'

'No!' Orla said, tongue lolling. 'No one's... speciality!'

'Orla, come on. I know how hot that is. Drink the milk and honey.' He offered the glass with a bit more insistence.

She shook her head. She'd dealt with this before. She'd taken part in a chilli-eating contest in Mexico for the sake of her writing craft and she'd survived, only needing a short course of antibiotics afterwards.

'Orla...'

'If you... offer me anything else to put... into my mouth... I will scream!'

Now she didn't know whether her face was on fire because of the ingredients of the jam or because she'd somehow made another lewd suggestion without realising. At this moment she didn't care; she just needed to channel zen-like energy and keep calm.

'Madame Voisin grows her own chilli peppers,' Jacques said, nodding.

'That's... nice.'

'No one really knows what category they are.'

'You... don't say.'

'The story goes that she grew them from one her grandfather brought back from Africa in the seventies.'

Orla shook her head as the heat continued. She looked around for anything to ease the burning *except* the drink Jacques was now holding like it was a beloved pet, fingers smoothing over the outside of the glass. Her eyes met the ground. The snow?

'Gerard had to be hospitalised for a week when she put too much in a sandwich.'

'OK! Enough! Give me the drink!'

He didn't need to pass the glass. She grabbed it. And drank and drank until it was all gone. *Better.* Everything inside her mouth still throbbed but there was relief.

'I am sorry,' Jacques said. 'I should not have put so much on your plate.'

'It's not your fault,' Orla answered, finally able to form a whole sentence all at once. 'And it's no big deal.'

'You are taking this very well.'

'Not my first chilli rodeo,' she answered with a nod.

And now was the perfect time, while his well-controlled guard seemed to be down, for her to ask about how he knew she had visited the coldest spot in the world.

'So, before, when we were fishing, you said that—'

'Orla! Jacques! Come quickly!'

It was Delphine shouting from across the square, arms fanning out like the feathers of an excited peacock.

'There is either a fire, or she has something to show off,' Jacques told Orla. 'It is the same expression.'

'Well,' Orla said. 'No one else is moving with any form of fear so—'

'It is the reindeer!' Delphine shouted again. 'It is here!'

## 31

Orla couldn't believe it. Despite her sole reason for being here being the reindeer, the fact it was actually here and right in front of her felt like a Christmas miracle.

'I've not seen a real-life reindeer before,' Erin commented. 'It looks bigger than the ones on Christmas cards.'

Tommy laughed. 'You would freak if you saw an elk. Those guys are a lot bigger and definitely meaner.'

'What's your brother doing?' Orla asked as she watched Jacques.

The reindeer was behind Delphine's café, having been moved away from the inquisitive villagers at Jacques's request. But he was now prowling around it like he was doing a pilot walk around the plane prior to captaining it into the skies. Any second now she expected him to attempt a reconnaissance of the reindeer's undercarriage.

'Getting closer to it than I would,' Tommy answered.

Orla watched him some more. He was touching its fur one minute, then standing back and assessing, then moving to another angle, running a hand down each leg in turn like it might be a piece of antique furniture he was considering buying. *The kitchen table.* Suddenly she was only thinking about furniture in the context of how Jacques had pinned her down and held her wrist. What would it feel like to have his fingers running up and down her leg? Erin's laugh broke through her thoughts.

'Are you scared of the reindeer?' Erin asked Tommy. 'I'm gonna tell Burim.'

'You talk about me to your boyfriend?'

'I'm going to tell him some weirdo I'm stuck here with is terrified of a reindeer. He will think it's hilarious.'

'O-K, if you wanna piss him off, I guess,' Tommy replied, putting his hands in the pockets of his coat.

'What d'you mean?'

'Well, Burim doesn't seem like the kind of guy to like the idea of his girl even looking at another guy, never mind talking about one. What was it he said when you mentioned that footballer? "Why you not talk to this guy instead of me"?'

Tommy had done some kind of Eastern-European accent and Orla's attention was now firmly with her sister and Tommy, learning as much as she could from this interchange.

'Have you been reading my messages?' Erin exclaimed.

'How can anyone not read your messages?' Tommy countered. 'When your phone is out of your hand it's going off every second with notification after notification.'

'So what? That doesn't give you the right to read them! And... and... Burim doesn't speak like how you did it!'

'Well, I think Burim's a jerk!'

'Well, I think *you're* a jerk!'

The reindeer made a noise like someone had blown an Alpine horn and everyone stopped focussing on anything else. Erin jumped towards Tommy who put his arm out to catch her and then, very quickly, Orla watched as realisation of the close proximity hit Erin and she swiped at Tommy like he was an annoying wasp.

Orla stepped towards Jacques. 'Is it OK?' she asked. 'It's not going to give birth yet, is it?' She paused before going on. 'I mean, obviously the sooner it gives birth the sooner I can go back to the UK but slightly nearer Christmas would be better for the online hits and GMB might pick it up.'

'It is OK,' Jacques said. 'And no, it is not going to give birth yet.'

'But there's something wrong?'

She could tell, by the way Jacques's brow was furrowed and because of the straight expression he was wearing and trying desperately to maintain.

'No,' he said.

'Jacques, you know I'm a reporter.'

'I need to speak to Delphine,' he said, finally stepping away from the reindeer.

'About what?' Orla asked, following.

'About the reindeer. It needs... care.' He carried on walking towards the front of the café/store.

'So there *is* something wrong with it?'

'No. I just need to speak with Delphine.'

'Great, I'll come too and ask her more questions about its origins. Where has it come from? Why has it been sent to Saint-Chambéry?'

'No,' Jacques said, putting a hand on her arm to stop her from making any more progress.

'Why not?' Orla asked, looking directly at him.

'Because... someone should stay with Erin and Tommy and stop them from killing each other.'

'But, when we left them alone before, you said Tommy was a gentleman and that they would be fine.'

'Orla, just let me speak to Delphine.'

'I will. And I will be there to listen to every word. I might even make notes.'

He sighed. 'This isn't going to work.'

'Why not?'

'Because...'

'What aren't you telling me?' So much for the man who didn't mince his words and loved to express an opinion! Now he was clamming up tighter than an oyster protecting its pearl.

'Nothing.'

'Liar.'

'OK, OK.'

He had his hands up now like it was some kind of surrender.

'So?' Orla said. 'I'm waiting. Or are you not talking so you can quickly concoct a fake story in your head?'

'The reindeer *could* be sick,' he stated. 'OK. I didn't want to say anything in front of the kids but, there is this illness they get, foot rot. It can be very serious.'

She hadn't been expecting that. 'Oh... well, can we fix it? Because I need to write heart-*warming* not heart*breaking.*' She paused. 'But, you know, obviously the health of the animal is paramount.'

'So, will you go back to the kids? Let me speak to Delphine and organise the vet?'

'Yes,' Orla replied. 'And I won't tell Erin or Tommy you called them kids.'

'OK,' Jacques said with a nod. 'And do not... touch the reindeer or... look at it too closely.'

'O-K,' Orla said, her suspicions raised. This was a little weird but she didn't know anything much about reindeer diseases. Was foot rot contagious?

'Good,' he replied and then he strode off.

## 32

'Delphine, I need to speak with you.'

She was behind the till at her store. For some reason, the fish barbecue meant apparently there was a run of people suddenly wanting to buy groceries even though the store was usually closed at this time.

'I cannot speak now. I am busy.' She hammered at the barely electronic till before addressing the customer. 'These biscuits are two for the price of one. I will fetch you another packet.' She came out from behind the counter and raced off up the aisle.

'Delphine, you cannot avoid me forever,' Jacques said, giving chase.

'I am busy. You can see. There are many people. You brought them here with your fish.' She began plucking packets of biscuits from the shelves, sending spirals of festive ribbons flying.

'You've also brought a reindeer that is not pregnant,' Jacques announced.

'How do you know that?' Delphine exclaimed. 'Did you... examine it?'

'Yes.'

'What? Internally?' Delphine asked, looking horrified.

'I did not need to examine internally. From the outside I can tell it is not pregnant. I can also tell that it can *never* be pregnant,' Jacques elaborated as Delphine stacked up biscuit boxes on her arms like they were a pile of logs.

She tutted. 'I do not believe that. How could you know that?'

'Because,' Jacques said, taking two boxes from her pile before they fell off. 'That reindeer is male.'

He watched and waited for Delphine to deflate. Except she didn't. She kept moving, pulling items from the shelves, stacking them high in her arms and walking back through the store.

'You are mistaken,' Delphine stated. 'I know you know animals but you are not an expert in the genitals of reindeer.'

'Delphine, I know the difference between a male and a female.'

'Well... as I said... you have made a mistake.'

'Delphine, I checked, thoroughly, *hoping* I was making a mistake.'

She slowed now, like the conversation was as weighty as the groceries in her arms. For a brief moment she looked unsteady on her feet.

'Delphine, slow down,' he ordered.

'I cannot slow down,' she said. 'If I slow down then things do not get done and who will be here when I am not here to get things done?' She sighed. 'Not Gerard, he has his hands full with the bar. Not Madame Voisin, she is older than me. Not you, you are still determined to keep a life alone and never move forward.'

An expression was crossing his friend's face that he had never seen before. It wasn't just frustration, it was deep concern, anxiety, maybe even fear. And it resonated in his gut. Something was wrong.

'Delphine,' he said, softly, tentatively maybe. 'What aren't you telling me?'

She lowered her voice to a whisper. 'I need you to make the reindeer pregnant.'

'What?'

'Not like that! Do not be ridiculous! Who do you think I am?' She sighed. 'I need you to let Orla think the reindeer is pregnant.'

'So you *knew* it was a male? That it was never pregnant?'

'I did not even know if I could get my hands on any kind of reindeer!'

Jacques shook his head. 'Delphine, you lied to *me*. And you lied to Orla. So much so she has flown here all the way from England with her sister because of this.'

'Desperate times call for desperate decisions.'

'My dating life is not a desperate time,' Jacques said.

'No,' Delphine agreed. 'But my having cancer is.'

Now it was him that felt unsteady on his feet. It was like someone was pulling at the tiles on the floor, ripping them away to reveal a gigantic sink hole he was going to plummet through. He couldn't function for a second, his mind processing but equally not *wanting* to process. Had he heard her right?

'Do not say anything,' Delphine ordered, still in hushed tones. 'I have customers to get back to and you have a reindeer to look after. Please, make the best kind of story for Orla, even if that is all you can do for me.'

'Delphine, let me... take some of those.' He reached out, wanting to relieve her of some of the boxes, lighten her load, if only in the here and right now.

'No,' Delphine ordered. 'Do not fuss! I have told you what I want you to do. The time for talking is not tonight when there are so many people in Saint-Chambéry and you have caught the

wonderful fish that has made this evening another special one.'
She smiled. 'Now, please, do what I ask about the reindeer.'

She did not stop for him to be able to give any answer
whatsoever.

## 33

'Shouldn't there be a horsebox?' Erin asked as the reindeer was led up a makeshift ramp and into a trailer that had been attached to the back of Jacques's truck.

'*Reindeer* box,' Tommy corrected.

'Shut up, stupid,' Erin snapped.

'I agree it's not ideal for the trip to your house,' Orla commented to Jacques as she helped encourage the animal up the wooden boards and it seemed to dig its feet in.

'We make do in Saint-Chambéry. That is how it works,' he answered. He put a hand on the reindeer's rear-end and gently suggested it comply.

'I'm getting to realise that,' Orla answered. 'But it's pregnant *and* it has possible foot rot. I don't want it falling out of this contraption on the way and getting hurt.'

'Well, what do you suggest we do?' Jacques snapped. 'Ride it back to my house?'

His tone was harsh and she was a little taken aback. She swallowed, not knowing how to respond. If she was honest his mood had been off since he had come back from talking to Delphine. When he'd returned he'd inspected the reindeer all over again and then gave them all an audible rundown of his findings. *It is in good health, despite the potential foot rot. The pregnancy looks to be progressing OK. It is not lame.* Orla hadn't been sure why she needed to know the last one unless it was entered for the reindeer Grand National equivalent…

It was the reindeer making a noise that broke the awkward silence that had descended.

'It doesn't sound happy,' Erin remarked.

'It sounds like you when Burim doesn't message for thirty seconds. Wait… twenty seconds… no, actually ten,' Tommy said.

'Just because you have no one in *your* DMs,' Erin countered.

'Ha! Yeah, whatever you think.'

'Will you two shut up!' Jacques roared, loud enough to cause an echo.

'OK,' Orla said calmly. 'I think the reindeer is going to be significantly overstimulated if this carries on.' She took a firmer grip on the halter. 'You two get in the truck and play nice. Jacques and I will *calmly*, get the reindeer in the trailer and we will be on our way.'

She wasn't going to beat around the bush. As soon as Erin and Tommy were out of earshot she was going to ask Jacques exactly what had changed his demeanour from happy-fish-catching-hero to this grizzly bear in front of her now.

She tugged a little on the halter. 'Come on, beautiful one.'

'It does not want to move,' Jacques stated. 'Complimenting its appearance isn't going to change that.'

'Well, do you have any better ideas?'

'Yes! We make a bigger barbecue and grill it like the fish!'

Orla gasped. 'You're not serious! You can't eat… a reindeer!'

'Why not? Because Santa Claus will disapprove?'

'People don't eat reindeer!'

'People will eat anything if they are hungry enough. You should know that. You have travelled.'

'OK, that might be true but... this one is pregnant! No one eats a *pregnant* reindeer!' Now was the time, before he came back with another ludicrous suggestion. 'What happened when you spoke to Delphine?'

'Nothing happened,' Jacques answered. 'I asked her about the foot rot and she told me she was too busy to talk to me. There were many people in her store going crazy for discounted cookies.'

He was talking quickly. He didn't do that. It was one of the many things she had noticed about him. He took his time. He considered. He didn't ramble or embellish for the sake of it.

'Why are you lying to me?'

'What?'

'Something is going on with you. I can see it.'

She didn't take her eyes from him, watched her words land and waited to see what they would do. But instead of doing what she had expected him to do – more small talk about Delphine's shop, perhaps denial that he was being anything other than normal – he did neither of those things. He said nothing. *Did* nothing. There was a glazed expression on his face now, a blankness in his eyes. It was like he wasn't even there any more. What did she do with that?

'Jacques,' she said tentatively.

No reply.

'Jacques,' she said, louder.

Then, he took a gasp of breath, almost like he'd been drowning. Colour was back in his face, eyes alert, but his hands were shaking. She didn't know what to say but when he met her gaze, looking at her with a good deal of confusion, she knew she had to say something.

'OK, we need to show this reindeer who's boss. Let's go. Come on.'

She leaned into the reindeer a little, a firm nudge with her body and a tug with the rope, trying to make out she was very much used to handling caribou on the regular. 'Come on,' she said again.

'*Allez!*' Jacques added, pushing from the rear.

Surprisingly, the reindeer decided now might be the time to comply and it retracted its stubbornness, along with its hooves, and finally made its way into the trailer.

'It won't jump out, will it?' Orla asked, as Jacques began tying the rope through the trailer and then to the back of his truck.

'If it tries,' he answered. 'It will hurt itself.'

'I know!' Orla exclaimed. 'That's what I'm worried about.'

He did some kind of magic with knots and then looked at her. 'You care about this animal already? Is it not just a story to you?'

She couldn't tell whether he was really asking because he wanted to know her answer or whether he was suggesting she wrote without feeling. Well, she *had* told him this article was important for hits and website views.

'I don't write about anything I don't care about,' she stated firmly. 'And you should know that... if you've read my article about Oymyakon.'

There. What was he going to say to that? Her words seemed to hang in the cold air between them, along with their visible breath.

'We should take the reindeer home,' Jacques said.

'Agreed,' Orla said.

'Right.'

'OK.'

She didn't wait for him to offer another nothing response before she turned away from the trailer and headed for the door of the truck.

# 34

## JACQUES'S HOME, OUTSKIRTS OF SAINT-CHAMBÉRY

He knew he'd had an episode. But, as usual, he didn't know what had actually happened. And Orla hadn't said anything about it. But she *had* mentioned her article about Oymyakon. He'd realised at the time when they were ice fishing that he had let that slip out, but he had thought it had gone under her radar. He should have known better. She was more astute than that. But he didn't know what to do about it if she pushed the agenda. He could make something up. Exactly like he was doing with this reindeer farce. Perhaps that was all he *could* do. Because the alternative was admitting Delphine had wanted to play some kind of matchmaker. Because she was sick. And he currently had nothing more to go on, and it was eating away at him. How bad was it? Was she having the appropriate treatment? She hadn't been absent from the store for any extended period of time. But maybe that was a good thing because seriousness always took place in Grenoble. He took a breath. All he could do right now was keep moving, keep doing.

He entered the code into the pad at the door of his barn then opened it, leading the reindeer inside.

'Oh my God! You have chickens!' Orla exclaimed, following him and the reindeer.

'Yes.'

'You have so many!'

'Thirty,' he replied.

'I love chickens!' Orla remarked, bending down and trying to encourage them to come to her. 'I had two hens when I was younger.'

'Two?' he queried.

'Well, a mid-terrace in suburban London isn't the best place to keep more than a couple.'

'We will keep the reindeer in here tonight and see how the weather is in the morning.' He would keep it tied loosely for the sake of his poultry.

'What are their names?' Orla asked.

'What?'

'Your chickens. What are all their names?'

'You think I have given names to birds I have to get eggs from?'

'You don't care about them?' Orla exclaimed, hand to her chest as she stood upright again. 'And there you were mocking me about my concern for a reindeer we have only just met.'

He shook his head. 'You are crazy. OK, why don't you name them?'

'All thirty of them?'

'And I guess you will need them to get into a line so you can individually identify them?'

'Are you telling me you can't? What kind of pet owner are you?'

He shook his head again. He could tell them apart. He knew each one from their markings and subtle differences, he just hadn't named them. It was a bit like with his old work days. You gathered intel, but you kept a distance, it was better not to personalise anything or get too close.

'OK, this one with the ginger bit by its beak is... Ginger.'

He couldn't help but spit out a laugh. 'Inspired.'

'And this one is... Baby because it is smaller than the others. And that one there is... Scary because it looks really fierce.'

He laughed again. 'Are you really naming my chickens after The Spice Girls?'

'No,' Orla said, quickly. 'This one is... Zayn.'

'None of them are being named after One Direction.'

'You know it's saying a lot about your music taste that you know these groups.'

'I think it says more about Tommy's.'

'*You* name one,' she encouraged.

He shook his head. 'No, I am enjoying your baptisms.'

'Perhaps thirty was a task too far.'

'Then maybe we should name the reindeer,' he suggested.

Why had he said that? The reindeer was not staying. It was actually irrelevant in the grand scheme of things.

'We? Or me?' Orla asked.

Now it felt as though they were about to name their child...

'I do not care about the reindeer,' he reminded.

'I don't believe that.'

'Why?'

She put her hand on the reindeer's fur coat. 'Because I see you care. Even when you think you aren't showing it. With Tommy. With the foxes. With Delphine.'

He swallowed, the worry invading again. He couldn't tell her. He had to simply bury it until he knew more.

'Let's call her... Noble,' Orla said. 'Because Grenoble is the nearest place and, well, she's a queen.'

'I like it,' he agreed, brushing his hand over the reindeer's fur.

'Do you?'

'I said so.'

'I know. It took me by surprise.'

'Why?'

'Because you don't admit to liking things.'

He let go of the reindeer and took a step back. 'That's not true.'

'You don't actually give away anything about yourself.'

'I could say the same thing about you.'

'OK, I will tell you something about me if you tell me something about you. And I'm not talking about your favourite crisp flavour.'

'I like Original Pringles. There.'

'I said not that.'

'Well, what do you want?'

'Something real.'

This was getting deep and he wasn't ready for it. Because being near her already gave him pinpricks up and down his spine.

'I thought we agreed the reindeer was the story, not me.'

'I don't think I agreed to that.'

He sighed. 'What do you want to know?'

'Where you went to when we were getting Noble into the trailer. When you went silent, when you stopped breathing, when your eyes glazed over.'

He bit the inside of his lip. He would rather have given her anything but that. But he also knew she wasn't going to stop asking. He stepped towards the door at the rear of the barn and with another input of a code, it slid open.

'Want a drink?' he called.

'What is this?' she asked as she crossed the barn to join him. 'A secret bar?'

'No,' he answered matter-of-factly. 'It's my memories.'

The second Orla crossed the threshold she gasped. It wasn't the biggest of rooms, but the walls were covered with thick books, like photo albums. There had to be scores of them and down each spine was a name and dates. As she stepped further in, Jacques produced a bottle of what looked like whisky from one of the cupboards.

'This looks like a bunker I was in once when I wrote about preppers. But with more books and fewer guns.'

'Yeah, and the guns your preppers had weren't the greatest, trust me.'

'So, you *do* read my articles!'

'Yes,' he admitted.

'You subscribe to the magazine?'

'I used to get the magazine delivered to Delphine's store. But, since the prices went up and, to be environmentally friendly, I subscribe online.'

She shook her head. 'You've read *all* my articles?'

'And you are so much better than your predecessor who had a fixation with putting advertorials in every piece he wrote.'

She suddenly felt bare in front of him. Yes, she knew thousands of people read her words but to know that he had read every word she had written... it was simply the weirdest feeling.

'Is that the something real you were looking for?' he asked, handing one of the glasses out to her.

'Well, I would have said yes when we were next to a reindeer and surrounded by chickens, but now we're drinking by bookshelves that look like they could hold the world's history, you obviously wanted to tell me something else.'

She watched him take a swig of the alcohol, like he needed it before he said anything more. Maybe she needed to start him off, let her journalistic tendencies take over.

'Were you in the army?'

'No.'

'So these files and books aren't intel on people you've killed?'

'Do you think I would do something like that?'

'No... I don't know. What are they? And why are they in here and not the house?'

He sighed. 'They are all people I have had to become, over the years. They hold information to keep me and my family safe, they are reminders of who I was when I was playing a part.'

'Different identities,' Orla said, her eyes going back to the thick books. 'You worked undercover?'

It would explain all this smart home business and the codes for all the doors. It also said something about his lack of personalisation in the rest of his home. He was someone used to holding things – and people – at arm's length.

'I was... in the police force.'

'Here? In Canada?'

She watched him shake his head. 'In Belgium.'

'O-K.'

'I was good at my job,' he said. 'Very good.' He took a breath. 'Some people thought a little too good.'

'You made enemies,' she guessed.

He nodded. 'And when you soak yourself in your undercover life and you reel people in and you make them believe you are their brother-in-arms, they get very pissed off when they find out it was all a lie and they are going to pay for it for the rest of their lives.'

She was getting it now. He was usually a man of few words because he'd had to be to survive. He had kept many secrets. He was guarded because he didn't know how to be any other way.

'They offered me another new identity, but what was the point? You cannot give somebody a new face and these people are powerful. They have connections all over the world.'

'I understand,' Orla said, nodding as she took a sip of her drink.

'Do you?'

'The bones of it,' she admitted. 'Obviously not the effect it's had. Is *still* having?'

'I am no longer in danger. So my superiors keep saying. People were imprisoned. People died. The organisation was in turmoil and they ended up selling out.'

'But you still keep yourself hidden,' she breathed.

'Because how do I know if it is safe? What happens if one day a godchild or second cousin of the men I helped kill or imprison decides that they want retribution? These people don't ever stop. Why do you think I live in this place? Why do you think I get scared whenever Tommy visits? Why I don't like visitors?' He swigged the drink back.

'You've imprisoned yourself.'

Her words seemed to bounce around the room, but had they

hit the target? Jacques was gripping his empty glass, eyes looking into it. This man was buried alive by his past. No wonder he was here in this desolate place choosing to dip into the quirky little village sporadically, not truly engaging, not making more than surface level connections.

'Yes,' he said finally, with a nod of acceptance and a sigh. 'That is what my girlfriend said before she left.'

*He'd had a girlfriend.* Of course he'd had a girlfriend. He'd already told her he didn't know what a situationship was. He'd had something real with someone. She was all at once jealous yet intrigued to know more. Although she didn't need her journalistic instincts to know if she pushed too hard he was in danger of shutting this conversation away and locking it up tighter than this room of memories.

'When... did that happen?' she asked softly.

'When did she leave? Or when did I start imprisoning myself?' He looked up from his glass then, put it on a shelf next to some boxes.

'Just... tell me what you want to tell me. *Only* what you want to tell me.'

He sighed, leaning back against a countertop. 'I don't want to tell you anything. I don't want to tell anyone anything but...'

'But?'

'I don't know,' he said, shaking his head. 'It is like your articles, no? What are these people's lives if they aren't shared with somebody? I mean, the places you go to, the people you meet, the animal kingdoms you grow close to, no one would know so much about them if their stories weren't shared.' He looked at her. 'And if their lives weren't connecting with others, how would they be able to inspire or encourage or change the thinking of the world?'

His eyes were locked on hers now and Orla was trembling,

but not on the outside, on the inside. His words had hit spots of her she had long forgotten about. Her passion for discovering the previously unknown and untalked about. People doing things outside of the norm in a rapidly changing world, animals on the verge of extinction that doggedly adapted and survived, phenomenon that was happening because of how the people of the world were screwing up, phenomenon because of this that some people still thought was punishment from the gods. What she had always wanted to achieve wasn't about website hits or magazine sales, it was so much more.

'You give those people a voice, Orla,' he carried on. 'And, in doing that, you're allowing all the people who read your stories an insight into something precious, a story that will change what they do or make them feel grateful for what they have. If those communities didn't let you in, if you didn't share their lives, the world would be a much poorer place.'

Her heart was pounding in her chest now, so many emotions licking her insides like flames around a bonfire. He was telling her her own heart, the one she had let get hidden amidst deadlines, heartbreak and family drama she was always expected to be the solver of... It was like having her eyes opened and her soul set free all at once. And it was completely overwhelming. So overwhelming that all her now heightened senses were dancing like revellers on New Year's Eve.

'And, maybe, if I don't tell someone something, there is no point to my story and everything I went through. Perhaps I will have imprisoned myself for no reason at all.'

He was being so raw with her now. She could see it in his face and she could feel it in the air. She had never felt so drawn to someone despite of, or maybe, *because* of everything that he had just confessed to her. Before her brain had any chance to redirect her emotions, she was crossing the space between them. And when her mouth met his it seemed it was as much of a shock to him as it was to her. For the briefest of moments she felt his lips hold hers and it was like a desperate ache being immediately soothed. But then the connection broke.

'We... can't,' he told her, his mouth still close but not attached.

'Why not?'

'Because this is... too emotional.'

As he said this sentence he reached up and held her face with those huge, beautiful hands. She looked into his eyes.

'What does that mean?' she asked, her breath in her throat.

'It means... we are not in control.'

'You're saying that like it's a bad thing.' She wanted to kiss him again so desperately.

'Orla.'

'What?'

Was she misreading all these signals she felt were firing like bullets all over her skin?

'Don't you want to kiss me?' she asked him. She didn't know if she was ready for whichever answer he gave.

'It isn't about that,' he replied, his face still so close.

'So you don't?' The signals were definitely turning from sharp sexy hitting-the-spot-ammunition to the potential to be misfires now.

'No! I mean, yes, but... I do not do this.'

'Do what?' The tingling was back as his thumb grazed her bottom lip.

'I do not casually kiss women.'

'Good to know.'

'Yes.'

'Right.'

This time his lips crashed onto hers and it was all she could do to stay upright. When her back hit the wall she lost all air from her lungs but she didn't care because his body was pressing into hers and his mouth was delivering a kind of passion she'd never experienced before. As his lips moved from her mouth to her neck and then back again she traced her nails across the back of his neck, up through his hair. This was sensual in capital letters. He lifted her by the waist and, on instinct, her legs wrapped around him, drawing his body closer until he was all she could feel. Then his mouth was on hers again, intense, deep...

Suddenly a loud bark cut through the atmosphere and she jumped, shocked. His mouth left hers and she slipped down from his hold as he broke away again. He was looking back at her now almost as if he didn't know what had just happened between them.

'It is Hunter,' he told her. 'But not his bark of high alert.' He sighed. 'It means Tommy or Erin must be coming.'

'OK,' she replied, straightening her clothes a little and trying to gather herself together. She was still shaking on the inside, her libido dancing a merengue.

'OK,' he said, unnecessarily. 'We should shut this room up and go to the house.'

'Yes,' she agreed. 'Let's do that.'

They both moved together, and the near clash was awkward.

'Sorry,' she apologised.

'No, no, it was my fault. You go first,' he said.

She smiled. Politely. Like this person whose tongue had just been in her mouth and marking the line of her collar bone was a representative of a company wanting to buy magazine ad space.

'Thanks,' she said, stepping towards the door and hastening out.

She sighed as she walked amongst the chickens and gave Noble a pat on the neck. It was one thing to now know a little about Jacques's past, another thing to feel that he really understood how she felt about her journalism, but it was something else entirely to turn all that into a... She didn't even know what it was, except a mistake. A delicious mistake maybe. But, fundamentally, still a mistake.

## 36

'Hi, Mum.'

It was early and Orla was sitting on Jacques's sofa, her laptop on the coffee table and a couple of hundred words on screen. Late last night, after she'd gone to bed, but been unable to switch off, there had been an email from Frances asking for an update and some 'teaser content', as her boss had called it. When Erin's phone finally ceased dinging at around 2 a.m. and the teen insisting she didn't want to 'get into it again' after their fractious chat before Noble turned up, Orla had chosen sleep and an early wake-up call to get these words down. Except concentration wasn't her strong suit when her mind was churning over other things – her mum and dad's stories that didn't match up, Burim, the fact she had kissed Jacques in a room full of police intel... She'd chosen to tackle one of her parents as soon as she knew her mum would be awake.

'What's happened?' Dana said without a pre-greeting. 'Is it Erin? She hasn't tried to pierce her ear again, has she? I've told her she's not to get a nook or a rook or whatever it's called. And when did the world start naming bits of the ear anyway? In my day you just had the lobe you got pierced and the rest of it was just called your ear.'

'Erin's fine,' Orla said, getting to her feet. 'She's still asleep.'

'Of course she is,' her mum replied. 'Because she will have been up until all hours doing a thumb workout with that foreign boy. Is she sending him photos? Because I told her if she sends him photos of her in her underwear she will see them come back to haunt her on one of those sites some of Prince Andrew's friends were into.'

'Mum, I spoke to Dad.' She walked to the window, taking in the view.

'No, you didn't.'

'I did,' Orla said. 'He was on a bus. With a dog.'

'Ah, so that's what the code words for the pub are now.'

Orla shook her head. 'No, Mum, he wasn't at the pub and… what he said has got me worried.'

'Talking nonsense was he? Three sheets to the wind already?'

'No, he didn't sound like he'd been drinking.'

'Well, he's well-practised at pulling the wool over everyone's eyes, isn't he?'

'Mum, stop,' Orla ordered. 'Dad's worried about *you.*'

'Like feck he is! That man worries about one person and one person only and that's himself. Always has. Always will.'

'Mum, he told me that you're pushing away your friends and that you've stopped going out. And he said he didn't do anything with the jewellery.'

'Well, he would say that, wouldn't he?'

'Why would he say that?'

'To throw the spotlight on someone else. To distract attention from what he's up to with whoever he's up to it with.'

'Mum, tell me the truth! Please,' Orla pleaded.

'No one wants the truth, Orla. You should know that with your writing. What people actually want is a *version* of the truth that's a little bit more palatable. Because if you hit people with out of the ordinary, they back away faster than a Tyson Fury opponent.'

'I want the truth, Mum. I want *your* truth.'

She looked out at the bright, white snow clinging to the pine trees and listened to the silence down the line to the UK. Until...

'You want the truth, do you? Well, here it is. Some days I want to kill him and that isn't right, is it?' Dana asked, her voice full of emotion. 'I mean, how can you be married to someone for this long and be constantly thinking about the best way to implement his demise?'

'I... don't know.' She swallowed. Her mum couldn't be serious, could she? Suddenly Orla was overwhelmed with an acute sense of fear and her usually methodical mind was battling to look for a logical explanation.

'See! You didn't really want to hear that, did you?'

'No, Mum, I did want to hear it.' No matter how unsettling this situation was she didn't want her mum to shut down letting this emotion out now it was unlocked. 'Keep going. Talk to me.'

Dana sighed. 'The doctor says it might be the menopause. *Might be.* How can you get up every day and function on a "might be" I ask you!'

'You've told the doctor about all this?'

'First time after I really considered putting slug pellets in your Dad's cottage pie.' There were tears now. More tears from the person who rarely cried. 'How could I be thinking these things? Wanting to do these things?'

'Mum, I don't think it's uncommon to have those feelings during the menopause.'

'How would you know?'

'Well, because I've researched it for the piece I wrote on Chinese women.'

'Oh yes, the Chinese women who float through middle-age like elegant, exotic butterflies with perky tits and perfect arses.'

'I don't think I wrote it quite like that but they do experience fewer symptoms of the change, yes.'

'So none of them are thinking about pushing their husbands off the ladder when he puts up the Christmas lights. Or wondering if arsenic will be untraceable when mixed in cranberry sauce.'

This was bad. She swallowed. 'Mum, you need to talk to the doctor again.'

'So he can offer me those anti-depressants again? The ones that space you out so you don't complain about anything? Make you think that that Lee Mack's actually funny?'

She felt so helpless when she was so far away and looking at the wintry wilderness outside Jacques's home only made it more apparent just how great the distance was between them. She needed to be back in the UK.

'Mum,' she said. 'We're going to be back before Christmas.'

'Really?!' Dana replied, her voice going up a few octaves and her joy evident.

'Yes,' Orla said firmly. 'I don't care what I have to do to make it happen… Help a reindeer give birth, get the magazine to order a private plane, whatever happens I promise Erin and I will be back for Christmas Day dinner.'

'Oh, Orla love, that will be grand. I mean, don't you worry about me, but your dad and Auntie Bren will be delighted and—'

'But I want you to be truthful with me now,' Orla interrupted.

'O-K.'

She took a deep breath. 'Does Dad have a drink problem? Did he really sell Granny's things?'

There was a silence on the other end of the phone until eventually Dana responded. 'No.'

'Which one?' Orla asked.

'Both,' her mum said. 'But don't get angry with me. He has a volunteering job and lots of new friends and he doesn't need me any more and I sold the things because when he leaves me or I kill him I will need money for solicitors... or bail... or a hitman.' More tears and rapid breathing ensued.

'Mum, it's OK,' Orla said, wanting to be there in person to comfort her. 'We are going to sort all this out when I get back.'

'But you shouldn't have to sort everything out. I asked you to help with Erin and I didn't want to do that when you have your career to think about. Work is important and there's *Time* magazine. Your dream.'

'Mum,' Orla said, watching as a group of chickens sprinted across the snow, heading towards the track Jacques's truck had carved over the past few days. 'Family is more important than anything else. Isn't that what you've always told me? People are more precious than things.'

She heard her mum sigh. 'Life before loot, your granny used to say.'

'Well then,' Orla said. 'That's settled. Christmas all together and we will get you feeling much more like your old self in no time.'

'If there's a choice I'd much rather feel like Sharon Osbourne than myself. Could there be a pill for that, do you think?'

The next thing to go past the window was Jacques and he was running.

'Mum, I'll come to the doctors with you and we'll discuss all the options. I'll call you again, OK? Let you know when I'm coming home.'

'OK, love and, really, don't you worry about me.'

With those words ringing in her ears, Orla headed for the front door where she had left her boots.

## 37

Jacques still didn't know how chickens could escape from a shed with more security than a bank vault but here they were, rushing away from him across the glistening white ground. Hunter had barked to alert him, then the dog had whined at the window of his bedroom and he had immediately seen what was going on. His first thought had been to fly out of the house and catch them but the next thought had been: how did you corral chickens with nothing or no one to help you except a dog who seemed to think you wanted to play?

'What can I do?'

Suddenly there was Orla, boot laces undone, coat open, no hat.

'Go back inside,' Jacques stated. 'It's too early. Too cold. You will freeze.'

'I'm not abandoning Ginger and Baby and Posh... or Zayn Malik.'

He shook his head. 'You are crazy.'

'So tell me what to do to get them back in the barn.'

'I have no experience in catching chickens. They have never

escaped before and when I move them into the barn for the winter it is a well thought out procedure.'

'Well, how do you do that? Can we think about it quickly before they run all the way down to Saint-Chambéry?'

'Food,' Jacques said. 'That is the only way. The feed is in the barn.'

'I will go and get it.'

'And I will catch the ones who have run furthest away.'

He watched Orla turn and head back to the barn before he set off in the other direction.

It took a while, but, by the time Orla had re-joined him, he had a chicken under each arm and a few were bobbing about by his feet.

'Sprinkle a little of the feed on the ground and we will keep going, like dropping breadcrumbs to lead them back to the barn.'

'OK,' Orla said, taking a handful of the feed and doing as he said. 'Come on, chickens, let's get you back somewhere warmer than this. Come on, eat the food.'

He watched her, dropping the pellets, her hair falling over her face, enthusiastically encouraging his poultry to comply and all his thoughts went back to last night. He had kissed her. Without any holding back. And it had been more than he could have imagined. Because that action, coupled with the fact he had opened up about his previous occupation and told Orla a part of what he had been through, was something he had never done, even with Katie. And it was something he never thought he was going to be *able* to do. Everything had been heightened ten-fold since last night when Delphine had said she was sick. Everything had at first felt insurmountable and then suddenly, with the kind of clarity bad news always brings arriving at top speed, his heart and head had been challenged to take a chance and trust his feelings. Except now, in the very cold light of day, he was questioning that decision-making all over again.

The birds in his arms squawked.

'So, how pregnant is Noble?' Orla asked him.

'What?'

'I looked it up. Reindeer are usually pregnant for around seven and a half months and, you were right, usually they give birth in May or June.'

'Oh, well,' Jacques began. 'I would say this one is... going to give birth...'

'Yes?'

Her expression was so hopeful. He knew he should tell the truth because, Orla wasn't stupid, she would work it out herself before too much longer. But he really needed a frank conversation with Delphine before he said or did anything. Finding out *her* exact situation had to be his priority.

'I would say any day now,' Jacques finished.

'Great!'

'But, I will need to speak to the vet in Grenoble. Take his advice on what to do, see if there is anything else we should be thinking of. Maybe he will come... if the weather stays consistent.'

'And as soon as the baby is born, Erin and I can get out of here and back to the UK for Christmas.'

He swallowed, gripped the chickens a little more securely. She was thinking about leaving. Of course she was. She wasn't even meant to be staying with him. He still didn't know if Delphine's windows were really being fixed. Saint-Chambéry seemed to be a whole web of white-lies right now.

'Sorry,' she apologised. 'I didn't mean for that to come out quite how it sounded. I've enjoyed my time here, of course, but my parents need me at home.'

'It has got more serious, with your parents' situation?'

'I just think someone needs to guide them through a few things.'

'And that is your job?'

'I can't exactly leave it to Erin.'

He nodded. 'For me it was the same. With our parents. I was the older one. The one expected to understand the problems and explain them in simple terms to Tommy. It is a big responsibility.'

'Yes,' Orla agreed, nodding.

'And you worry about Erin too. And this guy she is in a shituationship with.'

'*Sit*uationship,' she said, putting down more feed. 'Though perhaps your word is better. Yes, I worry about her too.'

'A lot of worry for one person.'

'Yes,' she agreed. 'But that's what happens when you care about the people in your life.'

It resonated hard. He cared about Tommy. He cared about Delphine. He was beginning to care about Orla. And he had always been someone who had shut down those emotions because, in his line of work, that's what you had to do. Katie hadn't understood that. Had called him cold. Maybe that's what he had needed her to see at the time.

'You are a caring person,' he told her.

'Not as much as I was,' she responded. 'Because if you care too much, people take advantage.'

'People have taken advantage of you?'

'Yes,' she answered with a sigh. 'Because I let them.'

'In your work?'

He watched her scatter the chicken feed and take a moment before she answered.

'In my love life.' She sighed and shook her head. 'Love life. That's a joke. No one actually has love in their life when they're dating these days. It's like that four-letter word really is a swear word after all.'

He wanted to say something heartening, something to dismiss her theory. Because how could someone who wrote so emotively about life feel so disheartened about connection? Except he usually had nothing to give in that arena. But he had given last night and both of them seemed to be ignoring that fact today. Perhaps he should be the one to address it now...

'Orla, about last night. I—'

'You don't need to say anything,' she interrupted, moving on as more chickens congregated.

'No?'

'No, I mean, you telling me about your past and then talking about my writing, that really made me realise what's important.'

'And that is?'

'Our sense of self,' she answered. 'Amid every situation we find ourselves in, the most important thing to remember is who is the story and who is the storyteller. I am a storyteller. A narrator for those who don't have a voice.' She sighed. 'And you were a storyteller too. You went undercover and played a part so you could report back the stories.'

He shook his head, gathering the chickens closer. 'I do not believe it is as straightforward as that.'

'What do you mean?' she asked as she crunched over the snow.

'You cannot always be the narrator,' Jacques told her. 'Sometimes you will be the person who is creating the content.'

'No, that's just how it is for me,' Orla said with a shrug. 'I'm the person backstage making things run smoothly for the lead roles.'

'But that means you are saying that you will never be the person who *is* the action.'

'I'm just saying that, for the most part, I know that I'm meant to be the helper of others and that's OK because I like that and I'm good at that. The minute I put the complete focus on me everything goes wrong.'

'No,' Jacques said, shaking his head and finding himself feeling angry. 'That is not all you should be. That is not all that you are.'

He put down the chickens he was holding, ripped the feed away from her, sprinkled a whole heap on the path and watched as the chickens all ran to the spot and began feasting.

'Maybe other people's action is enough for me,' Orla suggested. 'When you're in the spotlight you're just setting yourself up for someone to tell you you have no right to be there.'

'Someone has made you feel like that?' he queried, getting angrier by the moment.

'Someone made you feel like that too,' she reminded him. 'Maybe *I* should build myself a fortress in a forest and never come out.'

He grabbed her then, with a bit more force than he had intended, until her back was up against a fir tree. 'Don't you say that. *You* should never hide away. You are too beautiful, too clever, too charismatic to not be one of the biggest parts of this world. I can't believe someone would dare to try to make you think otherwise.'

He was breathing hard now, exactly how he had been last night before they had kissed. And she was looking at him with those beautiful eyes. It would be so easy to get caught up in the moment. But it would just be a moment...

'Orla,' he said softly, stepping back from her.

'Yes?'

'Can I... take you out to dinner?'

He was holding his breath now, waiting for her reply.

'Yes,' she answered. 'But... there is one condition.'

'What?'

'Can it be something we haven't had to catch first?'

He smiled. 'Agreed.'

'And can I just check? Did you just call me charismatic? Because, if you did, I might want to add that to my résumé.'

'If you carry on helping me with these chickens you might be able to add "farmer" too.'

She laughed. 'Just so we're clear, this is *your* story and I am merely the describer.'

'We will work on that,' he answered.

And as she picked up two chickens and the abandoned bag of feed, a warm feeling he hadn't experienced for a long while grew strong in his gut. He had slowed things down for now, disconnected the immediate intensity, but only because everything was telling him that he wanted more than a moment with Orla Bradbee.

# 38

## DELPHINE'S STORE/CAFÉ, SAINT-CHAMBÉRY

'What happened?' Jacques asked, elbow deep in tinsel with Gerard as they both worked to support Delphine's rummaging around in the biggest cardboard box he had ever seen. It was so large it could easily have homed all Santa's reindeer, the sleigh, gifts and Santa himself.

'She has gone crazy this year,' Gerard remarked, baubles rolling out onto the floor of the shop. 'There are three more of these boxes in my bar!'

'Delphine, come out of the box,' Jacques ordered. 'Tell us what you're looking for in there and we can find it.'

The last thing he wanted Delphine to be doing was getting overwhelmed by anything that could make her condition worse. Right now he wanted her to be in bed, resting and taking care of herself. Or, better still, letting someone else take care of her the way she usually took care of everyone else. He thought back to what Orla had said about people who worked backstage to let others shine...

'I am not finding anything specific!' Delphine called, voice muffled by mountains of Christmas regalia. 'I want it all out! It all has places to go!'

With those words said she made a high-pitched gasp and an avalanche of tinsel, bells on strings, angels, Santa Clauses, and enough baubles to fill the *brouette* three times over rolled out of the box, Delphine coming with it.

Jacques caught her as the decorations continued to come like they were being powered out by a leaf-blower.

'It is like a tsunami!' Gerard exclaimed, being forced back into the shelving of tinned goods.

Finally, it stopped and there it was, a mountain of festiveness blocking the entire aisle. Why had she opened it in the middle of here? Surely taking it into her stock room would have been much more sensible.

'Delphine,' Jacques said. 'Until this is moved you cannot have customers accessing this aisle. Someone will get hurt.'

'Or lost!' Gerard remarked, pulling an ornate Christmas cracker from his beard.

'Ah, is that so?' Delphine said, a twinkle in her eye. 'Yes, I fear you may be right. Isn't it lucky that I have you here to help me decorate?'

'Oh, no, Delphine, I have beer arriving in an hour and I need to move my stock around. They have put off the delivery for over a week because of the weather so I cannot miss it and Saint-Chambéry cannot run out of beer,' Gerard said, side-stepping a currently flat but very large inflatable angel.

'Gerard—' Jacques began.

'You must go, Gerard,' Delphine interrupted. 'Jacques can help me.'

Now he saw the woman's vision. She had deliberately unpacked this here knowing it would cause an issue that needed to be solved and that he would not be able to leave without assisting her. And Gerard didn't need to be told twice that he could escape from this mayhem. The bar owner had untangled himself from a string of coloured lights and moved like a cheetah towards the back of the store and freedom...

'I do want to talk to you,' Jacques said when they were alone, the conversation from the café area and light festive music the only sounds around them.

'I know,' Delphine replied. 'But you also know that this conversation will kill me quicker than any cancer. So, we will do it my way. While making this store look like a Christmas wonderland.'

She had planned this. Like she planned everything. He had no other choice, so he picked up a line of maids-a-milking.

'Where do you want these?'

\* \* \*

'So, you can ask now,' Delphine said, as Jacques, on a stepladder, tied another garland to the rafters.

'OK,' he replied.

'OK,' she repeated.

As they had begun decorating, Delphine had told him she did not want to start straight into talking about her illness, that they needed to do good work first and then she would be ready to confide in him. He knew there was no way he was leaving the shop today without getting his answers but he also appreciated how hard it must be for her. But with a whole stream of questions fighting their way to be first, what *did* he begin with?

'Are you in pain?' he asked.

'Sometimes,' she said with a sigh. 'But it is manageable.'

'You have medication?'

'I do.'

'What kind?'

'The pain-killing kind. The type that puts it in the background so I can live without it taking over everything.'

'Whereabouts is it? Do you have to have an operation?'

'My stomach. And nobody *has* to have an operation.'

'Delphine, what does that mean?' he asked, storming down the steps of the ladder until he was opposite her. 'Does it mean that you can have an operation to fix this, but you are refusing to have it?'

'There is no point. I will be away from the shop and the village for too long, the chances of it working are not high enough, then there will be more draining treatment and more time away from Saint-Chambéry so—'

'So you're just going to give up and... die?'

His heart was beating in his neck, throbbing so hard it was making the skin hurt. This was worse than the cancer itself. How could someone with so much vitality decide to just let that slip away?

'I have decided to do everything I can to live the fullest life possible until God decides it is time for me to stop.'

'Delphine—'

'Stop!' she ordered, stamping her feet. 'You can ask me anything but you cannot tell me what decision to make.'

'But Delphine—'

'Jacques! Please! Have some respect!' she shouted. Then she carried on, her voice a bit lower. 'When you first came here, did I question why you were sitting in the church soaking wet with only a backpack? Did I ever question your decision about where to build your house or make comment about how many ways there were to lock the doors?'

'No,' Jacques said, picking up a line of stars. 'But you asked me a thousand questions ranging from my mother's favourite recipe to had I ever been chased by a bear.'

'OK,' Delphine said. 'That is true. But I never ever asked you why you sometimes get official-looking letters from Belgium, or why when Tommy visits you're torn between feeling glad and looking terrified.'

Granted, this was true. And her apparent appreciation of the situation without having any direct knowledge had always been something he held in high regard.

'You are changing the subject, Delphine. We are talking about your illness.'

'We are talking about my life. *Mine*. And my wishes, which everybody knows, have to be adhered to before anything else. Because that is the one thing a dying person should be allowed to be a bit selfish about.'

*Dying person.* He didn't want her to be a dying person. She was a living person, a larger-than-life-itself person, one of his closest people. He swallowed and put a hand on the stepladder. 'What are your wishes? Apart from to make me have Orla and Erin at my house with a fake reindeer and even faker window replacements.'

Delphine put a hand to her chest. 'How can you say the reindeer is fake? You have seen it with your own eyes! How is it today? Settling in with your chickens?'

He shook his head. 'It is still a male.'

'And you have told Orla this?'

'Not yet,' he admitted. 'But I am not going to carry on lying to someone I care about and—'

'Someone you care about.'

He watched Delphine put her hands on either side of her face, fingers resting on her cheeks like he had spilt a secret code to the enemy. Why had he said that?

He cleared his throat as he picked up another garland from the very slowly decreasing pile. 'I care about them both having a good image of the village to take back to the UK and for Orla to write about in her magazine. Just like you said.'

'Oh, Jacques,' Delphine said, pushing her glasses up her nose. 'I do not think that is it. I see you two together. It is like a fire. One minute the flames are so hot and there is passion and singeing, the next there is that warm glow of the embers that is not as hot but sometimes even more satisfying.'

Her words trickled down inside him like the glittering streamers were now trickling down from the food shelves. *Was* that how he and Orla were together? He couldn't deny there were feelings there he was finding it hard to suppress. But their meeting had been planned by his friend. They had been literally pushed together...

'I know what you are thinking,' Delphine carried on, picking up a snowflake decoration. 'You are thinking that I am wanting you to get together with Orla, then marry and have children that will carry on all the traditions of Saint-Chambéry for generations to come.'

'Aren't you?'

'No,' Delphine said. 'Because I am not naïve enough to think that people will want to spend their whole lives in this tiny village when there is such a big world out there waiting to be explored.'

'Then, what *is* your wish?'

'For you to have the strength to leave here,' Delphine said. 'But for you to have the desire to also return sometimes.'

'Delphine,' Jacques said, sighing.

'What?' she queried. 'I am sick! What else is there for me to do but plan for other people who *do* have a future?'

He didn't want to hear this. That his friend, the person who had been more of a mother to him that anybody else, wasn't going to be here until she was almost as old as the legend of the *brouette*.

'I am not going to ask you to make me any promises,' Delphine said. 'Not about this village. Not about Orla.'

'But?' Jacques said.

'But, think about things, Jacques. Re-evaluate. If only for an old woman's sake.'

He knew he already was and had been from the moment all his carefully crafted routines had been turned upside down by the arrival of his brother and a reporter who had moved from the admiration zone to whatever was transpiring between them now. His mouth dried like someone had stuck it up to a Dyson Airblade.

'I... have asked Orla on a date.'

Delphine gasped. 'You have?'

'Yes. And... I have no idea where to take her. Grenoble seems cliché. But Grenoble is the only place with life around here and more choice of places to eat and I do not know the best places to eat or even what food she likes and—'

'Jacques,' Delphine said, smiling. 'Listen to yourself.'

'I would rather not listen to myself.'

'You are excited about this. You are not thinking straight.'

'Because I don't do this!' he reminded her, throwing up his hands and knocking tinsel into a pendulum swing.

'Ah, that is wrong,' Delphine interrupted. 'You have done this but all the times you have done this it is because I forced you to.'

'And might I remind you that you brought Orla here.'

'Maybe,' she answered. 'But you are the one who has asked her on a date.'

He nodded, internally regrouping.

'So, you need to not think about Grenoble,' Delphine told

him. 'You need to think about further and wider. Use your experience. Or, perhaps, use Orla's.'

He caught her wincing and he reached out, putting a hand on her arm. 'Are you OK?'

'Yes,' she insisted. 'I'm fine.'

'Because I can do this on my own if you need to...'

'Lie down?' Delphine asked him. 'I will have a long time to lie down when they bury me in the cemetery.'

'Don't say that,' Jacques begged. 'In fact, if I am going to do something for you, then I would like you to do something for me.'

'No,' Delphine said firmly.

'Delphine...'

'Ugh. What is it?'

'If I am to think about things and re-evaluate then, I want you to do the same.'

'That is unfair, Jacques.'

'How so?'

She shook her head, that valiant determination always appearing at the forefront of everything she undertook. 'Because it is different.'

Jacques put a hand on her shoulder then. 'You do not have to do this on your own, Delphine. Isn't that what you strive to make sure Saint-Chambéry is all about? Helping one another? Giving a place to those in need? Supporting those who suffer?'

He watched her wrinkle up her nose in disapproval. 'Do not use me against me.'

He shrugged. 'What choice do you give me?'

He could see she was thinking about his words, now trailing a skein of red and white ribbon through her fingers. All he needed was a bit of hope, the vaguest chance that he could get through to her, let him help her like she had helped him.

'I will think,' she said, finally. 'That is all.'

A warm feeling spread through him. It was something he didn't have before he'd walked in here. He wanted to hug her. And that kind of physical affection didn't come easy for him. He made the tiniest movement.

'Do not hug me!' Delphine exclaimed, her voice breaking a little. 'We have much to do here with these decorations!'

'OK,' he said, smiling. And he had much to think about when it came to his date with Orla.

## 39

### JACQUES'S HOME – THE OUTSKIRTS OF SAINT-CHAMBÉRY

*Calm.* That was how you got things done. It was no good eyeing up the coffee machine like it was an adversary. She was going to make friends with it. A smile, a gentle touch as she put a cup under the spout, a peaceful press of its buttons and...

The angry grinding started and Orla recoiled, jabbing a finger at 'cancel'.

'Oh my God!' Erin exclaimed, laughing. 'I wish I'd been filming then!'

'Why doesn't this appliance like anyone but you?' Orla asked, frustrated.

'What can I say?' Erin said, getting up from her seat at the kitchen table. 'It has taste. Do you want me to help?'

'Steady now, Erin,' Orla replied. 'You're almost sounding like someone who wants to lend a hand. Will your nails survive the manual labour?'

'If you carry on taking the piss I'll carry on letting you fight for your caffeine fix,' Erin said, hands on hips.

'Well,' Orla said. 'I was going to make *you* a coffee. I found some syrup at the back of the cupboard and—'

'You found syrup?' She took strides forward.

'Yes.'

'Wait,' Erin said, curtailing her enthusiasm. 'This is bribery and corruption, right? This is you trying to make up for being a bitch about Burim.'

'Well, I wouldn't exactly say I was a bitch but—'

'Oh, what's the point?' Erin asked, moving closer. 'You know you had me at syrup. OK, the trick to this machine is this.' She reached out and pressed what looked like a black blank space below the display screen.

'What does that do? Because it doesn't even look like a button,' Orla said.

'It cancels everything,' Erin said. 'Wipes clean everything everyone else has done to mess it up when they're repeatedly hitting this button and that button and making it confused.'

'It is just a machine, though, right? There's not a little coffee-creating cat in there or something.'

'I'm sixteen now, Orla. I don't need you to make up a fairy tale. So... get another cup out and I'll show you what else to do.'

Only a few moments later, ludicrously good coffee with a syrup refinement was in both their cups and for a short while they sat at the kitchen table, sipped and enjoyed without saying anything. Until...

'Dad doesn't have an alcohol issue and it's Mum who's sold all Granny's things,' Orla stated.

'What?' Erin asked, cream on the end of her nose.

'Yeah,' Orla said, contemplative.

'But... why would she tell me it was Dad? Like, lie?'

'Because sometimes people do and say things they wouldn't usually when they're under pressure,' Orla said.

'But she's always told us God can see your lies,' Erin said.

'I know.'

'And that the only thing worse than lying is stealing and murder.'

'Yes,' Orla agreed. Their mum did always say that.

'So, what, the rules don't apply to her?'

'As I said, sometimes, when people are in a difficult place themselves, they often blame others before looking internally.'

'What's wrong with her then?' Erin snapped.

'We don't know yet but, sometimes, people, women, get to a certain stage in their life and, well, it can feel like everything's turning upside down.'

Erin sipped her coffee. 'If she needs to get some anti-depressants you can just say.'

'I don't know what she needs yet.'

'To stop lying?' Erin suggested.

'Maybe a bit of compassion?' Orla offered as an alternative.

'Well, perhaps if she didn't lock up her feelings tighter than the tin for the good biscuits, she wouldn't be in this situation.'

And Orla had no answer for that. Because, as usual, Erin was astute in her analysis.

'Burim doesn't understand our family,' Erin continued, swirling her finger in the foam on top of her coffee. 'He says him and his family are always looking for a reason to get together. Like it's not just Christmas or someone's birthday if we can be bothered, it's most weekends or around sports events; they just love being together and spending time together.'

'Well, I expect Burim's family live close together. We have Auntie Bren in Norfolk and then the rest of them in Ireland.'

'And I've never seen the cousins in Ireland at all,' Erin continued. 'And you're talking about it like it's a country on the other side of the galaxy.'

'I don't know what to say,' Orla admitted. 'Lucky Burim?'

'Now you're taking the piss.'

'I'm not, Erin. It's just everyone's family dynamic is different. And, perhaps, ours is struggling right now.'

'No shit. It's kinda embarrassing. Burim's talking about all the Christmas plans his family are making and all I can say is if we can keep Auntie Bren awake long enough after the turkey dinner, we might have a game of Monopoly.'

'OK,' Orla said. 'So, you tell me about Burim. What are his Christmas plans?'

'You want to know about Burim?'

'I've always wanted to know, Erin. Yes, perhaps, when Mum first mentioned you were talking to someone I was suspicious, in a big sister kind of way but now, well, if someone is making my sister smile then I want to know all about him.'

'And you're not going to judge?'

'Of course not. I promise.'

She was holding her breath. Because she knew this was important to Erin and, perhaps, with everything up in the air back in the UK, maybe this situationship was something that could ground her sister while Orla helped work things out with her parents. Was she really thinking that? Because Henry might have been the one freshest in her memory but Craig, Joe and Salvatore had all done their best to convince her that men were an untrustworthy species whose priorities were as screwed as the Conservative party's opinion on trans rights...

'He says he loves me,' Erin blurted out. 'And I want to believe him.'

'O-K.'

Whatever Erin said, she had to remain calm. Her sister was opening a portal into her feelings and that deserved respect before personal opinion. Exactly the same way she respected the traditions of all the people she interviewed and reported on.

'And he wants to be a boxer. In the Olympics. And then to turn professional and be rich.'

'O-K.'

'Are you going to say anything other than "OK"?'

'I think so,' Orla said. 'Keep going.'

'He loves his family... and his cats... and he likes old hip-hop songs and he has a record player. He drives but his dad's Mercedes is really old and keeps breaking down. He goes to the gym and he doesn't drink alcohol and his favourite football team is Man United.'

'O-K... sorry, I mean, wow, can we get him to change from Man United? Get him giving Chelsea a look?' Orla suggested.

'And,' Erin began but paused. 'He's... Albanian.'

'Oh,' Orla said before she had thought about it.

'Now I *want* you to say OK,' Erin said, annoyance in her tone.

'Albanian,' Orla repeated. 'Are you sure?'

'Orla! Of course I'm sure! He lives in Albania with his Albanian parents.'

'OK, it's just... well, they don't have the best reputation for being...' How could she put this? There was only one word for it. 'Loyal.'

'I'm aware. Believe me, I'm served the "save her from the Albanian boy" TikToks on an hourly basis,' Erin replied, folding her arms across her chest and looking defensive. 'But *you've* always told me that we take people at face value. That we form our own opinions based on people's actions with us.'

She had said that. Many times when Erin was growing up. Instilling into her sister that you always looked for the good in people before anything else. That was the whole basis of her reporting. The feel-good stories, communities with different ways of doing things that we can all learn from. And her sister had remembered that... and was now using it to her advantage. She went to make comment.

'Orla, I know that Craig was a shit to you. I also know that Salvatore was punching big time and, by the way, he does not have a villa in Portugal. But Henry... I think he really liked you and I think that's why you stopped replying to him. Because it scared you.'

'What?' Orla gasped, putting her coffee cup down before she dropped it. She had no idea what her sister was talking about and... how did she know about Salvatore's villa in Portugal? Or, apparently, his *lack* of a villa in Portugal!

'You stopped messaging him back. It was quite a sad ending to something I thought had potential,' Erin said, unfolding her arms again.

'I didn't stop messaging Henry,' Orla said. Except her words were coming out stilted as if they couldn't commit to escaping from her mouth.

'Six messages he sent you over a period of three weeks and then you sent him one really bland effort when you got back from one of your African trips.'

'And he never replied.'

'Do you blame him? The guy was reaching out for weeks and getting nothing back. What's he supposed to do? Keep hanging in there?'

Orla's throat was dry. Was this true? Had *she* ghosted Henry and not the other way around? Suddenly the coffee was tasting sour.

'So I know you know what situationships are, Orla. But I think you've been making your own rules.'

She didn't know what to say. Her heart was beating hard, her head feeling a bit muzzy. Was this a newsflash? Or, deep down, did she know it was *her* avoiding commitment and not the guys in her DMs?

'OK, say something,' Erin urged, leaning forward and inspecting Orla like she had turned to stone. 'I thought you would... come at me with excuses or... have a go about me reading your messages or... be pissed about me kinda stalking your ex like Joe Goldberg.'

Her brain was firing around all kinds of scenarios now. Had she avoided a real relationship in favour of something she could manage around her work? Not really getting invested. Leading people on? Were there guys out there sad over the way *she* had treated them? Yes, she had always been the career girl, the girl who wasn't in the same country longer than a few weeks, but she was also the girl who cared. Caring for others was what she did. Her stories were proof of that. Her need to protect the family unit was undisputed evidence. But what Erin had just suggested was starting to loom large and grow roots.

'Orla! Speak!'

She opened her mouth and there was only one sentence that came out.

'Jacques has asked me on a date.'

# 40

## SAINT-CHAMBÉRY

'What happens to these gifts anyway? Or are they just empty boxes? I've always thought about it but been too scared to ask when Delphine's around.' Tommy took his eyes off the *brouette* and looked over his shoulder like the village stalwart might suddenly appear.

'They are donated to charity. Each of the tags gives an indication of the suggested recipient.' Jacques picked one out of the wheelbarrow. 'This one says... someone young at heart. OK, that was a bad example and I have no idea who is going to make a call on that one.' He put the gift back in the wheelbarrow.

Tommy picked a present up and checked the tag. 'This one says... I don't know... my French is bad lately.' He passed the gift to Jacques.

'It says "*quelqu'un qui offrira un foyer aimant à un petit ami*". It means "someone who can offer a loving home to a little friend".'

'Why are they so cryptic?'

'Because there would be no surprise if people write on the front what is inside.'

Tommy sighed. 'Isn't that a guide for life.'

Jacques caught the contemplative tone and he put the parcel back in the *brouette*, replaced the tarpaulin keeping the presents away from the elements and nudged his brother with his elbow. 'Talk to me.'

'Whoa, hold up, are you crazy?'

'What?'

'You've never said those words before. Actually, no, that's a lie. You have said those words before but they've always had "do not" in front of them.'

'Then you should make the most of this new opportunity,' Jacques suggested. He indicated the bench next to the Christmas tree they were meant to be putting more decorations on, despite it being loaded already. Tommy sat down and Jacques joined him.

'So, have you ever felt like you're at this crossroads in life and you don't know which way to go? Or even if any of the roads are real?' Tommy asked him.

'OK,' Jacques said. 'These are big questions.'

'Were you hoping I was just gonna ask if Santa Claus was real?'

'No, that is also a big question.'

'I don't know what to do,' Tommy admitted. 'I mean, I got my sports leadership qualification, but do I want a career teaching people how to be a team? And, you know, fixing to something means permanence, right? I'm not good at that. I like getting on planes or boats when I feel like it.'

'But Dad won't be able to support you forever, Tommy. You're eighteen now.'

'And he still feels as guilty now as he did back when Mom left. That's why he's still handing out the dollars.'

'And you shouldn't be taking them.'

Tommy shrugged. 'I never could turn down a free ride.'

'Except, when you get something for free it usually means you're not the consumer, you're the product.'

'Even when it comes to Dad?'

'Maybe.' He sighed. 'I don't know.'

There was a brief silence and Jacques watched Tommy making circles in the snow with his trainers. What advice could he give his brother? He wasn't exactly in the best position in his own life to hand down any kind of wisdom.

'I don't know,' Tommy started. 'I thought I might look into joining the police.'

Jacques's heart lurched. 'Are you serious?'

'What if I am?'

'Tommy, the police... it is not like you think. It is not eating doughnuts and running around putting handcuffs on bad people—'

'How old do you think I am? Seven?'

'No, but, you know how my time in the police was and—'

'You know, I don't,' Tommy said firmly. 'I don't know how your time in the police was because you never actually opened up about it.'

'With good reason.'

'But, Jacques, you say that with no context and when I asked Dad about it he just palmed me another fifty.'

He knew it was true. He knew he hadn't just shut Katie down when she had brought it up, he hadn't said anything about the dark depths of his job to his family either. He had just made moves on their behalf to keep them safe. Distanced himself here in Saint-Chambéry. Minimised contact. Discouraged in-person visits – would still be doing that now if anyone made the suggestion instead of just turning up. But were any of them safer *not* knowing? Wasn't forewarned being forearmed?

'I cannot tell you what to do with your future, Tommy,' Jacques began. 'But I can try to warn you about what not to do with it.' He sighed. 'Joining the police, it is a big commitment. Even from the very beginning it's something you need to be so sure of.'

'And you were sure of it for you?'

'I thought I was,' Jacques said. 'But, looking back, I don't think I was at all prepared for how it turned out.'

'You went undercover, right? I guessed that much,' Tommy said.

He nodded. 'More than once. In different places. The last one was for eighteen months.'

'Shit. So, when you said you were in Germany...'

'I *was* in Germany.'

'Yeah, but, I was imagining a little *wurst*, maybe some beer festivals and casual sightseeing...'

'I went to see Borussia Dortmund play,' Jacques stated. 'When I wasn't trying not to kill people unlawfully and keep my cover.'

'Man, your life is sounding like a movie right now. I see Keanu Reeves playing you in theatres.'

He sighed. 'It wasn't exciting. Most days it was terrifying. Until it became my normal and that's when it is the most dangerous and the lines begin to blur.'

'Was that what happened? Did you have to break cover before you... lost yourself?'

'No,' Jacques said bluntly. 'I was never going to leave until the job was done. No matter how things ended for me.'

He hadn't realised quite how blunt that sounded until the words were out of his mouth. But it was nothing short of the truth. He would have been prepared to sacrifice anything – even himself – to bring these men to justice.

'You had a purpose,' Tommy said quietly. 'I don't have that.'

'Tommy... you're still young.'

'Yeah, but I should have some fucking idea what comes next, right?'

'It doesn't happen overnight. Not everyone finds what they want to do with their life the second they leave school or college.'

'You did.'

'But, Tommy, look at me now,' he said, gesturing to their surroundings. 'Hiding in a cabin in the smallest village in rural France, having lost my purpose, sitting in front of a symbolic wheelbarrow and a Christmas tree.'

Tommy shrugged. 'Things could be worse.'

'Yeah,' Jacques admitted. 'Things could be worse.' He paused, looking at the scene in front of him. 'Hunter could be about to knock down that small child if they keep waving their arms like that.' He stood up and whistled hard. Immediately his dog stopped what it was doing and powered over towards them, dropping to sit at Jacques's feet. Jacques retook his seat on the bench.

'See,' Tommy said. 'You're a natural problem solver. Me, well, I just run away. You know, can't make a decision about my future, run away, Dad pisses me off, run away, Mom makes contact enough to piss me off, run away.'

He looked at his little brother then and got a glimpse of the vulnerable teenager beneath the outer shell of swagger he put on for the world.

'You don't run away from me,' Jacques said. 'You always run towards me, no matter what I try to do to prevent it.'

Tommy let out a breath. 'Yeah, well, that's because you're the only one who listens to me and because I know you need me maybe even more than I need you.'

And now the astuteness was kicking in and he was suddenly overwhelmed with the urge to... put an arm around Tommy's shoulders. He didn't think about it, he just did it, tightening his grip quickly and pulling him close.

'What the fuck, Jacques,' Tommy reacted. 'Is this a move you learned in the force because I'm having trouble breathing right now.'

'Oh, sorry,' he said, loosening the hold a little.

'Yeah, that's better,' Tommy said, coughing. 'Less of a reminder that I could really do with hitting the gym.'

'Don't force a decision,' Jacques told him. 'Don't think just because you're an adult now that you have to do anything or be anywhere or have career aspirations.'

'So, carry on living off Dad?'

'I didn't say that either.'

'I know I need to get a job but, you know, I don't wanna start something I can't finish. Just like you said.'

'Ah,' Jacques said, feeling older than he ever had. 'But that depends on whose terms you are working to. What is the finish line? Whatever you do, only you can decide that.'

'Jesus,' Tommy remarked. 'Now you're sounding like Delphine.'

Jacques swallowed. His friend. Struggling with her own crisis. And he couldn't share that with anyone yet. *Distraction.*

'So, I might have... maybe... asked Orla to go on a date with me,' Jacques stated.

'Whoa! Bro, are you for real?' Tommy exclaimed.

He took a breath and nodded. 'Yes.'

'Wow, I wasn't sure the day would ever come.'

'And that is why I have no idea what to do,' Jacques admitted.

'OK, that's bad.'

'Well, as your reaction suggested, it's been a long time.'

'And you're asking for my input? I've had two dates,' Tommy said. 'One of them we shared a pizza on the wall of a parking lot.

Her choice. The second one I went all out with melted chocolate and strawberries and the chocolate got too hot and almost gave us third-degree burns.'

'Now I am worrying about things I wasn't thinking about before.'

'OK, well, the key to a successful date according to most of the reels I get served on my "for you" page is "thoughtfulness". It's not buying two hundred red roses or something from Pandora, it's about having listened and absorbed the little things they've shared with you and delivering those in a romantic way.'

'OK,' Jacques said, nodding but already feeling the clench in his stomach that said he was so far out of his comfort zone he could no longer see the border.

'And your fit.'

'Yeah, I know, we established you need to spend more time in the gym.'

Tommy laughed and Hunter sat up and barked. 'No, man, your fit. What you're gonna wear to impress Orla.'

He frowned then. He dressed for practicality not for fashion.

'Oh my God, Hunter, right now I think you'd have more of a chance taking Orla on a date,' Tommy said, rubbing the dog's fur.

'I can't deny that,' Jacques answered. 'Although I would hope that I won't drool as much as Hunter would.'

'Over the food or over Orla?' Tommy asked, grinning.

'Hey,' Jacques said. 'I'm not comfortable with you making jokes like that.'

Tommy laughed. 'I'm an adult, remember. But, listen, bro, I got you. You work out where you're gonna take her and what you're gonna do and I'll make you look as fine as I can.'

Hunter barked then as if the suggestion was set.

'OK,' Jacques said, getting to his feet. 'Enough talking for now.

If we don't get these Christmas decorations up around the town then Delphine is going to be on the war path.'

'Yeah, and no one wants that,' Tommy agreed. 'Come on, Hunter. Let's go put some more tinsel up! Come on, boy!'

Jacques watched his brother run off, Hunter yapping at his heels and, as he looked across the village square, he sensed a little change in the air.

## 41

'Why are there so many chickens? Are they in battery cages? Because that could be another story. Heart-warming reindeer, mute guy doing evil deeds keeping the other nature cooped up.'

Orla was wondering if Frances was halfway down a bottle of Baileys already the way she was rattling out her responses over the Zoom link. Having emailed off her words, she had got a request from her boss for an online meeting and Orla had decided to take it to Jacques's barn now he had entrusted her with the pin codes for barn and house, but not what she was now calling 'the memory room'. And she hadn't actually told Frances that Jacques wasn't mute...

'No!' Orla said quickly. 'They're all roaming free. Outside usually, too far yesterday actually. It's very cold here though so they're inside and they don't lay eggs in the winter. Look.' She turned her phone to the barn so her boss could see Jacques's fowl strutting around the space.

'Ugh, disgusting. Granted it's not as disgusting as that place you showed me in Padang Bolak but literally, ugh.'

Orla laughed. For someone who worked on a destination

magazine Frances only had five-star, pristine locations on her mind. Everything else was on her personal to-don't list.

'Show me the reindeer! And hurry up, because Sonil has training in twenty minutes.'

She looked into the camera again. 'Oh, did you finally agree to the time-management course?'

'No,' Frances said, frowning. 'Training for the Cadbury's Heroes eating contest.' She lowered her voice. 'Two days ago I took him to my personal dentist and now he can widen his jaw an extra centimetre.'

Orla had no idea what to say about the degree of effort going into this.

'Show me the reindeer!' Frances reiterated.

'Right, yes,' Orla said. She turned her phone around again and this time focussed on the four-legged animal who seemed to have its head permanently in a trough of food since Jacques had set that up. 'Well, here it is.' She did a bit of a pan up and down the reindeer's body, ending at the head end and those crazy blue eyes. 'Do you see its eyes and how blue they are?'

'Is it AI?' Frances asked.

'No, it's how reindeers' eyes are in the winter. It's all to do with how they adjust to poor light. In the summer they're a golden colour and in winter they're like this.'

'Well, I want that. Surely the science is there! And you're saying we have to put up with coloured contacts?'

'I... hadn't really thought about it.'

'It's a bit sad looking though, isn't it? Mouth's a bit droopy. Is that froth around its nose?'

'It's cold here,' Orla reminded her. 'Well, not actually as cold as it was when we first arrived. Then it was almost too dangerous to be outside according to the locals. But they are resourceful, you know, they light fires, everywhere, and do crazy things with bean bags and make excuses to have community events.'

'It sounds *terrible*! I bet you'll be glad when it's pumped the kid out and you can get back to civilisation.'

Orla swallowed, her eyes going to the window of the barn. It was like a beautiful painting, the scenery outside framed to perfection – white glistening ground, tall spruces, sunshine through the clouds and those icy mountain peaks in the distance. Yes, perhaps it was barren in some ways, but it was also peaceful, with Saint-Chambéry only a short drive away. She shook herself. What was she doing? Daydreaming? She lived in London – a hive of what was hot right now, business, busyness, more baristas per square foot than anywhere else in the world – or that's what it felt like. And she was striving for somewhere even more metropolitan – New York. She regrouped.

'They're called calves,' she told Frances.

'What are?'

'Baby reindeer.'

Frances took a sharp breath. 'Don't say "baby reindeer" to me, I'm still so traumatised from the Netflix series I had to delete an email from someone in the Glasgow office just because they were called Martha.'

She turned the camera back to her face. 'Listen, Frances, if the reindeer takes a while to have the calf... I mean, if it doesn't give birth in the next... four or five days then... I might have to come back to the UK before it's born.' She held her breath. She had never tried to amend any plan before, never backed out on a story before its conclusion.

'What?' Frances asked, sitting forward on her office chair, eyes very close to the camera.

She swallowed. She just had to be straight with her. She was needed at home. She had made a promise to her mum to be there for Christmas Day. She'd never asked anything of the company before and she had dropped everything to fly over here in the first place.

'I really need to be home for Christmas, before preferably. My parents are going through something right now and I need to spend some time with them. I have taken loads of photos and videos of Saint-Chambéry, there's a lot more to the village and its traditions than we could have realised, the little shop and café are run by Delphine who contacted you about my coming here and it's so quirky and there's this bar that does its own cider and there's an ancient wheelbarrow and I've been ice fishing and I've fed foxes and—'

'Your *parents* are going through something?' Frances had said the word 'parents' like the consonants and vowels were foul-tasting food stuff on her tongue.

'Yes,' Orla answered. 'And I wouldn't say something unless I believed it was crucial I go back.'

'So, your parents are how old?'

Orla could already sense this was not going down well. And she knew Frances didn't really want to know her mum and dad's dates of birth.

'Frances, I wouldn't be asking this if it wasn't really important to me.'

'And why did your sister have to go to France with you again? Because couldn't she have stayed at home and looked after your *ageing* parents?'

Orla sighed and tried not to take this personally. Frances had no empathy, and she didn't even understand how it worked in others. 'Erin is sixteen.' And she knew what was coming next the second she'd said that.

'At sixteen I was running my own car wash business.'

How many times had the staff heard about her

entrepreneurial beginnings? Car washes, manicures, making clothes out of recyclables...

'I know,' Orla said. 'But not everyone is as motivated and inspirational as you. Sadly.'

'No,' Frances said. 'And it's a shame to hear that coming from someone I thought I was going to write a recommendation for *Time* magazine for.'

*Wow.* Orla bit the inside of her mouth and tried desperately to not show on her face how that dig had affected her. This was not a reflection on her professionalism. This was unfortunate timing, the like of which she had never had to face before. And she wasn't going to let Frances insinuate that this was anything other than a difficult situation for her family and one her employer should have a bit more sympathy over.

'It's OK,' Orla stated, firmly yet politely. 'You don't need to write me a recommendation for anything. So, I will book my flight back and if the reindeer doesn't give birth before the gate closes at Grenoble then I will work with what I have so far and make the best article I can.'

'I don't want the "best article I can"! I want this reindeer, on video, pushing that whatever-the-baby-is-called out into the world in its full gory. I want this being served on "for you" pages the way they serve up people having their deep-rooted blackhead spots removed!'

Noble grunted and Orla didn't disagree. This was turning into the kind of vulgar reporting she, thankfully, never got involved in.

'Oh... Frances... I... you... losing... signal.' Orla shook her phone around and dipped her head a little as she hid her lips, allowing her to make static noises.

'What's going on? Can you hear me? Orla!'

'Sorry... I... don't...'

With one extra loud noise of her scraping her boots hard on

the floor of the barn, Orla cut the call and took a deep breath. OK, that could have gone better. But actually, it could also have gone worse so she was taking it as a win.

She rubbed Noble's fur, taking solace in the warmth of its body and leaned in as the chickens ran around her feet.

'I am sorry about that,' she breathed. 'Us talking about the birth of your beautiful little one like you're part of a reality TV show.'

Noble moved its head and it was then that Orla saw it. She swallowed. This couldn't be right. A sick feeling started to rise up in her stomach as she made a closer inspection.

'Hold still, lovely,' Orla said, trying to get a good view of the base of the reindeer's antlers. She didn't like what she saw. And then her eyes moved down to its throat, and it gave her all the confirmation she needed.

## 42

'Erin! We have Thai takeout!' Tommy yelled as Jacques let them into the house. 'I remembered all your favourites! And, if I remembered them wrong then you get to try my favourites!'

Hunter ran ahead and then began whining. Jacques felt a prickle of tension spread across his neck. Something was wrong. He put a hand to Tommy's arm, stopping him from going any further and then he put a finger to his lips to quieten him.

'What's going on?' Tommy whispered, clinging on to the bag of takeaway food.

'Wait here,' Jacques said. He softly paced down the corridor to the inner part of the house, being guided by Hunter's sounds. His dog then arrived at his feet, licking his hand. He knew there was no danger now, but he still felt something was definitely off. And when he made it to the kitchen, he saw what it was. There were two cabin cases set by the door.

'Tommy, you can come in now.'

'I was always coming in,' he answered, already at his back. 'What's going on? Can we eat before this gets cold? Where's Erin and Orla? Oh... is that... their luggage? Are they leaving?'

As Tommy fired out his questions, Orla and Erin arrived in the space.

'Yes, we're leaving,' Orla answered. 'I didn't know when you were coming back so I've arranged for someone to come and collect us to take us to Saint-Chambéry.'

'What?' Tommy said, looking bemused. 'But we've got Thai food. This food truck comes through Saint-Chambéry once every freaking blue moon on its way to Grenoble and it came today!'

'You've got Thai!' Erin exclaimed, dropping her coat to the ground and striding towards him.

'Prawn spring rolls, panang curry, spicy beef strips, like five portions of noodles and—'

'Stop talking,' Erin ordered. 'I'll get plates.'

'Just get forks,' Tommy replied.

'Erin,' Orla interrupted. 'We're leaving.'

'Yeah, but I don't know why and you said Gerard was going to be an hour at least.'

'You have called Gerard to collect you?' Jacques didn't know why that was the first thing he had asked. They were *leaving*?

'Come on, Erin,' Tommy said. 'Bring the forks. We'll save you some. Or not.'

Before anyone could say anything more, Tommy and Erin had left the kitchen for the cinema room, taking the bag of takeout with them. Hunter let out another whine then spun around in a circle and went to sit on his mat. It was like the dog could sense the tension in the air.

'I do not understand,' Jacques said.

'No,' Orla said, folding her arms across her chest. 'And neither do I.' She sighed. 'I don't know, I thought you and I had reached a place where we respected each other. You told me a little about your past. I told you a little of mine. You did weird things to my ear and helped my tension headache. You even asked me on a date! Ha! What a joke! Because then I find out that you've been lying to me.'

*Lying to her?* He hadn't lied to her. He had told her as much about his life undercover as he had told his brother only today. OK, perhaps he hadn't told her the details of what had happened with Katie or his mom and dad's separation, but he hadn't lied.

'Why aren't you saying anything?' Orla demanded to know, throwing her arms up in the air. 'Because if that doesn't smack of a guilty conscience then I don't know what does.'

'I don't know what you mean,' he replied.

'Oh really!' Orla said, stalking towards him. 'You don't know what I mean? Well, how about I tell you exactly what you've lied about.'

'Please,' Jacques said. 'Enlighten me.'

'Why don't you tell me exactly what's in that barn!' She pointed a finger towards the window.

He was still unaware what this was about. Was it the books of his identities? Had she been in there without him? Read about the things he'd done? That was impossible without the code. Still...

'The information in the books?' he asked.

'Not the books!' Orla yelled. 'The reindeer! The *pregnant* reindeer who is supposed to be at the centre of my article! The one we called Noble because she's a queen! The reindeer who is never going to give birth on Christmas Day or Easter Sunday or fucking Doomsday... because *he's* a male!'

He closed his eyes. Ah. That. He opened his eyes again and looked at her. She was angrier than he'd seen. A whole different kind of angry from the first day they had met in the snow and even different to when she'd realised she was locked in his smart home. He turned away from her then, opened the fridge and extracted a bottle of white wine.

'How did you know?' he asked.

'How did I know?' she shouted. 'Is that really the first thing you're going to say in this moment? I was kind of hoping that you had no idea!'

'Well, it took me a while to tell. With reindeer it is not so easy. There is a subtle difference with the shape of the head. Then there is kind of a beard on a male. But then you have to look at the horns. Males, they have antlers that split at the base and face forward.'

'I know!' Orla yelled. 'Because this is not my first wildlife rodeo and as pissed off as I am that you've been lying to me, I'm equally pissed off with myself that I didn't spot it straight away!'

'Well,' Jacques continued. 'We were so relieved that there was a reindeer at all.' He put the corkscrew into the wine.

'What are you doing?' Orla snapped.

'I am opening a bottle of wine to go with the Thai food. If Tommy and Erin do not eat it all. And, if they do, there is bread and cheese and paté that it will go well with just as happily.'

'I'm leaving, remember,' Orla said as the cork popped.

'You have a flight?' Jacques asked. 'Tonight?'

Orla sighed. 'No, because there isn't one... for a few days but I will find somewhere else for us to stay in Saint-Chambéry, maybe even Delphine's. Because I'm sure her story about the windows is just as fake as the pregnant reindeer.'

'You will stay here,' Jacques said, getting out two glasses.

'No, I'm going.'

'No. You will stay here.'

'This isn't a negotiation, Jacques.'

'Good, then it is settled. You will stay here until you have a flight and then I will drive you to the airport.'

'That wasn't what I said.'

'No, it is what *I* said. And, like you *did* say, this is not a nego-tiation.'

## 43

Why did the wine smell so good? Even from this distance away, the scent was in the air as Jacques poured it into glasses. She needed some too, needed something to numb the news that this whole article was going to be so much harder to spin into anything Frances was going to need for her viewing figures when there was no calf in existence. He was holding a glass out to her now and of course she was going to take it. Even though she was furiously mad at him.

She took the glass and sipped. It was divine and she made a noise that gave away her opinion. 'This is lovely.'

'It is local. Infused with mountain wildflowers.'

She took another sip. It was *really* nice. And it was reminding her of something she couldn't quite put her mental finger on. Jacques had pulled out a chair and sat down and, before she knew it, she was doing the same. Then they sat, silently, sipping the wine, their eyes dancing with each other like it was some kind of challenge as to who was going to break and speak first. Finally, she gave in.

'Does Noble have foot rot?'

'No,' he answered. 'That was something I made up to buy myself time to speak to Delphine about the reindeer being male.'

'So, another lie.'

He shrugged. 'If you like.'

'"If I like". Well, no, I don't like. I don't like being lied to at all.' She swigged back some more wine.

'Are you not glad that the reindeer is healthy? Being a lover of animals?'

'Of course I'm glad he's healthy,' Orla said. 'But I would really rather he was pregnant.'

'And, when you first arrived here, I told you it was almost an impossibility that a reindeer could give birth at this time of year.'

'So that makes lying to me later OK?'

He shook his head. 'But I will apologise that I could not be honest with you.'

'You could not be?' She had jumped on his phrasing. She knew his English was excellent. That wasn't what it was.

'Yes.'

'What does that mean?'

'It means that... I am afraid the reason you are here in Saint-Chambéry is not because of the reindeer.'

'Or the mute guy who isn't mute.'

'Oh no, that *is* the reason,' he answered, his finger tracing the rim of his wine glass. 'I may not be mute. But, I *am* the reason you are here.'

'Explain,' she said. 'Because this time I'm not going to ask permission for questions.'

He cradled his wine glass in his hands and looked into the pale liquid as if in deep contemplation as to what came next. That was when Orla was shot with a dart of concern. This was the body language of someone on the very precipice of the fall to the hard truth and realising that fact made her sit up straighter in her seat.

'Delphine got you to come here because your writing is possibly the only thing I have looked forward to, smiled about or felt emotional about, since I came to Saint-Chambéry.'

His words jolted her. So much so she vibrated in her seat until she caught herself. 'What? I... don't understand.'

He sighed again. 'Delphine, she is someone who wants everyone to be happy.' He shook his head. 'No. No, it is much more than that. She wants everyone to live their lives to the fullest. To reach for their dreams. To let go of anything that is holding them back. To accept what cannot be changed and to move forward.'

She swallowed; his words resonated hard but it seemed a stretch in this scenario. 'Well, I'm not sure how that relates to making up a story about a pregnant reindeer and getting me to travel all the way from the UK just because you subscribe to *Travel in Mind* and like my stories.'

'No?' he queried, his expression all seriousness for a brief moment until he broke into a small smile. 'To Delphine it made perfect sense.' He put his wine glass on the table and elongated his body, putting his hands behind the back of his head. 'You would come here, the woman who I have talked to her about at length, you would have to move into my house because of her windows suddenly needing to be renovated, we would bond over the reindeer and, with the forced close proximity, how could we do anything else but... fall in love.'

*Fall in love*. The way he had said it with that endearing somewhat French, somewhat Canadian, accent sent goosebumps slithering across her skin. She needed to focus. She was leaving. And *love*... what even was love?

'You talked about me to Delphine?' Orla asked him.

'I talked about your stories. We would have coffee. She would ask where in the world you were this time. It... sounds weird now I say that. It wasn't weird. It was something else other than here. A chance to get Belgium and Germany out of my head.'

She knew he wasn't talking about Belgium or Germany in the sightseeing context.

'But, you know, I did not think for one moment that she would do something like this.' He shook his head. 'Actually, I do not know why I am saying that. This is exactly the kind of thing she would do. Last Christmas she told a story of ancient, buried cheese to a local reporter so that the next national cheese contest would be held in the village and the local businesses would thrive from the revenue.'

'But what happened when there wasn't any ancient, buried cheese?' Orla asked.

He raised an eyebrow. 'You think there was not?'

'*You* buried cheese! And passed it off as old!'

He smirked. 'The best cheese is old. We are in France. The *vin rouge* was opened. At the end of the day, people believe what they want to believe.'

Orla knew that was true. How many times had Frances made her alter things in her articles to make them slightly more tantalising? Orla hated even subtle adaptations or enhancements of the facts, but she also knew she wasn't in charge of the bottom line and even a hint of sensationalism sold. As long as the core themes and values of her piece made it intact she knew she had to swallow the slight sculpting of an editorial sweep.

'Delphine must care for you very much,' she told him, sipping her wine.

'That is the thing with people,' Jacques said. 'You can try to hold them back but some of them refuse to quit.'

She took a breath. 'Is that what happened with your girlfriend?'

'I guess,' he replied. 'But, sometimes you have pushed them so far away there is no reaching out to them and perhaps you realise that it is better to let them go.'

She swallowed. Was that kind of what she had done with Henry? She hadn't responded to his messages and she knew when she did decide to reply it would be too late. Perhaps she needed to own that truth.

'I think the hurt we feel about things can make us insular,' Orla told him.

'Agreed.'

'I think we can let past damage cloud our judgement on everything.'

'All the time.'

'And change us as people.'

'Yes.'

'Until we lose sight of who we are and what we want and what any of this is really about.'

'Well—'

She got to her feet and paced to the window. Hunter raised his head and pricked up his ears. 'And then one day we wake up and our parents are getting old and can't make decisions for themselves and our siblings are getting older and they *can* make decisions for themselves and you're working and working because there's a tiny chink of you that believes what you're doing telling other people's stories is vital to the world, yet you're sad a lot of the time and lonely more of the time and you look in the mirror and see the last layer of hope in your eyes fading faster than a winter sunset.'

'No,' Jacques said, getting out of his seat. 'No, don't say that.'

'That's when you really question the point of everything.'

'Stop,' Jacques ordered.

'Because, when all is said and done, it doesn't matter what's said... or done, it's all... just over and—'

Her breath left and whatever her next words were going to be they stayed confined as Jacques's mouth clashed with hers. It was so passionate and hungry, so sweet and intense and wildflower-infused that she got an immediate head rush. But instead of common sense catching up, Orla was riding this feeling of guard-dropping for the spur-of-the-moment it was. She kissed him back, harder, and coiled her arms around his neck.

'*This* is the point of everything, I think,' he whispered in her ear. 'Undeniable connection.'

'But,' she replied. 'What if it's misinterpretation?' She looked up at him, a knot of anticipation for his reply in her throat.

'But,' he said softly. 'What if it is not?'

He didn't say anything else, he just lifted her up into his arms and headed in the direction of his bedroom.

## 44

Where are you?

Wyd?

Hellllloooo

*2 missed audio calls*

Don't you want Thai food?

*4 missed audio calls*

Orla was reading Erin's messages as her phone began to ring again. Naked, and wrapped up in Jacques's bedcover, she didn't know what to do first – answer and get ready to lie, or not answer and get dressed and hope she could be more convincing a liar in person. At her age she shouldn't be in this position – or any of the positions she had been in no more than moments ago with Jacques...

'Leave it,' Jacques said, an arm snaking around her waist.

'I can't leave it,' Orla replied. 'It's Erin and if I don't reply the likelihood is she will be knocking on your bedroom door.'

She jumped as there was a noise at the bedroom door.

'Relax,' Jacques said. 'It is Hunter. He is not used to this door being closed and locked.' He dropped a kiss on her shoulder. 'So, do not worry. No one is coming.'

And that was in a complete contrast to the past hour also... She wet her lips, flooded with the hot memories, and then rapidly regrouped.

'I have to answer or she won't stop calling.'

He removed his arm from around her waist and lay back in bed.

She took a breath and answered.

'Hello.'

'Where are you?' Erin exclaimed. 'Didn't you get my messages and other calls?'

'Where are *you*?' Orla answered, playing for time as she eased herself off the bed, tucking her phone between shoulder and ear and searching for her clothes.

'What? Hang on, I asked *you* that question.'

'I know, but something's telling me you're not still in the cinema room with Tommy.' She pulled on her underwear, then her jeans and picked her jumper off the floor.

'And something is telling me you're not in the kitchen, the lounge, the bathroom, our bedroom, or the weird, locked room that Tommy says is a gym thing.'

'O-K,' Orla said, foregoing her bra for just the jumper for now.

'And I know that because I've been to all of those rooms and you aren't in them.'

*Think, Orla, think.*

'I'm in the barn,' Orla said.

'Oh really,' Erin answered. 'That's crazy.'

'Why?' Orla asked, turning to Jacques. He had his eyes closed, beautiful body still nude in the bed.

'Because I'm in the barn and you are not!' Erin screeched.

She'd been caught out. But a good journalist never let her integrity be compromised until at least the bitter end. She took a breath. 'Which barn?'

'What?'

'Are you with the chickens and Noble?'

'Obviously!'

'Ah, well, I'm in the other barn. Give me a second and I'll come to you.'

Before Erin could say anything else, Orla ended the call, grabbed her socks and shoes and began putting them on.

'Do you have another barn?' Orla asked.

'What?' Jacques said.

'Other than the barn with the chickens and Noble? Do you have any kind of barn-type structure I can pretend I was in?'

He didn't reply but she could feel he was moving in the bed, perhaps rolling that athletic body upwards...

'You would rather create an outbuilding than let anyone know you were in my bedroom with me?'

It sounded particularly horrible when he said it like that. But it wasn't like that. It was simply practical. Erin would think... well, she didn't really know what Erin would think; it could go one way or the other, from a whole cheer routine of support to a horrified child who had been told Santa wasn't real. And really Jacques couldn't want them walking out of here together hand-in-hand when nothing had been spoken about, when they hadn't even actually gone on the date he had suggested...

'Do you want Tommy to know we were here together doing... what we did here together?' Orla asked.

'I wouldn't want to tell Tommy the exact full and intricate

details of what we did here together but I'm also not going to make up agricultural storage like I'm ashamed of it.'

She tied her laces. 'I'm not ashamed of it.'

'Of what?'

'Of it,' Orla said. 'Like you said.'

'Orla...'

'What?'

'We had sex.'

'I know,' Orla said. 'I was there.' Yet her cheeks were now glowing as if they could light a path from here to Saint-Chambéry in the dark.

'Me too,' he answered, suddenly arriving from behind her and whispering into her ear.

She stood up. 'I have to go. Because if I don't then Erin will—'

'Know you were not in a barn that is not there?'

'Well, yes.'

She didn't know what else to say. It felt awkward. They had crossed a line and she didn't know what happened next. She hadn't thought, she had acted, emotionally and perhaps there was also a level of irresponsibility about it. She was here to work. Her very impressionable sister was with her. She usually ran away from connection. In a few days she would be leaving again...

'Can we talk about this later?' she asked.

'Really?' he replied. 'Because I get the sense that you do not want to talk about this at all.'

'No... well... I do but...' She was running out of words and for a reporter that was the very worst thing that could happen.

'It's OK, Orla,' Jacques said, springing from the bed and snatching up his underwear. 'You do not need to say anything else.'

'No, wait, I—'

But her words were met by the firm closure of the en-suite door.

# 45

## GERARD'S BAR, SAINT-CHAMBÉRY

'Whoa, OK, you've drunk that way too quickly and you said the peppermint one was the strongest.'

Jacques was already eyeing up the butterscotch vodka and the Christmas pudding flavoured one. Coming back into the village hadn't been the plan for the evening but he couldn't stay in the house watching Orla actively avoid him after what they had shared together. He picked up the next glass.

'OK, you wanna tell me what's going on here?' Tommy asked. 'Because as much as I love sitting in Gerard's bar with you, it's kinda turned into a grotto with all these decorations. And you lining up shots like you wanna make the décor of your insides the same as the holiday season shouldn't be a plan.'

'Why not?' Jacques asked him.

'Why not what?'

'Why should I not plan to make my insides "happy holidays"?'

'Because you're the good brother and I know you're half a bottle down of the Saint-Chambéry good stuff which is why you let me ride us here on your motorbike.'

He nodded. '*Santé!*' He held the shot glass in the air and drank it down in one.

'OK, enough,' Tommy said, picking up the other glasses of liquor and moving them further away.

'Gerard!' Jacques called. 'More shots.'

'*Non*, Gerard! *Arrêt!*' Tommy countered.

'You used French,' Jacques said.

'Yeah, I mean, I remember a little, I guess. But, please, Jacques, don't change the subject. What's going on with you and Orla?'

'*Rien*. Nothing.' He picked up the empty shot glass and contemplated licking out the sticky remainder.

'So you're gonna sit here and lie to me?'

'I don't want to talk about it.'

'Yeah, that's the story of our family, right? Do anything but talk.'

Jacques put the glass down and took a breath. His brother was right about that. Completely right. And what was he doing downing festive shots and avoiding reality? That was the behaviour of someone who was not in control of their emotions at all, someone who let other people's actions affect their judgement and standards. He wasn't weak like that.

'You like her, right? You asked her on a date.'

'Yeah.'

'Yet now you can't be in the same room as her without bitching about the noise her laptop makes? I mean, jeez, Erin's phone goes off 24/7 with that crazy Balkan guy blowing it up, and I've realised commenting on that only gets me yelled at.'

Had Jacques been rude about Orla's laptop? He remembered being annoyed that she seemed to be using the computer as a prop to establish zero communication between them since he'd rather childishly left her for the shower. She'd been gone when he got out, everything of her gone, the bed made, like what had happened between them hadn't happened at all.

'Listen, bro, I know it's hard but Orla's not Katie, OK? I can see that, even from the short amount of time I've spent with her.' He took a breath. 'Orla's a thinker. She's deep, you know. She cares about things. I mean, some of the things Erin's told me, it's like Orla's been her mother really.'

Jacques nodded. He had expected as much. Orla was the strong backbone of her family. The person they looked to in times of crisis. It was literally her love for her sister that had sent her hurtling from his bed and outside. He couldn't criticise that. But he also sensed her issues with connection were much more deep-rooted than that. She had started to open up to him and he thought they had acknowledged their feelings.

'My therapist says that you have to be able to separate your feelings about things from your reactions about things,' Tommy said. 'So just because something makes you feel a certain way you shouldn't let *their* actions become *your* actions.'

They were wise words. But his alternative was usually to shut everything down, lock it up and not make any response or reaction at all. That was why Katie had left. It wasn't his reaction or response to her feelings it was his *lack* of reaction and response.

'It's never too late, you know. Like, never,' Tommy said. 'Well, you know, death could kinda get in the way of things but apart from that...'

*Death.* Immediately he was thrown back to Delphine's cancer diagnosis. He had said he was going to respect her wishes but maybe he should explore her options without her knowing for the time being...

'You OK?' Tommy asked. 'Or are those shots getting to you?'

'I'm good.'

Another lie.

'So you're still not gonna talk about Orla? Even to me?'

'I don't know what to say.'

'Anything. It doesn't have to be that deep, just something.'

Now it sounded like Tommy was an actual therapist. Although not the kind he had seen. The ones provided by the police seemed only interested in making sure his brain wasn't so fucked up he couldn't get back to work.

'She writes about things she's passionate about,' Jacques said. 'But it's always other people's stories. She doesn't think she is special.'

He swallowed after he said the last sentence. That felt a lot.

Tommy put a hand on his shoulder then. 'Good job, bro. That's a start.'

# 46

'Hunter, sit. Hunter, beg. No, *beg*. Good boy.'

Orla was only half-looking at the dog-training Erin was attempting to do in Jacques's lounge. She was also only half-looking at the laptop screen in front of her where some of the photos she had taken since she had been here were displayed amid the inadequate words.

'He's getting better at taking the treats without trying to maul my whole hand,' Erin remarked as Hunter licked her palm.

'That's good,' Orla said. It had been her stock answer since Jacques and Tommy had left the cabin. That and 'wow' and a few 'well done's. She wasn't excelling with the vocab right now, neither on paper nor from her mouth.

'So have you and Jacques had sex?' Erin asked.

'What?' Orla exclaimed.

'That got your attention. And a "what" instead of a "that's good", "wow" or "well done".'

'Shock tactics, Erin? That's usually Mum's thing. But more often it's something random like—'

'Have you heard that they're making smoothies out of car tyres now?'

'Exactly.'

'But I wasn't saying anything random,' Erin stated, stroking Hunter on the head. 'I meant it.'

And now her sister's eyes were fixed on her in that way she had somehow perfected.

Orla needed to clear her throat as tension built up there. What was she going to say? She took a breath. Only the truth set you free.

'How did you know?'

Erin gasped. 'I didn't *really* know. But now I do. So that's why they've run away down to the village. Because he's now *avoiding* you? Well, I guess you were snapping at him.'

'Was I?'

'Well, he was snapping at you too. It was like watching Mum and Dad squabbling over *Pointless*.'

Great. So she'd given herself away and was now emulating her parents. She wasn't currently being such a great role model for her sister.

'So did it not go so well?' Erin asked. 'Are you a bit out of practice?'

'No! Well, yes, but...'

'Everything I've read says it's easy, like riding a bike, but I don't get that because they all have a million gears and some of them have actual batteries and a motor so not easy at all.'

Orla didn't know what to say to that. And it hadn't been difficult, it had been easy, effortless in all the best ways and full of heat.

'OK, I can tell from your expression it was absolutely nothing like mountain biking.'

Hunter barked and Erin rewarded the noise with a treat for some unknown reason.

'It shouldn't have happened,' Orla said. 'It was poor decision-making on both our parts. We are going back to the UK in a few days. It made no sense.'

'Unless you believe in love,' Erin said, waving her hand in front of Hunter and getting him to spin in circles.

'The type in fairy tales? I think we both know that's a stretch in this day and age.'

'But it doesn't have to be. You just have to give it a chance. Like I am with Burim.'

It was such an old-fashioned view she could almost see her sister playing with her *Sleeping Beauty* toy castle now. Dressing the dolls ready for a ball, believing in a first dance ending in a happy-ever-after.

'If you always think people are going to let you down then you'll never let anyone in,' Erin continued. 'Or, you'll end up thinking that they've let you down when really *you* might have let *them* down instead.'

*She had fled from Jacques's bed. Barely unravelled herself from his body before she was looking for an excuse to run.*

'You don't have to marry him, Orla,' Erin said. 'But anyone can see there's a vibe between you.'

'Really?' she asked.

'Sure. Tommy thinks so too. Apparently, Jacques had this girl-friend called Katie and she just didn't get him at all. And I know he can be a bit gruff, but Tommy says, if Jacques lets you get to know even a small part of the real him then that's a big deal.'

She did feel she was getting to know him, that he didn't open the door to everyone and that what was inside his mind was locked away as securely as this smart home.

'By the way,' Erin began, stroking Hunter behind the ears. 'I think Delphine has cancer. She has a horrible cough when she thinks no one is listening, she's definitely sick when she visits the bathroom and she has tablets in her handbag. I googled what they were.'

'What?' Orla exclaimed.

'I didn't know whether to say anything but, well, if Saint-Chambéry is as close-knit as it claims to be then everyone should already know, right? And she must be OK otherwise she wouldn't be running around organising events and bossing everyone around and telling me I have to be the Queen of the *Brouette* this year. I mean, I don't even know if we will still be here for the festival, but wearing a crown sounded kind of cool.'

Surely Erin had got it wrong. But, if she hadn't, suddenly now Orla's issues with romance didn't seem so high up on the agenda.

## 47

'Is Delphine sick?'

Jacques jumped at Orla's question. She and Hunter were in the hallway as he came in. He'd lingered a bit outside, made sure his motorbike was put away properly, the chickens and the reindeer were OK. Tommy had left him to it, interested only in riding the motorbike, not the aftercare. And now his heart was thumping from the immediate confrontation he hadn't been ready for.

'What?' he asked, petting his dog.

'Oh, Jacques,' Orla said, shaking her head. 'Don't lie to me. I've had absolutely enough of men lying to me. Particularly when someone with your history should be much better at it.'

He swallowed. Perhaps the fact she could read him was a good thing. Maybe it meant he could finally be normal, not a tightened up, buttoned down clone of him who didn't show an ounce of emotion. But then he wondered why she was asking? Had something happened? Was Delphine OK? They had only just come from the village.

'Is she OK?' he asked Orla as Hunter retreated into the kitchen.

'That's what I'm asking you.'

'Yes, I know,' he said.

'And? Or are we back to me having to ask permission to ask questions?'

'OK, OK,' he said. 'Just tell me she hasn't called here. That she doesn't need help right now.'

'No, she hasn't called here.'

'OK,' he said, shrugging off his coat and stamping his boots on the mat.

'So?' Orla carried on.

'She has asked me not to say anything to anybody,' Jacques said, hanging up his coat.

'So it's true!' Orla gasped. 'She has cancer?'

'Wait, what?' How did Orla know that?

'Erin saw some pills in her bag and looked them up online. She also said Delphine has an awful cough.'

She had a cough now? When had that started? Did it mean she was getting worse? He was already walking toward the kitchen before he even realised it. And when he started pouring the whisky that was on autopilot too. He passed her a glass then took a slug of his.

'She says she will not have an operation that could save her life.'

'What?!'

He nodded. 'She says that she would rather have this one last Christmas with everything perfect, with the people she cares about, than go through any pain and time at the hospital when the operation may not be a success.'

'But that's crazy!' Orla exclaimed. 'And operations on these types of things are so much more successful these days!'

'You have met Delphine. You know how she can be.' He leaned against the kitchen counter. 'She knows her own mind.'

'Hmm,' Orla said, shaking her head. 'Well, she hasn't seen how forceful I can be when I think there's a reason to be.'

He saw the fire in her eyes, the hot determination, like the passion he had seen reflected back when she had moved on top of him. He swallowed, the whisky burning his gut.

'We need to do research,' Orla said, slapping her hand to the counter. 'We need to find out exactly what she's facing and then we find out the facts and statistics. When people are presented with evidence it's much more difficult to decide the other way.'

Like with his job. The risks he'd had to take to get absolute proof so there was no get-out clause for the gangs he had infiltrated.

'And there's so much more to wellness these days! When I was in the Amazon rainforest I spent time with this family who had managed to create all kinds of alternative medicines and I mean so seriously effective that a pharmaceutical company wanted to do research and, you know, perhaps if we talk to Delphine about natural treatments then she will be more open to it.'

*Hope.* Orla was spreading hope right now. And that was another thing that was at the heart of all her writing. He sighed, pulling out a chair and sinking down into it like his body was suddenly full of heavy mountain rock.

'Why aren't you saying anything?' Orla asked him. 'Because you can't want this woman who cares so much about you to have one last Christmas and cease to exist? I mean, tell me I'm wrong, but she's pretty much the only thing that's been stopping you from turning into Howard Hughes.'

'You are right,' he answered, staring into his glass.

'Then, what's the problem? We should go now. Back down to the village. Talk to her.'

He shook his head. 'Because if we went down there now and told her all these things, that would be for us and not for her. She has said this to me herself.'

'Well, OK,' Orla said, pulling out the chair opposite him and sitting in it. 'I can see where you're coming from but, you know, sometimes when people are presented with a new angle, a different perspective, then they have an opportunity to change their minds.'

'I think the English word for this is "coercion", no?'

'I think that's a bit of an extreme take on it.'

He looked up at her then. 'I have spent a lot of time running around the edge of coercion, Orla. At the end of the day, no matter what we might think is for the best, people have to be able to make their own choices. Be it good or bad.'

'I know that!'

'Do you?'

'Of course!'

'Like when you are putting Band-Aids across your parents' marriage? Or when you are telling Erin how she should feel about the man in her phone?'

He watched her eyes cloud over at his words, the fire extinguishing like the flame of a candle when it's snuffed. He hadn't wanted to do that, he had wanted to jump on the wave of her enthusiasm and ride it with her.

'You think we shouldn't try to help people? Isn't that what you've also done in your job?'

'I didn't say we shouldn't try to help.'

'Then what?'

'Just that, "helping" is very different to "fixing".'

'You think I'm a fixer.'

'I think you find it hard to accept that sometimes, no matter what you do, people have to be allowed to make mistakes, to make bad choices, to fail even.'

'Oh, right,' Orla said. 'So you feel qualified to make these statements now just because we've slept together?'

He shook his head, inhaling through his teeth. 'Not at all. But at least you are acknowledging that it happened.'

'I didn't ever *not* acknowledge it,' she clarified. 'I just chose not to parade it around my impressionable sixteen-year-old sister.'

'Because you think it was something you should hide and be ashamed of?'

'Because we haven't known each other very long and I don't do that sort of thing and I've been trying to tell her not to think about doing that sort of thing with the Albanian in her phone.'

'Fixing,' Jacques said.

'You're really annoying me now!'

'Good! Because I have come to realise what is missing from all of your articles in the magazine!'

'Oh, right, so now you've finished attacking my plaster-giving personality, you're going to start on my career? You said you loved my writing!'

She got up from the chair and looked like she was either going to leave the room or attack him with something from the fruit bowl. It didn't matter either way. He was committing to this.

'You only write about what's good.'

'That's not true!' She had leaned on the table and spat the words at him.

'Yes, it is true. And I don't know if that's the inspirational, beautiful picture-painting that you're told to write, that perhaps your writing in its purest form is then censored somehow but—'

'What?'

'The people and the animals and the extreme places you write about must have elements of hardship to their stories.'

'Of course they do!'

'Then why do you only give the tiniest glimpse of that? Surely the more difficult the journey the stronger the happy conclusion will feel.'

'I write about difficult journeys all the time!'

'But you never connect with that part of it,' he told her. 'Your words wash over it and bring people away from bad stuff and draw readers' attention to the communities rising, or the animals reproducing, or the environment changing for the good.'

'If you want to read about how the world is all going to end only a few hundred years from now I can direct you to a very different publication.'

'You're not listening to me.'

'And you're just deflecting. Like you've done since I arrived. Anything to take the attention off you and your identities and your inability to face up to reality.'

'It takes one to know one? Is that not the saying?'

'Oh, so you think we're alike now?'

He stood up, moved around the table until he was closer to her. 'I think we both hide how we feel so we do not hurt anyone else but ourselves.'

'Not listening now,' Orla stated. 'And I don't have time for this. I stayed up to ask you about Delphine, I've done that and you disagree. You've slated my writing which is the one thing I take pride in and you've described me as someone who wallpapers over things instead of facing them head on and—'

He couldn't help himself. In an exact replica of the move he had made when she first came to his home, he had her flat on her back and silent on the table in a millisecond.

'You know I think your writing is incredible,' he told her,

leaning over and close. 'It's brought the outside world to me here in Saint-Chambéry.' He smoothed a hand down her hair as she looked up at him. 'But you shouldn't be scared to show the cracks, along with the repair and the resolution.'

She was shaking a little as she replied. 'No one wants to see the cracks.'

'Yes, they do,' Jacques told her. 'That's what I've only just realised. When I've started to want to know how you got broken. It's those unaffixed parts spiralling away from everything else that makes things interesting.'

'Really?'

'Yes, Orla. And it's finding out how that feels, to want to know the parts of someone that aren't perfect, that has made me see that I need to learn how to show those pieces of myself too.'

He was staring into her eyes now, seeing someone very different to all the other times he'd looked before. She was vulnerable in this moment, as raw as he had seen her. And he liked seeing that honesty reflecting in her eyes.

'And you want to show *me* those pieces?' Orla asked.

'Yes.'

'But what if I can't show you mine?'

'I think it's maybe a work in progress for us both. But that's OK.'

He was shaking a little as he lowered his mouth towards hers.

'Whoa! Looking away!'

It was Tommy coming in and Hunter leapt up with a bark. Jacques backed up, turning to face his brother as Orla straightened herself.

'What's up?' Jacques asked him.

'It's Erin,' Tommy said. 'She's texted me. She told me not to say anything but, you know, she's freaking crazy so...'

'Keep talking,' Jacques ordered.

'She's gone,' Tommy said bluntly.

'Gone?' Orla exclaimed. 'Gone where? She was in our room an hour ago.'

'She's gone to meet Burim.'

## 48

---

Orla's heart was in overdrive. Very much like the truck she was having to drive because Jacques had been drinking. She was panicking. For her sister. For her ability to keep this vehicle in any way steady on the layer of snow. She didn't even know if she was going the right way. She didn't know much apart from a rather short text Erin had sent to Tommy. Why had her sister texted Tommy? Why hadn't she come to her? OK, she might not be 100 per cent on board about the Burim situation but she would never want Erin to be afraid of telling her anything!

'There is a rabbit!' Jacques yelled suddenly.

Orla swerved, gasping for breath as they narrowly avoided the animal. 'Is there any location on her phone yet?'

'No.'

'Have you looked again?'

'I am looking.'

'You need to refresh it.'

'Orla, please, keep your eyes on the road.'

'Please keep your eyes on the phone. She never has it off. She must be hiding her location! And that's dangerous because she doesn't know around here and there's literally nothing here except wilderness and wild animals and what if I'm not even driving the right way? What if she's gone walking the other way, further from Saint-Chambéry and civilisation?!' She could feel hyperventilation was only a few pants away.

'Listen to me,' Jacques said. His voice was firm yet calming. 'Right now it doesn't matter what way she has gone.'

'What? Of course it matters! She has an insubstantial coat that has probably got worse after the hot wash it needed when she was sick! It's still cold, it's dark... she can barely navigate her way out of her bedroom some days.'

'Orla, she's going to be fine,' Jacques said, his hand on her shoulder now. 'The reason it does not matter the way she is gone, is because as soon as we get to Saint-Chambéry we can ask others to help. Then we can come up with a plan and send more people different ways.'

That made sense. Except when he said "others" he really meant the village stalwarts of Gerard and Delphine and Delphine had too much going on without being called on to assist in the search for Erin.

'OK,' Orla said, her breathing steadying a bit. Then the thoughts came thick and fast. Should she call her mum or her dad? No. Not yet. She didn't know anything. How far could Erin really have got in an hour?

'Tell me about this guy, Burim. What is his last name?'

Orla was distracted by the question, eyes on the sloping ice road but mind revolving like the whisks of a KitchenAid. 'I... don't know.'

'Tell me what you do know,' Jacques said.

A quick sideways glance and she saw Jacques had his mobile phone in his hands. 'What are you doing? Are you putting something on social media?' That was a good idea. Except her Auntie

Bren was on Facebook more than LadBible and she would see it and tell Orla's parents.

'I do not have social media,' he reminded. 'But I know a lot of people. Tell me what you know.'

*Think, Orla, think.* 'He has brown hair... I think... not dark brown, not light brown. He wears Lacoste underwear.'

'Does he have a car?'

'I don't know. Wait, his dad has... an old Mercedes.'

'Job?'

'Him or his dad?'

'Both.'

'I actually don't know.' She sighed, racking her brain. 'He lives in Albania. He goes to the gym. He wants to be a boxer. He likes avocado. Argh! Why is all that so important to Erin and so no help in helping us?'

'It's OK,' Jacques said, reassuringly. 'We will find her.'

'*Chocolat chaud.*'

Delphine was pressing it into Orla's hands before she even really knew it. The café/supermarket was a hive of activity now with Jacques in the centre of everything dividing up sectors on maps and briefing everyone as to what Erin looked like and what colour her coat was. It felt suddenly real. Her sister was missing. Yes, it hadn't been that long but as every minute ticked by Orla was becoming more and more concerned. And she knew this was her fault. She hadn't listened long or hard enough, hadn't paid attention to the details, the depth of Erin's feelings for Burim. Because she'd made assumptions about the 'situationship' based on her own experience of them. An experience she was starting to realise that she had driven into non-existence.

'Orla, you must drink this,' Delphine insisted, taking Orla's fingers and wrapping them around the mug.

As divine as the hot chocolate smelled and as much as she was shivering from both the cold and nervous fear, she knew she couldn't stomach it. But she looked up at Delphine and gripped the mug as instructed.

'She will be just fine,' Delphine said, pulling a chair out and guiding Orla down into it.

'I can't sit,' she said, catching herself hovering above the seat.

'You *must* sit,' Delphine ordered. 'Because when that girl gets back here she will need you to stand to straighten her hair or check that her skirt is not higher than her underwear.'

'But I can't rest and drink chocolate when there are people over there, *strangers*, preparing to do their utmost to find my sister.'

'*S'il te plaît*. For only a moment. Jacques has it under control. And these people are not strangers. When you come to Saint-Chambéry a part of you belongs to Saint-Chambéry.' Delphine smiled. 'And the village looks after its own. That is how I know that Erin will be just fine. She is going to be the Queen of the *Brouette* this year.'

Orla swallowed. 'But, Delphine, you know we have to leave soon.'

The woman sat down too and waved a dismissive hand. 'Did I not just say that the village looks after its own? Perhaps this is a reason that you have not been able to get on a flight already or that Erin has gone to find her love.'

*Love*. Erin couldn't be in love. They hadn't even met. But, right at this moment, Orla didn't care about anything except making sure her sister was safe.

'You know,' Delphine said. 'Don't you?'

Orla didn't know how to respond. Was she talking about her

illness? Noble being male? Jacques struggling with the fall-out from his job? Saint-Chambéry might look after its own but it certainly also held many secrets. She stayed quiet, hoped Delphine would elaborate.

'Jacques told you, about my cancer.'

'Well, I—'

Delphine sighed, letting go of an uneasy breath and reaching for a trail of tinsel on the back of a chair, running it through her fingers. 'I knew he would. If he felt about you the way I believe he does.'

'It isn't like that,' Orla defended. 'I made him tell me. Erin actually—'

Delphine waved a hand again. 'It does not matter. Everyone will know soon enough. But you are wrong, you know, about *it* not being like that. I see how Jacques is with you. How you are together. It is that relationship that everyone seeks but is so very rare.'

Orla swallowed and her eyes went back to Jacques. He was next to one of the large Christmas trees, writing things down on pieces of paper he was handing out, pointing towards the exit door, his expression deep seriousness.

'You are alike, but you are also different. You are both independent creatures. But, for both of you, this is a form of protection. Him because it has been built into his nature by his job and the horrors he has seen there. For you because you have been let down when you have been vulnerable and you refuse to acknowledge your sadness so you spend time trying to mend other people's.'

*A fixer.* Why did the people in this village seem to know more about her than she wanted to acknowledge herself?

'Jacques, he holds himself at such a distance from everything. In the time that he has been here the pieces of him have only been given to me little by little.' She sighed, her eyes on the tall, broad man taking charge of this situation. 'But inside of him is this balloon of pure goodness. Once it was big and buoyant and now circumstances have let it shrink and it is like all the air has gone. But it does not go away, it is still there, the goodness, it just needs to be reinflated again.'

She was still shaking. Thinking about Erin out in the cold, thinking about her frozen emotions, thinking about how she had led herself down this work-focussed, solitary path, only indulging in company when there was a problem to be solved...

'Drink the chocolate, Orla,' Delphine said again. 'There is nothing that cannot be made better with something sweet.'

Orla put her lips to the cup and took a sip. Erin would be fine. *Please let Erin be fine.*

## 49

Jacques felt responsible. He had been too busy taking his eye off the ball, letting himself develop feelings for Orla that someone under his roof – temporarily under his care – had gone missing. *From his safe house.* The absolute irony of that. And, to top it all off, he had stupidly drunk too much to drive. He should be leading the search, taking one of Gerard's snowmobiles and getting Erin found. As resourceful as he suspected she was, as much as he knew exactly what Tommy would do in a similar situation, the French mountains could be brutal, the temperature drop was severe and it was pitch black now. He zipped up his jacket and petted Hunter on the head. He really hoped he wouldn't have to use Hunter's skills in finding people under snow...

'I'm coming with you,' Orla said, appearing at his side.

'No, Orla.'

'You can't say no to me, this is *my* sister we're talking about.'

'And when I bring her back here she will be cold and tired and she will need you to do all the things with hair-brushing and soft talking that I am not equipped for.' He looked at her with all the seriousness he felt.

'Delphine said something like the same thing.'

'And Delphine is almost always right.' He swallowed. 'So, let me do what I am equipped for.'

Hunter let out a bark as if he was warning Orla too.

'Sometimes,' Orla said, picking up a hat from a pile on the table and pulling it down over her head. 'We have to do things outside our comfort zone. And often we find that there are elements of it that we thought were more difficult than they actually were. Embracing the cracks, right?'

He didn't know if she was talking about her or him. But he sensed she was not going to listen to his advice. Perhaps it was better to accept that, stay focussed and give her instructions like he had given to his team of volunteers.

'OK,' he said. 'But out there you do as I say. It is dangerous and—'

'Can we go?' Orla asked, checking her phone screen for the billionth time and refreshing Find My Phone. 'Because it feels like we've been sat for way too long and, fuelled with determination, Erin can be a fast walker.'

'Orla, I am serious.'

'So am I,' she replied, heading for the door.

\* \* \*

Hunter let out a bark. It was one of his 'unsure' repertoire. Something was amiss enough for him to make a sound, but not so urgent anyone needed to panic.

'OK, Hunter,' Jacques said, petting his head and paying attention to the ground around his dog.

'What is it?' Orla asked. Her teeth were chattering around her words.

He examined the snow-covered ground. There was something there that shouldn't be there. Biscuit crumbs. No, not biscuits. *Cookies. Delphine's* cookies.

'Jacques,' Orla said. 'What is it?'

'Crumbs from Delphine's cookies.'

'Erin loves them. Delphine gave her some more yesterday.'

'She has been this way.'

Hunter barked again, a few paces further on.

Jacques stepped forward. 'There are more here.'

'Do you think she's leaving a trail?' Orla asked, rushing forward.

Jacques put out his arm. 'Do not run. You will disturb the ground and anything else we might find.'

'I just want... to find her,' Orla said, a tremble to her voice.

'I know,' he answered. 'And we will.'

'I can't lose her.'

He took her arm then, caught between steadying her and wanting to give her solidarity. 'You are not going to lose her.'

She was struggling. He could see it in her eyes. He wanted to draw her closer, wrap his arms around her, tell her it would all be OK...

Suddenly there was a whistle. One blast. Then another. And next a third.

'What's that?' Orla asked, wearing a haunted look now.

'The team ahead of us have found something.'

'Something?' Orla said, looking more terrified than relieved. 'Like what?'

He knew the instructions he had given. Three blasts was serious.

'Like what, Jacques?' Orla repeated.

'Come on,' he urged. 'Come, Hunter. Let's go.'

\* \* \*

Orla's heart was hammering against her chest as Jacques tried to call the team ahead of them on a walkie-talkie. Why they couldn't communicate with mobile phones she didn't know. All the white noise and garbled voices were unintelligible. She was powering as fast as she could over the snow, Hunter running close then getting in her way as if he was stopping her from being in front. She wanted to be ahead. She wanted to be the first person to get to whatever this was that had necessitated three loud blasts of a whistle.

'I cannot hear you. Repeat. Over.'

Jacques was still trying to get sense out of the two-way radio and Orla was starting to realise just how desolate the area was around Saint-Chambéry. All the trees looked the same. All the snow looked the same. You could only differentiate the sky from the ground now because it was night. And there were spooky sounds from the forest – the call of owls, the howl of goodness knows what, cracks of branches.

'Can we just hurry up? There was only one team in front of us, right?' Orla said, side-stepping Hunter again and elongating her stride.

'Orla, wait,' Jacques said. 'There is no use rushing. And if we have to backtrack, if we do not know what the other team has found, we will tear up this area and then there will be no further clues.'

'I don't care right now! If they haven't found my sister then they've found something *relating* to my sister and I want to know what it is.'

She stopped talking the second she heard Jacques's walkie-talkie crackle into life.

'*Nous avons trouvé quelqu'un. Sur.*'

'What does that mean?' Orla asked.

'They have found someone,' Jacques informed.

Orla gasped and grabbed for the radio in Jacques's hands. 'Who is it? Who have you found? Over.'

Jacques grabbed the radio back. 'You have to press this button.' He pressed it and spoke. '*Est-ce la fille? Érin?*'

Orla was holding her breath so hard her ribs were tightening like she was wearing a *Bridgerton*-style corset. Why was it taking so long to get a response?

'*C'est un homme. Il dit qu'il est Albanais.*'

She knew the French for 'man'. It wasn't Erin. But as her heart began to plummet, the sound of the last word began to morph in her mind. Before she could ask the question, Jacques had translated.

'It is a man. He says he is Albanian.'

Could it be... Burim?

## 50

Orla wasn't quite sure what she had expected Burim to look like, but it wasn't this person in front of her, sat on the tailgate of a flatbed truck, shivering under the flag of Albania wrapped over his black puffa jacket, the ripped jeans he was wearing wholly inappropriate for the French winter. She had imagined him taller, broader, with maybe a predatory look in his eye. But this boy – this young man – was all of five foot seven, with a buzz cut and a slit razored into his eyebrow. But she could also see what had attracted Erin. He was very good-looking, with the kind of lips women tried to replicate with overlining and his eyes were light brown, not quite amber, not quite hazelnut.

'Here, drink this,' Orla said, handing him a plastic beaker of something Jacques had given her before he left to continue looking for Erin once it was established that Burim did not know where she was.

'What is this?' Burim asked, looking at the offering as if it might be poison.

'It's coffee, I think.'

'You think?'

'Please, you're cold. Just drink it.'

'There is no alcohol?'

'No.'

He took the cup then, drinking it down as if he hadn't had anything for hours. He probably hadn't.

'Listen, Burim, I know I asked you this already but do you know where Erin is?' Orla asked.

'No,' he said, his voice laced with concern. 'I tell you before. We made a place on the map, halfway from where she stay and the airport. But, when I get there she is not there and I cannot contact her. I call her forty-eight times until my battery dies.'

'OK,' Orla said. 'So you walked all the way from Grenoble to here?'

'For some of the time I run.'

Was he for real? She knew how far that was. It was a crazy decision to make. A decision you would only make if you were utterly stupid or... in love. She swallowed.

Burim handed back the cup. 'We need to go now.' He jumped down from the back of the truck.

'You can't go,' Orla said. 'You've been out in this weather for hours and—'

'I am not sitting when Erin is out in cold. Why is she not where she say? Why is her phone not work?'

'I don't know,' Orla said. 'But maybe her battery has died too.'

'We need to find her.'

She definitely didn't disagree about that, but Jacques had told her to stay here until the team had thoroughly searched their quadrant.

'Burim, is there anything else Erin said about meeting you that might help us know whereabouts she's gone?'

He was pacing now, that nicked eyebrow raised like it was helping his brain deliberate. 'She say that Saint-Chambéry is a safe place. That everyone is welcome. That there is a nice lady who likes Tarantino and has a shop that makes hot milkshakes. She says that it is quiet but that sometimes quiet is nice.'

Orla swallowed. Erin had told Burim all this about the little village she assumed would not have enough going on for her always-in-need-of-entertainment sister.

'She said there was no place to make her nails nice.'

OK, that sounded more like Erin.

'I said I did not care about her nails.' And then Burim growled and it took Orla aback. 'Where is she? Do you think she is with someone else? Because if she is with someone else I will have to fight him.'

Suddenly Orla's phone erupted into life from the pocket of her jeans. *Jacques.*

As Burim began swinging punches in the air like he was practising for some kind of duel, Albanian flag still around him like he was actually about to enter a boxing ring, Orla pulled out her phone and answered.

'Hello.'

'I know where Erin is,' Jacques said simply.

'Oh my God! Thank God! Is she OK? Where is she?'

'She called Tommy. I have her location. I'm in a truck coming back to get you.'

He hadn't said she was OK. *Why* hadn't he said she was OK? Now her heart was thumping harder than ever.

'Jacques, is she OK? Please tell me.'

'She is OK, Orla. I promise. Tommy is heading there now. Now, save your battery on your phone.'

'Why do I need to do that?' she asked, confused. 'What aren't you telling me?'

She heard his intake of breath and so many scenarios began fluttering into her mind. She was going to have to call the emergency services. She was going to have to call her travel insurance company for an evac back to the UK. She was going to have to call her parents.

'Orla,' Jacques said. 'Erin's found a pregnant reindeer. It's about to give birth.'

## 51

'I don't like it. She's too quiet now. She wasn't quiet before.'

'Tommy, relax. She is fine. She is taking her time. And we need to keep our distance.'

'We should push her stomach? Make the baby come?'

Burim's comment earned him some surprised looks from Jacques and Tommy, and then Orla's focus went back to stroking her sister's hair as they sat on camping stools next to a fire that Jacques had made more rapidly than Ray Mears on a mission. They were hopefully far enough away that the reindeer didn't feel uncomfortable but close enough should she require assistance.

Orla couldn't be happier that Erin was OK but she was still going through everything that might have happened. And, apart from talking about the reindeer, before letting Jacques take the lead, Erin had said very little. It was Burim she had run to when they'd arrived and the hug between them that had looked like it was going to last for all eternity had brought a tear to Orla's eye. The couple's first IRL meeting and it was on a mountainside in front of a reindeer in labour. Perhaps it wasn't the most romantic scenario one could envisage but it was certainly unique.

'I know you're mad at me,' Erin said, breaking the silence between them.

'I'm not mad,' Orla replied.

'Orla, you're my sister. I know all your feelings. I sense them before you do half the time.'

'I just... why didn't you tell me you had plans to meet with Burim?'

'Do you like him?' Erin asked, suddenly animated and turning to face Orla. 'I know he can be a little bit weird but... I like that.'

'I don't know him yet,' Orla answered diplomatically. 'And, I asked you why you didn't tell me you had plans to meet him.'

'Why d'you think I didn't tell you? Because you would have told me I was crazy, locked me in that secret room in the barn and taken away my phone.'

'No,' Orla said straight off. 'That's what Mum would have done. I might have not reacted so severely.'

'You know you would have. *I* know you would have. I couldn't take that chance. Burim can't come to the UK, I was in France, it made perfect sense. We've been talking for months and we had a chance to actually *touch* each other and look into each other's eyes.'

Orla looked to Jacques then. He was the first person in so long that she had made an in-person connection with. She had touched him, looked into his eyes...

'And do some of the things we've talked about together.'

'What?' Orla said, breaking out of her reverie.

'Not that. Not quite yet. Maybe.' Erin sighed. 'But, I told him about here. Saint-Chambéry and all the weird shit that goes down. Throwing beanbags and putting Christmas presents in a wheelbarrow. Jacques's cinema room and Delphine's hot milk-shakes.' She paused. 'Delphine is going to be OK, right? Because I know she's annoying and opinionated but when I'm not here I need to imagine her here and obviously when we come back to visit she needs to be here and—'

'When we come back to visit?' Orla said.

'Yeah? What's weird about that? I mean, I know we need to go back to the UK and Mum and Dad are in the middle of some relationship mid-life crisis shit, but of course we're going to come back. There's you and Jacques for a start. Unless you've invited him to England. And Tommy comes to visit here and although he's really annoying most of the time, he's also quite cool. And you heard me say "hot milkshakes". Burim's going to love those.'

Orla didn't know what to say at all. Revisiting Saint-Chambéry had never been on her agenda. Up until recently she hadn't known the village existed. She had been to many places in the world but she'd never gone back. Suddenly that hit her full force. Was it like everything else in her life? She dipped in and out, taking what she needed at the time, but disregarding the bigger picture? Was that also what her sister thought she did? *Was* that what she did?

The reindeer made a noise and Erin jumped from the stool, rushing towards Burim who put a protective arm around her shoulders. Orla got up too, moving towards the scene.

'The baby comes now?' Burim asked. 'This is so cool, Erin.'

'I told you it was cool here,' she answered, hugging him close.

'It's not cool,' Tommy interjected. 'It's freezing!' He blew out a breath. 'But what is cool is the fact that now you two are actually together we don't have to listen to Erin's phone making noise all the time.'

'Why don't you three go back to the house?' Jacques

suggested. 'Take Gerard's truck back to the village and pick up mine. Make some food.'

'But what if something happens and you need the truck?' Tommy asked him.

'I will call you. Come on, Tommy, Erin and her friend have been outside for hours. Make a fire at the house, make some food. I will let you know what's going on,' Jacques reassured.

'Who is your friend?' Burim asked, looking confused.

'He means you,' Erin said, laughing.

'But I am your boyfriend, no?'

Erin gasped, putting her hands to her mouth. 'Did you just ask me to be your girlfriend?'

'We marry one day,' Burim said. 'I think you know this.'

Erin squealed and wrapped her arms around him again.

'Oh, wow,' Tommy said. 'Can't wait to get back to the house and be a third wheel.'

'Chaperone, please, Tommy,' Orla said seriously.

It was so much quieter once Tommy, Erin and Burim had left. Only the crackling of the fire and the occasional sound from the reindeer broke the night air. She had taken photos for the magazine but somehow, despite this being her ultimate mission, her reason for being here, it felt altogether intrusive.

'I cannot believe this,' Jacques said, sitting on the stool next to her.

'I know,' Orla said. 'Burim coming here all the way from Albania.'

'Oh... I was talking about the reindeer but—'

Orla smiled. 'I know you were. Tonight has been... a lot.'

'Yes,' he agreed.

'Is everyone OK?' Orla asked. 'Everyone who came to help look for Erin. I feel bad that they did that and she was absolutely fine.'

'You prefer that she was not fine?' he asked, his eyebrow raising slightly.

'No, of course not, I just... don't like to put anyone to any trouble.'

'Orla,' Jacques said, his angular jaw lit up by the glow of the fire. 'The thing you have to understand most about Saint-Chambéry is that nothing is too much trouble for people that care.' He elongated his legs and stretched his arms above his head. 'I find this hard when I arrived here. Look at my house. I built it with the intention of no one coming near, let alone inside. But, even here, on the very edge of a community, they get you.'

She laughed. 'You made that sound like you've been captured.'

'Well,' he said, turning to look at her again. 'Maybe I have.'

Both his expression and his words had her stomach churning.

'But there is a difference this time,' he continued. 'In the beginning I was determined not to be captured, by anything, by anyone. Now I feel that the choice I made then was the choice of a different person, a person that was so broken he thought he could never start to repair.'

'And now?' Orla asked softly.

'And now I see myself worrying hard about Delphine, wanting Tommy in my life more, wondering if the time has come to speak to my mother and try to understand my father... to open myself up to a writer from *Travel in Mind* magazine.'

'Oh, really,' Orla said, her cheeks hot not from the fire.

'Orla, I do not know the rules here. I do not know if I am built for any kind of relationship, but I know that if you left here and I did not say this then I would regret it forever.'

Her heart was burning but no words were coming.

'I want to know you, Orla. I want to know everything about you. All the tiny pieces that make you who you are. Even the ones you maybe have not recognised are there yet.'

'Jacques—'

'No, let me finish.' He sat forward on his seat and took hold of her hands. 'I do not recognise many of my pieces, Orla. You know about that more than anyone else. But the change now is... I do not want to be scared of them any longer. I want to know them. Even the difficult, misshapen ones that have no business being in my jigsaw at all.' He took another breath. 'And, even if I am calling this wrong, even if you do not see a way forward for us together, you have helped me get to a place where I can see a future where I am not afraid to be the only identity I want.' He took a breath. 'Jacques Barbier.'

She squeezed his hands in hers. She knew how much that meant for him to say and how deep-rooted those feelings were.

'Jacques Barbier is a beautiful person,' she told him. 'Inside and out. His look is wolf meets bear with a touch of YSL eau de parfum billboard man. But inside he's fire and caramel... rock and bubbles... hot coffee and iced champagne. His heart is surrounded by Kevlar but behind that wall is a divine purity found so very rarely.'

'I do not know this person,' he replied.

'You *are* this person,' Orla said. 'And that was part of the next page I was going to send my boss for the article for the magazine.'

'What?' he exclaimed.

'I know you're not mute and I know that was my initial remit. The mute man and the pregnant reindeer. But when I didn't have a pregnant reindeer I had a choice. I could lie. Or I could write a very different article. One about you and everything you've been through. Tell your story to the world. OK, it's not the Christmassy uplifting vibe Frances was looking for but I think it's better than that.'

He shook his head. 'Orla.'

'No, listen, I'm not saying it right. It's not *really* about any article, OK? It's about me feeling the way I feel about you and writing it down. That's what I do when I care. I write. And I've written five thousand words about you already. To be honest with you it could be a whole magazine on its own, or even a book and it's really great writing, some of my best work but... if the only person who ever reads it is you then that's more than OK with me.' She slipped off the stool, onto the snow and knelt in front of him. 'You were right about me. Everything you said. And I know my jigsaw needs fixing too so, maybe, we can work on it one corner at a time.' She squeezed his hands. 'I want to know all your pieces, Jacques Barbier. And I want to help you put them back together again.'

She looked into his eyes, hoping that her bravery in this moment was going to pay off. And when he kissed her, his mouth warm and wet, his tongue so wonderfully smooth, any doubts she had evaporated into the mountain night.

## 52

'Orla, wake up.'

Her eyes were gritty and her cheeks felt hot as she came to and remembered where she was. Huddled up to Jacques, lying on groundsheets under a sleeping bag he had pulled from a back-pack that seemed to have all the contents of a go-bag. Except she wasn't benefitting from his body heat right now because he was stood, gently shaking her shoulder.

'The baby is coming,' he told her.

'It's not Christmas Day,' Orla said, rushing to get out from the cover and stand.

She didn't know why she had said that. Frances's desperate spin to win viewers was no longer important. And Jacques had already reiterated again how reindeers gave birth in the spring and the fact that this reindeer was doing something so out of whack with nature was nothing short of a miracle.

'No,' he agreed. 'But it's a birthday and we could call the baby Jesus.'

'Inappropriate in so many ways. No.'

She got her phone from her pocket, ready to take photos.

Frances had said she wanted the birth in its full gory and this was a woman who enjoyed TikToks of blackhead popping after all and was training a colleague to fit a multitude of festive sweets into his mouth...

'She's not sitting down,' Orla remarked.

The reindeer was actually pacing a little and there were definitely signs of something coming from her rear end.

'Reindeer do not sit down to give birth,' Jacques said. 'When they are ready to calf they actually move away from the herd, separate themselves from the others. When they do this it can be a few hours or a few days until they have the baby.'

'Really? So, do you think she has been in this area for a while?'

'I do not know. Maybe. See, now she is moving around again. And there, the baby is appearing more.'

'Is everything OK do you think?' She wanted everything to be OK and the urge to get closer, to be nearer should anything need to be done was immense.

'Everything is OK.'

'But can you be sure? I don't know if I can sit here and then something bad happen. I mean the fact that the reindeer is giving birth now is very rare so what if something unexpected happens with the labour?'

'Orla,' he said, linking their hands. 'I am not going to let anything happen to these reindeer. I promise you that.'

She believed him, wholeheartedly. He was not the type of person to make a promise and not intend to keep it.

'I know what I said about the foxes but... take your photos for the magazine,' he encouraged.

She went to use her phone again but then she stopped herself. There was something about this moment that was calling her to be present, completely present, not looking at this wondrous act of nature through the screen of a phone. The reindeer had made its way from its herd for privacy, privacy they were already invading simply by being in the vicinity. Suddenly she thought about the thousands of readers consuming this personal, special moment with their Christmas morning Buck's Fizz and bacon sandwich. It felt like a violation of everything this birth represented – the stark, barren mountainside, a mother and child hidden amid the imposing trees, a dark starlit December night above them. It was soft and delicate and it wasn't something she wanted to share with the masses. She put her phone away.

'It is coming now,' Jacques said, putting an arm around her shoulders. 'See?'

'Yes,' Orla said. 'I see.'

Holding on to Jacques, she watched as the baby reindeer fell to the snow and the mother started to lick its fur. For a second Orla held her breath as the baby didn't move. But then it responded, wriggling its slick body and looking for attention. And, suddenly, in what she felt was a life-clarifying moment, Orla had never been so sure of what came next.

## 53

---

SAINT-CHAMBÉRY

*Three days later*

'Sit down, Delphine,' Erin ordered.

'*Mon Dieu*! You talk to me like you are in charge!'

'I am the Queen of the *Brouette*!'

'An honour bestowed by me and the rest of the Saint-Chambéry committee.'

'Which is you.'

'And Gerard. And Madame Voisin.'

'Who do as you tell them.'

Delphine gave a sigh of acceptance and dropped to the chair in the guest room, passing the hot hair tongs over to Orla.

'I don't know if I should have curls,' Erin said, surveying herself in the mirror and swishing the crinoline skirt of the Saint-Chambéry gown from times long ago like it was Prada and she was about to go on a runway. Orla was actually terrified, given her sister's penchant for spilling food and drink or getting items of clothing stuck in places they shouldn't be. Delphine had told a very long and complex tale about how the dress had come into existence and how many versions there had been. This particular one sounded like it was at least a hundred years old.

'What?' Delphine exclaimed. 'But we have spent almost an hour looking at different styles and deciding the curls.'

'But the Queen of the *Brouette* has to be perfect.'

OK, now perhaps Erin was taking this role a bit too far. Orla checked her watch. There was only forty-five minutes until the parade started and there was still quite a bit to do. But she couldn't make Delphine start to panic. Delphine had not liked giving up the tiniest bit of responsibility for the final preparations for the festival but Jacques really hadn't given her any choice. Perhaps it was against her initial wishes but sometimes people who had always led didn't know how to do anything differently and needed to realise that they didn't always have to be strong alone.

'Ah!' Delphine announced, looking ready to spring out of her chair again. 'There is only forty-five minutes until the start of the parade!'

'It's fine, Delphine,' Orla said, hopefully making her voice sound the very essence of calming and meditative. 'Jacques and Gerard will have it covered and Tommy and Burim are in charge of coffee to make sure the brass band don't get chilblains.'

'Madame Voisin will eat some of my cookies,' Delphine said, folding her arms across her chest.

'And, we agreed,' Orla said. 'That you have to let the small stuff go. Because people do what people do and if even 50 per cent of their intentions are good then that's OK.'

'I am agreeing to too much,' Delphine answered, sounding salty.

Orla wasn't sure that 'agreeing' was actually the right term but she had reluctantly listened when Orla and Jacques had spoken to her about her illness. It was as if the birth of that reindeer had triggered something inside Orla and a whole new perspective on the world had been unlocked. Things didn't have to tread a certain pre-determined path. She didn't have to react to things in the same way she always had. A new story could be written. In that way, her and Delphine were quite similar. Delphine couldn't see past the weeks and months she might be battling to what could be a brighter future, she could only see the here and now and the changes being to her detriment – her ultimate detriment in a worst-case scenario. But Delphine had agreed to let Jacques come with her to see the consultant in Grenoble and Orla had already devised a diet full of natural ingredients that were meant to promote well-being and encourage the body to repair itself.

'Hello!' Erin exclaimed. 'The Queen of the *Brouette* here! With her hair basically like ringlets! It's not a vibe!'

'Because we have not finished,' Delphine said, standing up again. 'They need to be eased into position.'

'Well, if I don't look good, I can't see me being eased into any kind of position with Burim.'

'O-K!' Orla jumped in before Delphine could say anything to that comment. 'Why don't we loosen the curls a little and see how we feel about it then.'

'Give me the tongs,' Delphine insisted.

Orla held them captive. 'Did you drink your plum and pumpkin smoothie this morning?'

'I did.'

Orla wasn't convinced and made an expression that suggested as much.

'I did,' Delphine insisted forcefully.

'Waiting for the truth here,' Orla continued.

'I did... except it was a bit *fade*. So I added some sugar.'

'Delphine! Natural! Honey if you had to!'

'What's *"fade"*?' Erin asked.

'It means tasteless,' Delphine explained. 'Yuck.'

'I think "yuck" is an international word. Burim says it too.'

And Burim was still here. Now with the knowledge of his parents thankfully. Although he was an adult, flying solo to another country without telling the people you live with and care about was nothing if not discourteous and Orla had been unhappy about the situation until Burim had put it right. But what happened with him when she and Erin flew back to the UK tomorrow she still didn't know. She had to admit the way he cared and showed affection for her sister was nothing short of princess treatment, but was this all a short-lived exciting adventure for him? She took a breath and handed Delphine the tongs. That was the old Orla thinking. Did it matter if it was short-lived? Nothing was guaranteed after all. Perhaps you just had to exist in the moment. Besides, she didn't really know what the future held for her and Jacques.

Suddenly her phone began to ring and she took it from the pocket of her jeans and rapidly moved to the other side of the room as Erin and Delphine began verbally sparring about the hairstyle again.

'Hello, Frances.'

'OK, Orla, I'm confused. I have this article you've sent me and apart from one paragraph about the reindeer there's nothing that says "festive", "Baby Jesus", "heart-warming" or "viral".'

Orla took a breath and stood next to the window covered in black sheeting. 'Do you like it?'

'No, I don't like it! For all the reasons I just stated!'

'But have you actually read it?' Orla asked, hand going to the sheet as she remembered furiously writing the words that were pouring from her heart.

'I skimmed it. It's the festive season. We're all trying to do three people's jobs because all the crazy people who didn't take all their annual leave in summer are taking their annual leave now! And you're in France, writing stuff that doesn't hit my remit and I'm starting to wonder what the fuck happened to you there.'

Orla smiled. She kind of knew the reaction she was going to get from Frances about the story she had gone for. Much more about the small community of Saint-Chambéry and finding yourself than it was about the miracle birth. But it hadn't really mattered what Frances's opinion was, she'd *had* to write it. She'd felt compelled to write it. And it was the first time in a long long time that she had experienced that feeling.

'Did you get my other email?' Orla asked her.

'What? No? I don't know,' Frances said. 'Did you not hear the part where I said we are all doing the jobs of three people?'

'I think you should read the other email,' Orla said.

'Ugh, Orla, I don't have time for this! You're just going to have to tell me.'

'Well, I—'

'Because this piece needs a complete re-write by tonight and I want better photos! I mean, what the fuck is this ugly wooden wheelbarrow all about?'

Now Orla was overcome with a feeling of defensiveness. Yes, she might have thought the *brouette* was weird when she'd first arrived here, but it meant so much to the people who lived here. It was part of the history and, yes, it may not be a beautiful golden statue, but it was just as important and its humble roots actually made it more so.

'Dear Frances,' Orla began. 'Please take this email as my resignation from my position with *Travel in Mind* magazine.

Although I have enjoyed my time with the company it's time for me to have a fresh beginning.'

There was silence at the other end of the phone line until:

'Are you joking? Has Alan put you up to this? Because yesterday he tried to prank me that the plant Moira has on her desk and waters every day is fake.'

'I'm serious,' Orla said. 'In fact, I've never been more serious.' She ran her fingers down the fabric over where the window should be.

'Is this about money?' Frances asked. 'What am I saying? Of course it's about money! It's always about money! Well, obviously I can't sign off on the intricacies of it but I am positive we can work around a... 10 per cent increase?'

'It's not about the money.'

'Twenty per cent!'

'Frances, you're not listening to me.'

'Is this *Time* magazine? Did they manage to poach you in the end? I thought I'd put paid to that the last time they came sniffing around but—'

'What?' Orla exclaimed. Had she heard right? Had her publication of dreams tried to headhunt her somehow? And Frances had intervened?!

'I didn't think they were serious at first but, well, I guess they were... and now this! So, when are you heading to New York?'

As quickly as the shock of this news hit, it dissipated just as fast.

'I don't have another job,' Orla answered.

'What? Are you insane?'

'No,' Orla said. 'I'm actually thinking more clearly than ever before.'

And with that said, she looked a little harder at the black sheet in front of her, blowing a bit with the breeze. *I wonder...* She pulled it back and there was the reveal. A perfectly intact window, a small fan moving left and right and creating the impression of outside air.

'Delphine!' Orla said. 'You were never having your window replaced!'

'Orla? Have you actually gone mad? Who is Delphine?' Frances called down the phone.

# 54

'Not gonna lie but Burim is putting me to shame in the gun show,' Tommy remarked as he and Jacques helped to coordinate the festival outside. It was remarkably mild today, actually a few degrees above freezing and some of the snow on the ground was beginning to thaw. This apparently called for Burim to be dressed in nothing but a vest on his top half as he and Gerard stacked the gifts made to the *brouette* around the central stage.

'Hey,' Jacques said. 'The dojo is open for you whenever you want to use it.'

'Thanks, bro. Now I know I need it.'

'And you know that is not what I meant.'

'Yeah, I know. Just feeling very single right now. Erin and Burim. You and Orla. Madame Voisin and Gerard.'

'What?' Jacques exclaimed in shock.

Tommy laughed. 'OK, I made the last one up, but can you imagine?'

'Yeah, no,' Jacques said. 'And I do not want to.'

'So, what *do* you want to imagine?' Tommy asked, straightening a row of bells along the fencing.

'World peace. Us getting through this festival with no one being struck by lightning like last year. Orla not winning the bean bag tournament because I will never hear the end of it.'

'She would have to yell pretty loud about it if you're gonna hear her from the UK.'

And there was Jacques's reminder that tomorrow, Orla and Erin were going to leave and go back to England. He'd known it was inevitable from the very beginning but so much had changed. Except in the whirlwind that had been the last few days, having Burim as an additional guest, tackling Delphine and getting her to think about changing her mind about her treatment and making sure the festival was on track so Delphine had a bit less on her plate, there had been no time for discussion about what happened next.

'I know,' he replied to Tommy.

'What does that mean?' Tommy asked, picking up a discarded paper cup from the ground and crushing it in his hands.

'I don't know.'

'So, you know or you don't know?'

'Tommy, we have a lot to do here. We have only thirty minutes before the Queen of the *Brouette* is meant to come with a flaming torch and light the beacon.'

'Knowing how much product Erin wears on her hair she's probably gonna set light to that before anything else. Unless the lightning gets to her first.' He laughed. 'Then Burim would have to have a duel with the lightning 'cos that's what Albanians do he told me.'

Jacques looked at his brother, adjusting Christmas décor, picking up litter, handing out sweets as they checked the perimeter fence where villagers and tourists alike were accumulating ready for the festivities. He was *good*. Inside him was the purest heart. He may not have a pre-determined life path yet and be worried about that but as far as Jacques was concerned his brother had so much time to work out what he wanted. There was no rush.

'So, do you know?' Jacques asked him. 'Or are you making plans the way Burim makes plans? Just, with, slightly smaller biceps.'

'Hey!' Tommy said, striking his shoulder.

'I am kidding,' Jacques replied.

'Well, I thought I'd let you cook me turkey. Stay for New Year too maybe,' Tommy said.

'I don't know if we will have turkey. I do know that Gerard has promised Delphine lobster this year. I have no idea if he will be able to make this possible but—'

'Delphine should have what she wants though, right?'

The way Tommy had said it was poignant and the threat to his dear friend's life was still very much hanging in the air amid the wonderful, over-the-top Christmas decorations she had co-ordinated around the village. However, Delphine had moved slightly on her first stubborn stance, thanks to Orla. He had watched as Orla's 'subtle' had moved to 'encouraging' and then to 'very direct' in exactly the right kind of increments and Delphine was open to receiving help and advice on the next steps. It was definitely a much more hopeful situation than it had been.

'Delphine always gets what she wants,' Jacques reminded him as they walked back and headed towards the main Christmas tree. 'She will still be getting what she wants when this version of the *brouette* is worn out.'

He looked at the wheelbarrow full of gifts and the surrounding plinths piled high with wrapped boxes for the charity, the sparkling trees covered from their bases to the glittering stars at the top with every ornament and trail of tinsel you could imagine. It was very nearly Christmas in the village he had made his home. *Home.* A word that had been unrecognisable in his world for so very long.

'I thought, you know, after New Year, I could stay a little longer maybe,' Tommy continued. 'I mean, I don't wanna get in your way or anything and I know we don't know how things are gonna go with Delphine but, I could, help with the café or the shop and take care of Hunter.'

'You don't have to do that, Tommy,' Jacques said, as they shifted back behind the barricade.

'I know I don't *have* to do it,' he answered. 'Maybe I want to. Maybe I want to take a minute and think about what comes next. Maybe I want to take a minute and think about what comes next from Saint-Chambéry.'

'Yeah?' Jacques asked.

'Yeah, I mean, why not. And maybe Delphine is gonna have to teach me to how to make the hot milkshakes so good.'

'OK,' Jacques said, slapping a hand to his back. 'It's a plan.'

'Well, hold on, I said that was what *I* wanted to do. It doesn't have to be *your* plan. Because I'm guessing your plan involves Orla, right? And that's good. And, like I said, me and Hunter will be just fine.'

He didn't know what came next for sure. He knew how he felt about Orla. He hoped he knew how she felt about him but the practicalities were quite a different thing.

'Got it,' Jacques answered with a nod. 'So, I am going to catch up with Madame Voisin, why don't you give Burim a hand?' He started to stride away.

'Jacques! You're leaving the conversation! Don't do that!' Tommy called after him.

## 55

Every inch of Erin looked regal as she arrived – very slowly – in the village square on a bucket-shaped add-on to nothing more than a decorated tractor. But everyone applauded and threw flowers or glitter and the band led the tractor in a circuit of the village centre playing an old French Christmas carol that sounded slightly dark to Orla. But her sister was beaming – mainly at Burim – who was waving until he seemed to catch himself and adopted a more nonchalant, slightly gangster-esque pose involving his hand on his chin. Someone else who was beaming was Delphine. Orla watched her, clapping her hands, buoying up Madame Voisin with a little good-natured elbow jostling, singing furiously along with Gerard, light and life shining from every inch of her. This woman had been born and raised here, married here, buried her husband here and then dedicated herself to keeping the community and its traditions going as well as reaching out to bring the magic of Saint-Chambéry to tourists. And then there was the fact she had lied about a mute man and a pregnant reindeer to get a reporter from London to come here and be matchmade.

As Erin held the fiery torch aloft like it was an Olympic flame, Orla's eyes went to Jacques. She had never met anyone like him. Except perhaps her own self. Although, the fact she was only really starting to recognise who she was spoke volumes too. In stripping back *his* layers she had been put into a position where she had no choice but to peel hers back too. It was terrifying yet liberating. Getting to know your own soul when you seemed to have been acting a part for others for so long felt like the ultimate kind of freedom. And Jacques had helped gift that to her. As she felt that now close-to-familiar warming up of her insides that came from just being in his presence, his eyes met hers. And there was her heart rate, hitting high heights as a plethora of thoughts lashed down like a Saint-Chambéry snowstorm. She was already smiling when he smiled at her. Both of them knowing.

* * *

'Oh, Erin! You look like a princess!'

'I'm a *queen*, Mum! The Queen of the *Brouette*!' Erin shouted over the FaceTime call. 'Now, I know it looks like a wheelbarrow but it's really important in the history of Saint-Chambéry. Like *the* most important thing. Almost like the London Eye.'

Orla winced a little at the analogy but had to hold her phone steady. Even though they were going to be seeing their parents tomorrow, Erin wanted to show off her status and the regal gown. And her official duties didn't begin again until she was presenting the prize to the winner of the beanbag competition later on. As competitive as Orla usually was, she really had no delusions of championing that. Plus, Delphine had told her Philippe had been coaching the other finalist – Sebastian – long into the night since Orla had beaten him...

'What a lovely Christmas tree,' their dad piped up. 'They didn't get that from the place next to Aldi, did they?'

'Dad, this village is literally surrounded by Christmas trees!' Erin yelled. 'And, yesterday, I found a reindeer in the forest and it had a baby!'

'Erin!' Delphine called. 'There are children who would like a photograph with the Queen of the *Brouette*!'

'Coming!' Erin grinned at the screen. 'Sorry, I'm in demand today but I'll see you tomorrow!' With that, she scooped up her dress and began running across the square towards Delphine.

'It looks very bustling there, so it does,' Dana remarked. 'And Erin sounds... happy.'

'I think she *is* happy, Mum,' Orla agreed, her gaze flitting over to the square where Erin was being handed a baby to be photographed with like she was a parliamentary candidate.

'Good,' Dana answered. 'So I take it the Moroccan has done what they all do and left her.' She frowned. 'If you can leave someone you've only sent word messages to. Don't they call it something? Spirited? Ghouled?'

Now there was only one person Orla's eyes went to. Burim. Perched on a stool, right elbow on a table, currently unbeaten in an arm-wrestling contest Gerard was taking bets on.

'Um, about that, you see, the thing is—'

'Well, we weren't going to say anything until you got home but... we're going to counselling,' her dad interjected.

'Oh, really?'

'Two different kinds, actually,' Dana added. 'One for my perimenopausal anger issues and one for our marriage.'

'We laugh,' Dalton said. 'About the best things coming in threes and what we should sign up for next.'

'We do,' Dana agreed. 'Because if you don't laugh, well, I don't know but things always seem better if you laugh, don't they?'

'They do,' Orla said, nodding. And then she really looked at her parents. They were close together – possibly because they had to share the screen for this call, but it seemed more than that – they were mirroring each other's body language and there was a definite lessening of tension.

'So, what about you, love?' her dad asked. 'Has everything come together for your article? Your mum was telling me.'

She nodded. 'Absolutely. You know me, stories fall into my lap wherever I go.'

There would be time to tell her parents about her professional decision to quit *Travel in Mind* but, for now, she wanted to leave them looking forward with positivity and knowing that she and Erin were happy enjoying this special day for Saint-Chambéry. Besides, she hadn't even told Erin or Jacques about her resignation yet...

'Oh, by the way, the heating's fixed,' Dana said.

'Terry got hold of a part for a good price and wouldn't take any money for his time. I even offered him my golf clubs,' Dalton said.

'That's great news.'

'Don't tell Erin just yet though,' Dana said. 'The second she hears it will be back to wearing crop tops and turning the thermostat up.'

'OK,' Orla agreed. 'Listen, I have to go now. I have a beanbag contest to take part in.'

'A what?' Dalton asked.

'I'll tell you all about it when I get home,' she said. 'Let's hope I can fit a trophy in my cabin bag.'

'We can't wait to see you, love,' Dalton said. 'Can we, Dana?'

'No, we can't wait to see you,' Dana agreed, looking a little tearful but smiling. 'I can definitely wait to see Bren now she's told me she's bringing some board game about whether you look like your dog or not. I mean, we don't even have a dog.' She sniffed. 'But you and Erin, well, you need to see these festive lights do all their twenty-nine different things, don't you?'

'We do,' Orla agreed. 'See you tomorrow, Mum. Bye, Dad.'

She ended the call and put her phone away. Turning, she smacked straight into something. Or rather *someone*.

'Oh! Sorry! I didn't see you there!' Orla gasped, just managing to keep her balance.

'*Désolé*. Sorry.' Jacques smiled. 'It is like when we first met.'

'When Gerard hit you with his car.'

'Yes.'

She smiled, the sound of a much cheerier carol coming from the brass band now rising up around the village square. 'A lot has happened since then.'

'It has,' he agreed. 'But there is one thing that has not happened since then.'

'Oh?'

He took her hands in his, drew her a little closer. 'We have not had our date.'

'Oh,' Orla said, nervous anticipation flowing through her. 'Well, I just thought that events had kind of superseded that and—'

'Oh, *non, non, non*,' Jacques stated. 'I do not say things that I do not mean. I had a lot of time doing that when I was being other identities but now... it is just me, saying things I want to say.'

He squeezed her hands. 'So,' he began. 'After you have won the beanbag contest we will have our date.'

She couldn't lie, his beautiful voice saying 'our date' did things to her. A real date. Like their real connection. Not a text message in sight.

'Where are you taking me?'

'That will remain an undisclosed location for now.'

'OK, I thought you were done with the undercover covert stuff now.'

'Allow me a little mystery, *non*?' He paused. 'But, I do not ask… perhaps you do not want to go now and—'

'*Non*. I mean, no. I mean actually yes!' Orla said. 'Of course yes.'

'Good,' he answered. 'Then, it is a date.'

## 56

Orla had no idea why she was holding her breath. This beanbag contest was just for fun. There was nothing riding on it except a trophy – a miniature *brouette* carved with the different shaped beanbags – and the kudos of being the 2024 champion. Except her supporters – Erin, Burim, Jacques, Tommy and even Hunter – seemed intent on her victory. It was unlikely, obviously. She had only played the game once before and that last time she had almost set fire to Gerard's bar and a hole had been burned into her coat. Perhaps that was why the final was being held outdoors, a firepit the centre of everything now the brass band had returned their instruments to homes and its members joined the evening festivities. She looked at the beanbag in her hand. Pentagon-shaped like the lake. The worst shape according to Jacques. He had advised her not to clutch one side but to take the whole shape in her hand and toss that way. She'd had a hard time not spitting out a laugh at that suggestion said with the utmost seriousness...

'Time!' Gerard called gruffly.

Ugh. That meant she was on a ten-second countdown until the beanbag had to leave her fingers. She adjusted her stance, looked up at the steeple of the little church across the square and tried to remember how the fire pit looked and how far away it was. *It doesn't matter. It doesn't matter.*

She swung her hand forward once and then propelled the beanbag over her shoulder. There was drumming from feet on the ground, hands on tables and fencing, until a universal shout. Not celebration. Not commiseration. Not one thing or another. Orla spun around. Her beanbag had landed on the very rim of the firepit. Not in the flames. Not out of the flames. Like the outer bullseye at archery or on a dart board.

'Five points!' Gerard declared as Orla made her way back to their table.

'That was great!' Tommy said, slapping her on the back.

'It was very great!' Burim agreed, slapping her slightly too hard.

'You only need another throw like that and you will win,' Jacques told her.

'Really?' Orla asked.

'Sebastian doesn't look happy,' Erin remarked. 'And he's going over to Gerard. Do you want me to go and find out what's going on in my capacity as queen?'

'No,' Orla said. 'It's OK. Why don't you come with me, and we'll get some more drinks for everyone.'

'You want me to help?' Jacques asked.

'No, no,' Orla said. 'It's fine. We can do it, can't we, Erin?'

'I'm the freaking queen. I can do anything today.'

Orla led the way to Gerard's bar and Erin pulled at her arm before they had even got to the door.

'OK, what's going on? Because this isn't nervousness about the beanbag-throwing final, is it?'

'No,' Orla admitted. 'I just... there's something I need to tell you before I tell Jacques.'

'You're pregnant?'

'Oh my God, Erin! Shh! We're in Village Gossip Central here!'

'So, you are!'

'No! Are you crazy? Of course I'm not pregnant!'

'Ohhh, I'm disappointed now.' Erin laughed. 'OK, what else boring is it?'

'Well, I've handed in my resignation. I'm not going to be working for *Travel in Mind* any more.' It still felt weird to say it.

'Is that it?' Erin asked. 'Well, that's dull as fuck.'

'Is it?'

'And, not gonna lie, I don't think they appreciated you anyway. You always worked far too hard, all hours of the day, all days of your life, so now you can get a job you enjoy more.'

*A job she enjoyed more.* Hadn't she enjoyed what she did? Or was it more a case of starting out enjoying something and then losing that feeling along the way?

'So, shall we get the drinks now?' Erin asked, as unperturbed as ever.

'No, wait, there's one more thing.'

'I'm getting baby fever...'

'No, it's Burim.'

'*He's* not getting baby fever, is he?'

'I really hope not. Not yet anyway. And he's unlikely to be discussing that with me.'

Erin laughed. 'You like him though, don't you? I can tell.'

'I do like him,' Orla agreed. 'He's very polite. He's very opinionated, particularly when it involves football or anything Tommy has to say.'

'Ha! Yeah, I've noticed that. But it's good to keep him on his toes.'

'And I can see how much he cares for you.'

'And here's the bit when you turn into Mum and tell me all the pitfalls of a long-distance relationship and ask if I know that Auntie Bren once dated a submariner.'

'No,' Orla said, leaning against one of the large barrels outside Gerard's place. 'I wasn't going to say that. I was just going to say that we're going home tomorrow and—'

'Burim's going back to Albania tomorrow too,' Erin said softly. 'He has a flight a few hours after us.' She sighed. 'He can't come to the UK yet. I get that. And don't worry, I'm not going to abscond to Albania or anything. It is what it is, and we'll just have to see how it goes.'

This was Erin being as mature as it got, and Orla's heart went out to her. She put her arms around her sister and drew her close. 'I love you so much, Erin. You know that, don't you?'

'I know that,' Erin answered. 'I also know that you're going to crease this dress if you keep hugging me and I don't want it creased *and* stained when it's given back to Delphine.'

'You've stained it?' Orla said, letting her go.

'It wasn't *my* fault. The baby literally poured its bottle on me.'

Orla shook her head, but she was smiling. Both the Bradbee sisters had done some growing since they had been in Saint-Chambéry.

'Orla!' A collective shout from their table volleyed around the square.

'Looks like it's your turn to throw again,' Erin said. 'I'll get the drinks. Then, when you've beaten Sebastian, you'd better get ready for your date.'

'What?' Orla asked. 'How do you know about that?'

Erin laughed. 'Just go and throw your beanbags, Orla Orange.'

Hearing her little sister say her nickname pulled at her heart-strings but apparently there wasn't time for sentimentality when there was a contest to win and a gorgeous guy to go on a date with.

Jacques was nervous. The kind of nervous you might get if you were waiting outside a church for a very different reason. But, to him, this date felt more important than any other kind of union he'd had before. And he knew that this place was where he wanted Orla and him to have this first proper date together. He blew into his hands to ward off the cold and checked his watch again. He'd text her. *The chapel at midnight*. It was three minutes to.

'The church,' Orla said, suddenly at his shoulder.

'You are early,' he remarked, turning to face her.

'And you've been standing here for five minutes already,' she answered.

'You've been watching me?'

'I was making sure the Queen of the *Brouette* had a chariot to get home in. And by "chariot" I mean your truck, driven by Tommy with Burim and Hunter squeezed into the back. I'm not sure how we get back.'

'We will find a way,' Jacques answered. He took her hand. 'Come on. Let me show you the chapel.'

He pushed open the tiny wooden door and, as always, he had to bend significantly to get inside. But, once over the threshold, the chapel ceiling rose into an A-frame and wooden beams with golden fairy lights entwined around them made up the roof space. The flagstones were covered with wooden pews and, as Delphine and her helpers had promised, a table set for two was at the far end, just below the pulpit, opposite the building's one stained-glass window and right next to the original, centuries old *brouette* in a glass case.

'This is so beautiful,' Orla remarked, walking with him down the aisle and taking everything in.

'It looks exactly as it looked when I first saw it,' Jacques told her. 'Apart from this table of course.' He pulled a chair out for her, and she sat down. There were plates, glasses, one candle flickering in its centre and a bottle of wine.

'Thank you,' she said.

He sat down too, more nervous than ever, but also never more certain about the things he wanted to say. The red wine was open, and he poured them both a glass and watched Orla take a sip.

'Saint-Chambéry magic grapes again?' she asked.

'I believe so.' He smiled at her. 'Orla, you look so beautiful tonight.'

'Even though I'm a beanbag loser?' she asked.

'A beanbag second place,' he reminded.

'I don't mind,' Orla insisted.

'I know,' he agreed. 'Because you let Sebastian win.'

She shook her head but there was a smile on her lips. 'The pentagon slipped out of my hand. You were right about those shapes, you know.'

He shook his head and smiled again.

'So, why the church?' Orla asked. 'Is church important to you?'

'*This* church is important to me,' Jacques admitted. 'This was the very first place I came in Saint-Chambéry the day I found myself here.'

'Really?'

He nodded. 'I had been driving and driving for hours, across borders, with no care for a map, no plan, no idea, just a head full of messed up thoughts and terrifying versions of my future and my truck just stopped right outside here.' He sighed. 'It had fuel, there was nothing wrong with it that I could identify, but it did not want to go any further. So, I got out and I pushed the door, and I came inside.' He shivered as the memories washed over him. 'And when I stepped onto those old stones it felt like something was holding me up, guiding me to sit down in one of the pews. I can't really explain it, but it was like the universe was taking control for me because I had lost control for myself.'

She reached for his hand, her fingers wrapping around his, so delicate and soft on his skin.

'I sat here for an hour, maybe two, just quiet and still, no thoughts, no feelings, just existing and this church just let me exist in it, sit with it.' He smiled. 'And then Delphine burst in with the rest of the choir and it got very noisy after that. In fact, I don't think my life has ever been as quiet as it was that first night here... before Delphine made me listen to that rehearsal.'

'And the rest is history,' Orla remarked.

'Yes,' he agreed. 'And it is crazy you should say those words because this is what our date is about. So...' He stood up and went over to a wicker basket that was on the front pew a few steps away. 'I remember you wrote about a man in South America. He only ate soup, and he went to the same restaurant every day and had five bowls. One to signify everyone in his life that he had lost.'

Orla gasped. 'You remember that article.'

'I told you I had read them all.'

'I know but there's a difference between reading them and remembering them.'

'Is there?' he asked her. 'If you have read them in the right way?'

He took out a Thermos and two bowls and placing the bowls on the table he filled each one with the most delicious soup. He knew it was delicious because it was one of his favourites. He sat down again.

'But, as much as I loved the article and as much as I respected that South American man, I do not want us to eat things and be sad about people who are no longer in our lives, for whatever reason,' Jacques told her. 'So, our three courses tonight will be one for the past, one for the present and one for the future.'

\* \* \*

Orla could already feel the tears pricking her eyes. This man was everything in this moment. He was strong and gentle, considerate and caring; in fact, there weren't enough words to describe what he had come to mean to her.

'Jacques,' she said. 'There's something I have to tell you.'

'You don't like soup?' he asked, almost panic on his expression.

'No, no, I love soup, and this smells so good,' she said. 'I just... I want you to know that, well, I won't be writing for *Travel in Mind* any more.'

He didn't say anything, and she watched his face as the news hit. His expression now wasn't giving anything away.

'You have a new job?' he asked. 'You deserve that. You will be incredible with whatever comes next. You will be able to—'

'No,' she said, reaching for his hand again and slipping her fingers between his. 'No, I haven't made any decisions about what I want to do yet. And that feels really good to say. I've always had this path I've been set on and I've never actually stopped to think if it's the right one, or whether I should deviate or change direction completely because I've never made time to just exist, to sit with myself.'

She looked at the stained-glass window, the moonlight flooding through the depiction of the fox, the fish, the wolf and things had never seemed clearer.

'Like you said when you first arrived in Saint-Chambéry, the church let you simply exist in it and that's what I need to do in life.' She smiled. 'I want to find out who Orla Bradbee is when she isn't a worldwide roving reporter. I want to know who she is as a woman. I want to know who she is as a sister and a daughter without any other demands on my time for a while. And, well, I'd quite like to find out who she is as... a girlfriend.'

'Really?' Jacques asked.

'If, you know, you know someone who might like one. And, by someone I don't mean anyone in Saint-Chambéry because Sebastian did tell me he was single earlier.' She took a breath. 'I mean you.'

Her heart was skipping more beats than the brass band had earlier, until it hit hard and strong as Jacques got to his feet and came to her side of the table. He pulled her up and out of her chair and put his hands on either side of her face, cupping it gently.

'I don't want a shituationship,' he told her.

'Neither do I,' she breathed. 'I might be going tomorrow but, Jacques, I'm coming back. I promise you, I'm coming back.'

'Then, Orla Bradbee, would you allow me to find out who I am as a boyfriend... to you?' he asked her.

The way he had asked was so perfect. She smiled. 'Hmm, let me think... if I say no, will you have to pin me to the table?'

'I may do that no matter what you say.'

'Then, yes,' Orla answered. 'My answer is yes!'

His mouth found hers the second the words left her, and she wrapped her arms around his neck and let him hold her tight. What had started as an assignment she hadn't even wanted to take had ended with a new beginning she could never have imagined.

# EPILOGUE
## SAINT-CHAMBÉRY

*Spring*

'We are gathered here today to say goodbye to a true servant of the community. Many have gone before and many will go after, but we will remember your time with us, always.'

Madame Voisin sniffed and wiped a tear away at Gerard's words to the group of villagers gathered in the square.

'This is the weirdest funeral I have ever been to,' Erin remarked a little too loudly. 'Is it even a funeral? Like is there a burial or a cremation or something else?'

'I think they just chop it up and put it on the fire,' Tommy said. 'That's why Jacques is up there with the axe.'

'Savage,' Erin answered.

'Shh,' Orla said. 'The other villagers are looking at us.'

Erin's phone beeped once, then twice, then a third time.

'Aw, man, it's like Burim's with us,' Tommy said.

'We commit this friend of the community, our friend, into the arms of our forefathers,' Gerard continued.

'Delphine,' Erin said, bending a little towards the wheelchair. 'Can you see OK?'

'I can see that nothing is as it should be and Gerard is making far more of his part than necessary. That is because he built this version of the *brouette,* and it has lasted the least amount of time of any in my lifetime!'

'Well,' Tommy said. 'Jacques and I have made the new one and there's plenty of your lifetime left to see how long it lasts, right?' He put his hands on her shoulders.

'Not if I have to eat any more kale,' Delphine moaned. 'Or watch you burn any more croissants. They are not meant to be toasted, I keep telling you!'

'I like them burnt,' Erin remarked. 'With cheese.'

'Yeah, me too,' Tommy agreed. 'Burim actually made one into a pizza last time he was here. That was epic.'

Orla smiled at the banter going on as the *brouette* that had held all the gifts at Christmas time was retired from service and committed to the wood pile, its replacement ready to be sworn in. A lot had happened during the weeks that had followed her pre-Christmas departure. She and Erin had celebrated Christmas Day with their parents and Auntie Bren and, as soon as all the bank holidays were over she had helped her parents prepare for their counselling, talking through some of their issues, and getting them to agree to go forward with compassion and respect for each other at all times. Then, after a failed attempt at the Cadbury's Heroes eating contest, Sonil had actually broken a Guinness record for Celebrations eating claiming his Achilles heel in the festive contest had been the Dinky Decker. That party night had been a chance for Orla to say goodbye to her colleagues and have a happy farewell to her time at *Travel in Mind.*

In late January she had returned to Saint-Chambéry for

Delphine's operation and helped Tommy and Jacques keep village store/café and sometime bed and breakfast going.

A couple of weeks later, for February half-term, Orla had brought Erin back for a treat and Burim had visited. Erin was never going to be Miss Academia, but she was trying with her A-levels and now things with their mum and dad were becoming much more stable the environment was a lot healthier all round. And it seemed her sister and Burim were stronger than ever despite the distance.

And here they were now in March, Delphine still going through treatment, but the signs that there was a chance for complete recovery were excellent. Her griping and moaning were definitely accelerating back to near normal levels so that had to be positive.

'...and with one mighty swing, we give thanks, but condemn you for all eternity!' Gerard roared.

Jacques swung the axe, the *brouette* broke in two and Hunter let out a bark.

* * *

'Cheese! Cheese!'

Jacques laughed as Orla galloped across the snow-specked grass towards the cave, unafraid, eager, so unlike the first time he had brought her here to see the foxes. And, within seconds, there they were, five of the animals now, coming to receive the treats.

'We ought to give them names,' Orla said as one of the foxes took some cheese and then had a lick of her fingers.

'No,' Jacques said sternly. 'We talked about this so many times. They are wild animals. You cannot touch them or hug them. They need to keep surviving without us.'

'Speaks the man who still has Noble in his shed with his chickens.'

'Not through choice,' Jacques replied.

The vet had visited after Christmas to check out Noble's condition and deemed him almost fifteen years old – quite an age for his species. He had also confirmed that he was fully domesticated and therefore letting him go into the wild would only lead to his demise. With Delphine having enough to worry about there was no other option but to keep him.

'Anyway, they all think their names are "cheese",' he teased.

'What does a name matter anyway?' Orla said. 'It's the person that counts. Or, should I say, the fox.'

He got her meaning completely. With him having had so many names over the years he had almost lost sight of who the real person was. But, in time, with strength, he knew he was going to enjoy rediscovering every genuine thing.

'You know,' he began as the foxes looked for more food, weaving between their legs as they stood at the cave viewpoint. 'There are some good reasons why a name would matter.'

'Really?' Orla asked. 'Wolf.'

He smiled. 'I mean, it would matter if you were, I don't know, performing a legal transaction.'

Orla gasped. 'Are you buying into Gerard's bar? Because he asked me and he was very insistent that the name would not be changing so—'

'I am asking you if you would like to find out who I am as a husband.' He swallowed. 'Badly. I think.'

She gasped again, looking at him with wide eyes, blinking. Saying nothing. Maybe it was too soon. He just knew it was harder and harder when she had to leave, and he missed her every second she was gone.

'I... don't know what to say,' she answered.

'Is it wrong for me to ask?' Jacques said. 'If it is too much pressure too soon we can pretend I meant investing in Gerard's bar.'

'No,' Orla said, shaking her head. 'It's not that.'

'Tell me.'

She sighed. 'I just want to enjoy every part of my new journey, each second of *our* journey together and I don't want to rush, I want to savour.' She smiled. 'And we only know how we are with each other in Saint-Chambéry. We've not been anywhere else... we should travel together, see all the places, I mean, what if I don't like you in Japan?'

'You would hate me in Japan. I cannot use chopsticks.'

'Oh my God! Stop!'

'You might hate me in Canada. When I take you on a tour of all the places Tommy broke bones.'

'I want to know if I'll like you in London,' she told him seriously. 'I want to know if you'll like my parents.'

He sighed. 'I think I should be more worried if they are going to like me.'

'I have no doubt about that,' she said, reassuringly, putting her arms around his neck.

'So, you're saying no?' he asked, raising one eyebrow.

'I'm not saying no,' Orla said, smiling. 'I'm saying "one day". Definitely one day.'

'Did you hear that, Cheeses?' Jacques asked the foxes who were noses to the ground sniffing for scraps. 'She said "definitely one day".'

'You're crazy,' Orla said, looking into his eyes.

'And you... are everything,' he answered, his heart full.

He kissed her then, with every ounce of passion he possessed and all the love that had grown between them since they had first met. It may have started as one winter in the mountains, but there were many chapters of their story just waiting to be written.

# ACKNOWLEDGEMENTS

Thank you to these wonderful people who always keep me focussed and motivated:

**Tanera Simons** and **Laura Heathfield** of **Greenstone Literary** – my fantastic agency team who always have my back. I can't wait to continue this journey with you both!

**Boldwood Books** – for publishing more Mandy Baggot books than anyone ever before and being super-fantastic!

**Robin Baggot** – for all your amazing hard work on my social media!

**All my readers** – thank you for continuing to love each and every story and allowing me to have the best job ever creating these romantic novels!

# ABOUT THE AUTHOR

Mandy Baggot is a bestselling romance writer who loves giving readers that happy-ever-after. From sunshine romantic comedies set in Greece, to cosy curl-up winter reads, she's bringing gorgeous heroes and strong heroines readers can relate to. Mandy splits her time between Salisbury, Wiltshire and Corfu, Greece and has a passion for books, food, racehorses and all things Greek!

Sign up to Mandy Baggot's mailing list for news, competitions and updates on future books.

Visit Mandy's website: www.mandybaggot.com

Follow Mandy on social media here:

facebook.com/mandybaggotauthor

x.com/mandybaggot

instagram.com/mandybaggot

bookbub.com/profile/mandy-baggot

## ALSO BY MANDY BAGGOT

Under a Greek Sun

Truly, Madly, Greekly

Those Summer Nights

In the Greek Midwinter

One Christmas in Paris

One Greek Sunrise

One Hollywood Sunset

One Greek Summer Wedding

Mr Right Now

Love at First Slice

One Wish in Manhattan

One Winter at the French Chalet

LOVE NOTES

*LOVE IN EVERY CHAPTER*

WHERE ALL YOUR ROMANCE
DREAMS COME TRUE!

THE HOME OF BESTSELLING
ROMANCE AND WOMEN'S
FICTION

 WARNING:
MAY CONTAIN SPICE

SIGN UP TO OUR
NEWSLETTER

https://bit.ly/Lovenotesnews

# Boldwood

Boldwood Books is an award-winning fiction publishing company seeking out the best stories from around the world.

**Find out more at www.boldwoodbooks.com**

Join our reader community for brilliant books, competitions and offers!

Follow us
@BoldwoodBooks
@TheBoldBookClub

Sign up to our weekly deals newsletter

https://bit.ly/BoldwoodBNewsletter

Printed in Great Britain
by Amazon